I0794056

DEAD END

Recent Titles by Joan Lock in this Series

DEAD IMAGE
DEAD BORN
DEAD LETTERS *
DEAD END *

* available from Severn House

DEAD END

Joan Lock

This first world edition published in Great Britain 2004 by
SEVERN HOUSE PUBLISHERS LTD of
9–15 High Street, Sutton, Surrey SM1 1DF.
This first world edition published in the USA 2004 by
SEVERN HOUSE PUBLISHERS INC of
595 Madison Avenue, New York, N.Y. 10022.

British Library Cataloguing in Publication Data

Lock, Joan
    Dead end
    1.   Best, Ernest (Fictitious character) - Fiction
    2.   Police - England - Fiction
    3.   England - Social life and customs - 19th century - Fiction
    4.   Detective and mystery stories
    I.   Title
    823.9'14 [F]

    ISBN 0-7278-6043-7

Typeset by Palimpsest Book Production Ltd.,
Polmont, Stirlingshire, Scotland.
Printed and bound in Great Britain by
MPG Books Ltd., Bodmin, Cornwall.

Acknowledgements

G rateful thanks for assistance from the Newcastle-upon-Tyne City Library; the Tyne & Wear Archives; the Museum of Methodism; St Giles's Christian Mission; The Women's Library at the London Metropolitan University; the Metropolitan Police Museum; the National Police Library; London Metropolitan Archives; the British Library (both Printed Books & Newspapers) and the National Monuments Record.

Individuals to whom I am indebted are Judy Faraday, the John Lewis Partnership archivist, for guiding me through the records of Bainbridge & Co.; the Reverend Terence Hurst for his splendid material on the history of the Brunswick Methodist Church, Newcastle-upon-Tyne; David Wright, curator of the York Railway Museum for some useful advice and John Slater, editorial consultant to *The Railway Magazine*, for pointing me towards that rarity: descriptions of how railway passengers fared in late-Victorian times (there is heaps about rolling stock and engines!). Also to my brother, Eric Greenslade, for his research assistance.

One

1874

The cry that jolted Henry Macdonald awake was one which he dreaded.

'Fire! Fire!'

Frantic whistle-blowing and the pounding of many running feet drove the message home.

Any fire at sea could be disastrous but Second Officer Macdonald knew that fire on this vessel could prove particularly terrible.

He leaped out of bed and, without stopping to dress, rushed up to the deck. There, to his horror, he saw dense smoke issuing from the forecastle. The cry was that it came from the boatswain's store under the forecastle head – a tinderbox packed with cans of paint and kerosene, coils of rope, casks of fat and buckets of tar. Ideal fodder for the flames.

He was relieved to see that the canvas hoses of the splendid new fire appliance, especially acquired for this journey, were already being unfurled and the suction end dropped into the sea.

Only the previous evening it had seemed that the luck of the *Cospatrick* had at last changed, a blessed relief after the trials of the journey so far.

The ship had left Gravesend at 5.00 a.m. on the 11th September and even before reaching Biscay had encountered atrocious weather. Then the notorious Bay had done its worst. There had been a short respite while they ran down into the Tropics but they came to halt as the Doldrums ensnared them.

The twelve-thousand-ton sailing ship, laden with 429 emigrants, had lain becalmed, drifting aimlessly. As the pitch on the deck melted and bubbled in the heat, steerage passengers nearly suffocated in their crowded accommodation. Water became scarce and the food ever more rancid.

After seventy-two hours of this hell, the wind and sea had at last relented. Passengers and crew cheered as the sails began to puff up then billow out to carry them steadily down into the vast empty wastes of the South Atlantic towards the Cape of Good Hope.

The stifling heat had dispersed to be replaced by pleasant, cool and invigorating weather. What's more, they had reached the halfway mark in their journey. Only 8,000 more miles to go before they reached New Zealand!

On the 17th November the wind dropped again to a light breeze, which slowed progress, but this was held to be no bad thing. That night the ship's concert was to be held. It proved to be a marvellous evening full of music and song, English West Country accents blending with Scottish and Irish voices, out on deck under the magical, starry southern skies.

So far on the voyage eight of the emigrant children had died, but that night, at 10.00 p.m., a baby was born. It seemed like a good omen.

Faint strains of celebrations reached Second Officer Henry Macdonald, who was on first watch on the poop deck. The last melodies faded away as midnight approached, after which Macdonald went off watch and climbed into his bunk.

The wonderful new fire appliance supplemented by a bucket and chain water supply failed to quell the flames.

With the ship's main sails furled to prevent them catching alight the efforts of the crew to turn the ship around to blow the flames out to sea were defeated and the smoke and fire were driven further along the ship.

The main deck was alight and fire shot up the rigging, which became a gigantic torch.

Panic set in.

Two

The buzz of conversation and clatter of cutlery on plates grad- ually ceased as the diners began to eat. Best took a bite of pork and pickle then peered around gingerly at his neighbours. Many of them looked fearsome. Some seemed familiar.

Halfway down the table to his left a grizzled old man with gaunt, pockmarked cheeks was wolfing down his food as if he had not eaten for a week. Was that Harry Edgars? The burglar who had escaped the scaffold by a hair's breadth after persuading the jury that he had not struck the householder but, indeed, had tried to save him as he stumbled and fell? If so, it was a much older and sadder looking Harold Edgars.

Opposite Best to his right was another face which he could not quite pinpoint. That of a burly man with protruding ears and buck teeth. Coining, was it? When Best was serving back on N Division? By the look of the bruiser it might have been something rather more violent. But, then, even coiners could defend their territory in nasty ways.

The man suddenly turned his head in Best's direction, thereby exposing his left cheek down which ran a deep, puck- ered scar. Not a coiner then, after all. He was Stephan Herschfeld, a member of one of the foreign gangs that terror- ized the East End, though Best couldn't recall whether Herschfeld was a Bessarabian or one of the Bethnal Green mob. And next to him, wasn't that Schoner, his murderous partner?

They were all villains, for sure. All from London's lower depths. But one thing was certain. No matter how villainous, none of them has done anything as bad as me, Best thought bitterly. I'm in the right company here.

Initial hunger pangs satisfied and thirst slaked with a few

3

swigs of tea, the diners began to glance around them. Mainly, Best felt, in his direction. Was he imagining lips tightening at the sight of him? Some might be taking in his single-breasted, black cutaway jacket and red cravat and contrasting it with their own shabby attire. Others could be recognizing him. All doubtless wondering what such a man was doing amongst them.

Herschfeld suddenly caught Best's eye, inclined his head to the right in dry acknowledgement then nudged Schoner. He, too, gave a sardonic bow. Best nodded in return. This seemed to please Herschfeld, who allowed a slight grin to spread across his face making the scar lift his lip grotesquely.

As the meal finished, shouts of recognition rang out between old cellmates and partners in crime. This raised the noise level once again, sending waves of sound echoing around the arches of the lower gallery. Not only was this a very odd event, thought Best, but so was the venue.

A distinguished-looking gentleman who sat at the centre of the top table commanded silence once again by rising to his feet, holding up his right hand and lowering it gently several times.

'Gentlemen,' he said, his object achieved, 'shall we adjourn?'

Almost as one, the men rose and began shuffling up the stairs to the ground floor of the chapel, where they quietly took their seats in the rows of benches facing a raised platform. They had eaten their fill and in return were now obliged to have their souls saved. But they did not seem to mind.

The popularity of this bizarre event never ceased to amaze Best. He knew that tickets for the 'thieves' supper', or, more properly, the Annual Supper for the Criminal Classes, were almost fought over and that the space could be filled six times over.

Best was still trying to find Detective Chief Inspector Cheadle among those at the ends of the benches, when the distinguished gentleman, now at the centre of an array of distinguished gentlemen on the platform, got to his feet once more and rather unnecessarily introduced himself as Mr George Hatton. Everyone knew who he was. One of St Giles's Mission's leading thief reclaimers.

'Please welcome,' Hatton continued, 'our current chairman, Mr Howard Vincent.'

A slim, dapper man rose to acknowledge the applause. He had a high-domed forehead and a long nose that sat like an exclamation mark atop a particularly luxuriant walrus moustache.

Some of Best's colleagues claimed that that moustache had been adopted to make Vincent appear old enough to be doing the job he had been given: that of Director of the new Criminal Investigation Department of Scotland Yard. However, despite its presence, the thirty-one-year-old Vincent still looked younger than all the other worthies on the rostrum that evening.

As his chief gazed benignly around the audience, Best was once again seized by a feeling of unreality.

'You have all been criminals,' Vincent announced in his elegant, patrician tones. 'But do not think that on that account you belong for ever to the criminal class. There is no such class in the natural disposition of social grades. No man was born criminal.'

Quite a clever opening for someone in his anomalous position of gamekeeper among poachers.

St Giles's Mission had begun their bid to guide criminals away from the downward path by meeting them as they came out of prison and inviting them to breakfast. Then they had taken to supplying long-termers with clothes to replace those handed out by the prison. 'Lunatic suits', the prisoners dubbed them, since they resembled those worn by asylum inmates and not only made them look foolish but instantly proclaimed their criminal past. The mission also helped the men find work.

The mission then inaugurated these annual criminal suppers with their accompanying soul saving, whipping in both the judiciary and the police to grace them. Too late for them to save my soul, thought Best. I'm bound for hell.

'Defective education, evil influences, drink, bad companionship and very likely real want led you into crime,' Vincent went on kindly. 'Then, you joined the criminal class by your action!' he proclaimed dramatically, making them all sit up. 'It is free for each one of you to leave it in a like manner. I trust many have done so.'

Aid was available from this mission, he continued in less dramatic tones. The Scotland Yard Convict Office would help them to find honest work or to emigrate to the colonies, where there was a call for their muscular arms.

'There you may rise to wealth!' he finished with fervour.

Well, not quite. His enthusiasm was running away with him again, thought Best. In fact, the colonies were making it plain that they didn't want any more criminals thrust upon them.

'Society is not against you,' Vincent added with a friendly smile, 'if you do not war against it.'

Well, I wouldn't disagree with that, thought Best.

As Vincent's place on the floor was taken by an enthusiastic ex-criminal who began describing how he had been saved by the mission, a malodorous old man to Best's left poked him on the arm and leaned close enough to insert a knife between his ribs.

''Ere,' he wheezed, pointing over to the far end of the row. 'That fellow, there, wants you.'

Best glanced across to where a large, agitated-looking man was beckoning to him.

Cheadle, at last.

He was pointing towards a side door and frowning as though it was Best's fault they hadn't met up earlier. Well, at least now he might find out why he had been dragged here.

Three

'Sorry to 'ave to drag you 'ere,' said Cheadle. 'I knows you've 'ad an 'ard day.'

An apology *and* sympathy from the chief inspector. Cheadle's new-found consideration was disconcerting. Ever since the terrible business at the Crystal Palace the chief had been changing his attitude to Best, although now and then he couldn't help letting the old sarcasm creep back.

'I was waiting for you at the Yard,' Cheadle went on, 'when Mr Vincent grabbed me and dragged me 'ere with 'im. Thinks it looks good if old 'ands like me take an interest.' He snorted but his tone was tolerant.

Best knew the reason for that as well. Vincent, Cheadle's old enemy, was sticking by three police officers and a woman searcher who had been accused of acting as agents provocateurs while trying to catch an abortionist. In consequence, the Director of the CID had suffered another press onslaught about his tendency to adopt 'odious foreign practices'. It was certainly true that Vincent's over-enthusiasm was partly to blame for the situation arising in the first place, but his solidarity with his troops had clearly gone down well with Cheadle.

'You got to go to Newcastle,' said Cheadle bluntly.

What was the man talking about?

'Newcastle?'

'That's right.'

'Newcastle under Lyme?'

'No. On Tyne.' There was none of the delight that Cheadle would previously have shown at sending 'that fancy fellow, Best' to a mucky, freezing coal town in the dead of winter. 'They've a case they can't 'andle and wants us to sort it out.'

Best lowered his head and passed his hand over his weary eyes. The last thing he needed now was a long train journey to take over some messed-up investigation from resentful local men who would make damn sure he got no assistance and if possible fell on his face as well. Couldn't blame them really. Nor their chief for wanting to hand on an insoluble problem.

He looked up at Cheadle. 'When?'

'Tomorrow morning.' Cheadle paused. Best knew that the chief inspector realized that he was on the brink of chucking it all in or even doing something more final. 'Change will do you good,' he announced suddenly. Best had to feel sorry for the man. Handling coppers gently did not come easily to him.

'How about Littlechild? He's finished that big long firm job.'

'Off to Paris. Rumours about some new Fenian activity.'

Oh, trust Littlechild. Paris.

'How about . . .?'

Cheadle shook his head. 'Only you available.' He paused then added, 'You got to do it,' with a firmness he clearly didn't feel. 'Be at King's Cross at nine in the morning.'

Best said nothing.

'I'll send Smith up after you,' Cheadle threw in. 'Soon as I can.' He patted Best on the shoulder. 'Good luck. Not as bad as you think up there, you know.' He turned and left.

Clever sod. The chief inspector had left him no option but to go – or let the side down.

Best strolled out among the stinking slums of St Giles and thought, well, maybe Newcastle won't be any worse than this.

The morning had the damp chill of late November, and the approaches to King's Cross railway station were, as usual, a scene of chaos.

Passengers struggled down from heavily laden cabs, omnibuses and private carriages. Below them, shouting and shoving porters jostled to grab their travelling trunks, portmanteaux, bags, rugs and 'discreet railway urinals' and pile them on their barrows. By the careful way some of the male passengers were moving Best guessed that they had already attached their patent railway conveniences. The joys of travel,

8

he thought, as he hurried by keeping a firm hold on his own dressing case and Gladstone bag.

Inside, the station, as usual, resembled bedlam. Passengers crowded the smoky, too-short platform. At least the local goods and passenger trains no longer jockeyed for space there now that a separate line had been created for them. But the place was still a byword for delay. Too many trains, too little space.

When I was a boy, Best recalled, this toy fort of a building was the largest and most impressive railway station in the world.

The nearby St Pancras was not only newer, quieter and less crowded, it smelled better too. The Midland Railway used the milder Nottingham coal while the Great Northern trains were fired by the fierce products of the South Yorkshire mines. The raw reek of the smoke they produced did nothing for Best's delicate early morning stomach.

I'm getting old, thought Best. Travel used to excite me.

He was late. The train left at nine o'clock and it was already eight fifty-six. Four minutes to go. If he didn't hurry he wouldn't get on the train. Thank goodness he didn't need to find a food basket. His landlady had packed him enough to sustain him on a Himalayan trek. The woman was a saint, refusing to blame him for what had happened, despite his obvious guilt. She clung to him even.

He pushed through the mêlée surrounding the guard's van, where the last of the trunks and wicker travelling baskets favoured by aristocrats were being edged aboard. The procedure was not helped by the pack of yapping foxhounds being shepherded aboard by their foxy-looking keeper.

Best dodged the trays carried by the noisy sandwich-sellers and newspaper-hawkers and sidestepped the trolley loaded with carriage warmers. Really, he thought angrily, the railway police should get better control of all this mess! Wasn't it bad enough that, even if he found a seat, once aboard he was going to have to endure being crushed up against who knows whom?

All the compartments he peered into as he rushed alongside were full. Two minutes to go! The engine was already sending out clouds of warning steam, puffing and snorting at the starting gate.

One minute to go. The puffing had built into a crescendo, a whistle screamed and carriage doors slammed shut one after the other like shots from a rifle.

He was just going to have to push into one of the already crowded compartments despite objections. Later he'd try to move to one that was less packed. At least the crush of bodies should keep him warm.

An apple-seller thrust his wares into Best's face, so startling him that he tripped over the lead of a toy poodle about to be lifted up into his seated owner's arms. The animal yelped and snarled at him as he tried to recover his balance. A hand steadied him from behind. He looked up into the face of a young railway policeman.

'Inspector Best?' the fresh-faced lad enquired. 'Getting worried about you, sir.' He pushed Best unceremoniously towards a compartment that had drawn blinds and a reserved sign in the window, opened the door and shoved him in.

'Got you a warmer and a bottle for the necessary,' shouted the constable above the din.

'How did you know who I was?' Best yelled.

The young man grinned. 'They said you looked a bit foreign, sir – oh, and,' he added cheekily, 'that you was on the slick and handsome side.' He began closing the door as the puffing grew more urgent. 'Good hunting, sir!'

The door slammed shut just as the panting engine reached its peak and the train began moving off. Thank heavens for the railway police, thought Best. Splendid fellows.

He assuaged his feelings of guilt about having a carriage to himself by deciding that he would remove the reserved sign – soon. Passengers further up the line would be overjoyed to find an almost empty carriage and he would be doing them a favour.

Meanwhile, he would make the final decision about what he was going to do about his life. He sat back wearily in his seat and promptly fell asleep.

Four

Best was drowning again. A huge ship loomed above him. Helen, Martha and Mary Jane were struggling in the water close by. He tried to reach all of them but every time he grasped one pair of hands the others slipped away. Finally, he managed to get hold of all three women, but they began to pull him down, down. He was drowning. As he shook himself free the long, plaintive whistle of a boat in distress intermingled with their terrible cries.

He awoke, sweating despite the meagre heat thrown out by the warming pan on which he was resting his feet. A nightmare. Thank goodness. His relief soon turned back to despair when he remembered the real fate of two of those women.

The chuntering diddle-le-dah of the engine was speeding up. He glanced out of the window just in time to glimpse the final Peterborough station sign. Damn. He'd missed one of the stops where he might have gone to the toilet and had a hot cup of tea – though managing even one of those was often impossible.

Never mind. At least I have a urinal and the privacy to use it, he comforted himself. Not to mention all that food. He saw to the first priority, steadying himself as best he could against swaying of the carriage. Then he inspected the food: a bottle of ale, a chicken leg, some ham and pickle sandwiches and a round of shortbread. That should set him up nicely until the forty-five-minute dining break at York.

When he had finished eating he wiped his fingers and took out a cigarette. What a clever railway policeman putting him in a smokers' compartment. Before getting down to the docket, which Cheadle had admitted, 'ain't got much in it', he opened one of the two old copies of northern newspapers he'd found on the luggage rack: the *Newcastle Daily Chronicle* and the *Newcastle Daily Journal*. It was always wise to find out as much as you could about an area before you arrived, and he'd had no chance so far to even think about his destination.

Best's impression of Tyneside, like that of most schoolboys, was centred almost entirely around coal. Coal, coal and more coal. He was aware that the combustible, carbonaceous rock was found there in abundance and, when extracted from the ground, was sent forth around the world by train, barge and ship.

Indeed, it was one of these coal-carrying ships, or colliers as they were called, which had given him the worst experience of his life. Two years earlier, a Newcastle-bound collier having unloaded its cargo at a Thameside gas works had accidentally rammed the *Princess Alice* pleasure steamer on which he was a passenger. Within minutes, six hundred and fifty men, women and children were drowning in the murky Thames.

Their cries had still invaded his quiet moments and haunted his dreams until replaced by the latest horror.

Every schoolboy also knew that the North East was the birthplace of the railways, and Best was aware that Newcastle and Sunderland were ports. But, to him, Newcastle had still signified coal until he'd had to handle a recent, very odd and very sad, murder case involving two middle-aged northern ladies attending the Police Fête at the Alexandra Palace.

I'm getting morbid, Best thought, and turned his attention back to the northern newspapers.

London's local papers always gave the impression of a city steeped in sin and sorrow – largely of the inhabitants' own making. But, good grief, their sorrows had nothing on those of the North East. Here the populace seemed to have tragedy endlessly visited upon them. The place was awash with death and destruction, but it was not, it seemed, the fault of the average working man – just their fate.

Mining accidents, large and small, fought with shipping disasters for print space. A pitman had died in a gas explosion and another been badly burned at Benwell Colliery, while at another mine a man had been killed by a fall of stone. All hands had been lost when a Hartlepool steamer foundered at sea between Odessa and Bristol, and four of the crew of a Sunderland barque had drowned when it had run ashore in a gale off the Philippines. There seemed to be no end to it.

But, of course, the incident which was still given the most space was the recent, terrible, Seaham Colliery explosion in which one hundred and seventy miners had died. The youngest were fourteen-year-old boys, the oldest a seventy-one-year-old 'shifter' by the name of Thomas Cummings. Some families had lost several members.

Then there were the reports of another local girl going missing.

Best gazed wanly out at the flat, wet Lincolnshire fields. No doubt about it; his destination was a vale of tears. How fitting. How apt. Just what he needed.

He shivered and pulled his overcoat around him. The compartment was getting colder and his hot-water tin had lost most of its warmth. Just his luck not to get a carriage with the new steam heating installed.

York railway station proved a revelation to Best and lifted his spirits a little. The place was so light and bright and airy and had an optimistic air befitting its current status as one of the most elegant and exciting of the grand new railway stations.

The sun had emerged from hiding and was flooding through the roof's arched glass panels, which curved to follow the graceful sweep of the platforms far below. The magnificent roof was supported by handsome iron pillars with tracery spars, all following the same dominant curves.

The billowing steam even managed to look ethereal against this background, and the sooty dust motes drifting down the shafts of sunlight seemed almost magical. If only Helen could see this!

The engines of the North Eastern Railway trains scattered around this grand junction were also a revelation. Each one, puffing up in readiness for journeys to Berwick, Edinburgh, Carlisle and Scarborough, was painted a different shade of bright green, but what caught the eye was their incongruous embellishments.

Here, a transfer of the head of Queen Victoria decorated the circular front. There, clinging to the side of the driver's cabin, a favourite female beauty or a scenic painting. One engine chimney even sported a pair of polished brass-antlered stags, giving the locomotive a distinctly cavalier air.

Extraordinary. Best had not expected such levity in the North, which he imagined to be a dour and uncompromising place. He could not help smiling.

This time, after the refreshment stop, Best had to find his own seat, but passenger traffic proved light. This didn't surprise Best. Who in their right mind would want to go north in the middle of winter? He found an empty compartment without too much trouble and settled back to concentrate on that day's *Northern Echo*.

Its pages, carrying long columns on the case that was taking Best north on this interminable journey, were obviously trying to make much of little information. They fell back on describing two of the key characters in detail: Sir George Threapleton and his daughter Phoebe – the latest missing girl. She had not been seen since yesterday afternoon.

Good heavens, it hadn't taken them long to get on the electric telegraph to Scotland Yard. Could that possibly be, wondered Best cynically, due to the importance of the girl's father? Surely not?

It seemed that fifty-five-year-old widower Sir George was a man without stain. A ship and mine owner with many railway interests, he might not be of the stature of the North Eastern industrial giants, Armstrong, Parsons and Swan. Nonetheless, he had brought much employment and prosperity to the Tyne and bestowed bountiful charity upon his birthplace of Newcastle.

Eighteen-year-old Phoebe was comely, suitably innocent, modest and also without blemish. Her fate was one of the deepest mystery. It was rumoured, reported the paper, that the chief constable was considering appealing to Scotland Yard for assistance in solving the case.

Best groaned. Already alerting the guilty and putting up the backs of the local constabulary.

The train stopped at Darlington, but until the very last minute it seemed that Best might retain his privacy. However, shortly after the guard had slammed the door shut again, a flustered red face appeared outside the window. The door was wrenched open again and an out-of-breath, middle-aged gentleman, wearing a flapping Inverness overcoat, clambered aboard.

'Only just made it!' he exclaimed unnecessarily, as he sat himself down opposite Best, threw back one wing of the coat's checked cape and withdrew a large briar pipe from his pocket. He contemplated it silently for a moment as he regained his breath, then began the business of filling and tamping, before muttering, 'Hope you don't mind old fellow?'

Best shrugged. 'No. That's all right.'

'Such a rush. I'm afraid I became too absorbed in the local sights,' he laughed.

Best was surprised. He imagined that Darlington was an industrial town. Iron, steel, railways and all that. He'd certainly glimpsed enough belching chimneys and glowing foundries. Perhaps it boasted some monument to the world's first passenger railway, which had run from Stockton to Darlington in 1825.

The man laughed at Best's puzzlement, causing his extravagantly long and wavy side-whiskers to tremble like a waterfall cascade. He drew in his first intake of tobacco smoke and exhaled slowly, filling the air with a curiously sweet aroma, and said, 'Ecclesiastical, old man, ecclesiastical.'

'Ah,' murmured Best. 'There's a historic church here?'

'Exactly right. Exactly. St Cuthbert's. Twelfth century. Built by Bishop Hugh de Pudsey – Earl of Northumberland, one of the Prince Bishops. Important man in these parts. Did a lot for Durham, and its cathedral. Now there's a sight for you – coming up soon. Magnificent, quite magnificent. You're going to see one of the best views in England. Lucky man!' He glanced out of the window where heavy clouds were drifting back over the sinking sun. 'If the light holds out.'

His voice was deep and rich with only a trace of Northern accent. The man was garrulous but he had a cheerful ebullience and enthusiasm about him. Best thought he might have drawn a worse companion to help pass the last weary fifty miles or so.

'As soon as I tell you,' the man instructed, 'you must look to the right and keep looking. You won't be sorry.'

He proved right. Perched on top of a wooded bluff that rose steeply from the river below was a magnificent Norman cathedral and castle. The late sun caught the western end of the nave and transept of the cathedral and spread a golden glow over the walls and baileys of the castle. The whole aspect seemed like a ridiculously theatrical display staged especially for them and it quite took Best's breath away.

'Wonderful,' he said sincerely.

The man looked pleased, as though he, alone, was responsible for such wonders. 'Resting place of Saint Cuthbert,' he enthused, pointing towards the cathedral. 'Brought here in 995 by Lindisfarne monks fleeing from the Vikings. The building's eleventh century. The Prince Bishops ruled from that castle right up until, well, less than fifty years ago.'

He's speaking as if I'm a complete stranger to these parts, thought Best. As if I knew nothing of these matters. And, of course, he's right.

'By the way, Arnold's the name, Eustace Arnold.' He held out his hand.

Best took it and introduced himself. 'Best, Ernest Best.'

On reaching Newcastle Best was greeted by more amazing views – along the Tyne as they crossed George Stephenson's remarkable double-decker bridge: railways on top and road below.

Below them, to the left and right, into the distance, was a scene of unfettered industrialism, commerce and decay. Climbing up the steep banks of the River Tyne was a jumble of factories and warehouses; puffing chimneys and belching iron foundries; glowing glass works; flour and timber mills; giant coal staithes, filthy slums and, down by the Quayside, handsome soot-blackened buildings.

Down there, also, piles of barrels and crates jostled for space as constantly bowing cranes fed the cargo on to puffing steam ships and sailing barques and lighters and tugs bustling around them. Hanging over everything, a grey pall stretched as far as the eye could see. Evidence that coal, Tyneside's chief export and the substance largely responsible for its growing prosperity, was also put to great use here. It was a terrible but awesome sight.

Seconds later, they pulled into the monumental Newcastle Central Station – a palace for the worship of the steam train.

As he stepped off the train Best was met by a harassed-looking detective sergeant, who announced bluntly, 'We've found her.'

Five

The missing girl was found. Best tried to suppress a relieved sigh. Wonderful. As soon as he had had a night's sleep he could return home. The expression on Detective Sergeant Clegg's face quickly disabused him.

'What about the others?' he asked.

Clegg shook his head. 'No sign,' he said abruptly as he took Best's dressing case and led him towards one of the hansom cabs waiting in line in the station's colonnaded forecourt.

'Detective Inspector McLeod has gone straight there an' he wants you to come down,' said Clegg, adding with a slight note of sarcasm, 'If that's all right with you – sir?'

Best nodded. 'Of course.'

He was a squat, muscly man with a thatch of straw-coloured hair, a pugnacious expression and large fists that must come in useful quelling gangs of drunken miners. He was making little attempt to hide his resentment at the indignity of this interloper from Scotland Yard arriving on the scene before they had even had an opportunity to look for this daughter of an important person.

However, Best realized, Clegg was sensible enough not to be downright rude to a senior officer. His feelings would doubtless surface in the usual manner – petty, untraceable obstruction and the subtle thwarting of his action plans.

He didn't blame the man for feeling angry. His presence was probably not in the least necessary to aid a force that, unlike some, not only had its own, albeit small, detective branch but also a detective superintendent in charge of it. He was here, he realized, to protect the chief constable and the Watch Committee from accusations that they had not done everything possible. Also, to act as a suitable scapegoat.

18

'I think that man there wants you.' Clegg pointed one of his chunky fingers in the direction of the cab that was stopping alongside them.

Eustace Arnold was leaning out, proffering his card, his long, silvery side-whiskers wafting in the brisk east wind.

'Please call on me if you need any assistance with your "business matter",' he smiled, using the expression with which Best had explained the purpose of his journey north. 'I know one or two influential people.' He winked, tapped the cab roof, saluted and was off.

'It's just up the road here,' muttered Clegg as they started off. 'She was in bed.'

At least that's what Best thought he said. He found he could only catch half of Clegg's words and of these much of their meaning failed to penetrate until after he had digested them.

It's a foreign language, Best thought, panicking. How am I going to be able to work here when I can't even understand what they are saying?

Phoebe was in bed? Where? At home? Was she still alive then after all? It was too much for his weary brain to assimilate.

Fortunately, the rattle of the cab wheels, the clatter of the horses' hooves, the jingle of their harness and the surrounding traffic noise prevented further attempts at conversation. Dodging the horse trams they proceeded along a wide thoroughfare flanked by tall, solid-looking banks and business premises on one side and a solid-looking church on the other.

Dusk was falling fast and it had started to rain. The street was now bordered with tall, brightly lit shop windows, which reflected radiantly in the wet road and pavements. Ahead, Best could just make out a huge column, topped by a statue. Before reaching it they turned sharp right then made a dangerous diagonal dash across the road in the face of the oncoming traffic.

They came to an abrupt halt in front of a drapery emporium that had tall arched plate glass windows displaying a sumptuous array of silks, satins, velvets and furs.

Best scarcely had time to digest this puzzling new scene before an ashen-faced but erect floor walker whisked them through the main entrance.

'I'd be obliged if you gentlemen would maintain a calm demeanour,' the tail-coated gentleman murmured before hurrying them through Hosiery, Millinery, French Fancy Goods and Artificial Flowers.

The displays, brilliantly lit by chandeliers equipped with the powerful new albo-carbon gas jets, were reflected many times in myriad mirrors – to dazzling effect.

As they rushed on Best glimpsed other departments to the left and right: Dress Materials, Bedding, and Gents' Outfitters. What a place!

They proceeded deeper and deeper into the shop until brought to a halt before a handsome oak staircase, which they ascended. On the second floor they were faced with a jewel-coloured stained-glass partition with an opening that allowed them access to a handsomely decorated and furnished dining room.

Placed here and there among the furniture were lifelike models wearing what were obviously the latest evening fashions from London and Paris. Some were standing, some sitting and some were about to take their seats as though at a real dinner party. Extraordinary!

On they went through a narrow passageway, carefully guarded by more grave-faced shop walkers, then into a glass-walled and roofed gallery – probably the longest room Best had ever seen. Indeed, he couldn't even see the other end.

Every variety of dining- and living-room furniture was on display from the heavy, fussy traditional in dark woods to the new, plainer styles in light oak and elm. Deep-buttoned plump sofas sat alongside games and side tables, writing desks, sideboards and cabinets.

Bedroom furniture was next. At the centre of the groups of washstands, dressing-tables and tallboys stood a parade of currently fashionable metal bedsteads. It was around one of these, a French brass tester with elegantly turned pillars decorated with a riot of curlicues, that a huddle of white-faced men had gathered.

The four-poster was shown 'dressed', and the canopied bed hangings, now drawn back by tapes like theatre curtains once the show had commenced, were made of heavy white cretonne decorated with pastel-coloured flowers.

The sheets and pillows were of the purest white linen and the quilt was of glowing ivory sateen.

'Oh my God,' exclaimed Best when he saw Phoebe lying between them.

She, too, was quite white – and obviously quite dead. Her flaxen hair was splayed out on the pillow like that of a maiden in a Pre-Raphaelite painting. Beside her head lay six long-stemmed white silk roses. She could have been asleep, though scarcely so white and so still.

Somehow, Best found the scene more shocking than even the most violent and blood-spattered he had seen. It stressed, in a heartless manner, just how young and beautiful Phoebe had been and how cruel therefore was the taking of her life. Not for the first time Best felt a loathing of his fellow men. How could they?

The question soon recurred – in a more practical sense. Indeed, how could they? In the midst of this busy, well-run emporium, how were they able to place a body and arrange it like this? There was nothing rushed or careless about this scene.

To the left of the bedhead stood an impeccably dressed, middle-aged man with a stunned expression on his face. The shop owner or general manager, Best assumed. Standing slightly back from him was a uniformed policeman.

To the right of the bedhead, a bespectacled, middle-aged man was leaning over the body dictating quietly to an earnest, moon-faced young fellow to his left.

Clegg cleared his throat. 'Sir?'

The man glanced up, finished his sentence, straightened and walked over to Best, his right hand extended.

'Inspector Best. Welcome,' he said warmly. There was friendliness in his manner and a hint of relief in his voice. Another familiar initial reaction. Someone to share the burden and maybe take the blame. 'Glad you're here. I'm Inspector McLeod, Newcastle CID.'

Thank goodness the accent was a familiar one. As his name suggested, the Inspector was a Scot. The Metropolitan Police recruited heavily both in the Highlands and Lowlands.

Thank goodness, also, that he was not an ambitious young

man anxious to make his name by solving the case. McLeod had greying hair, half-spectacles, a benign expression and the relaxed air of someone who felt he had little left to prove.

'How do you do,' said Best, shaking his head sadly at the sight before them. 'This is a very bad business.'

McLeod nodded. 'Aye. Her father will be heartbroken. She's his only bairn.'

'What can I do to help?' he said.

McLeod looked a little taken aback. He thought I was going to march in and take over straight away, thought Best.

'Well,' McLeod contemplated the body, 'I'm waiting here for the doctor and the chief.' He hesitated. 'If you wouldn't mind questioning the assistants in this department while Sergeant Clegg here talks to Mrs Walker – she's the woman who found the body.'

'Certainly.'

'Do you think you'll be able to understand them?' Sergeant Clegg asked, raising an impertinent eyebrow. He had sensed Best's problem. He'd have to watch his back with this fellow.

'Our assistants are in the habit of conversing with all kinds and classes of people,' put in Mr Barker, the floor walker who had greeted them at the front entrance. 'Many foreign visitors and Southern businessmen come here to visit our factories,' he explained to Best. 'If you have any difficulties I will be nearby.'

Barker fell into customer-ushering mode, moving Best gently forward with his arms outstretched. Before allowing himself to be swept along, Best took one last glance at the scene. He was pleased to see that McLeod was recording the details before it was disturbed, but hoped that he would remember to inspect underfoot before it became even more trampled.

McLeod followed his glance. 'I'll be taking a note,' he nodded.

The dazed-looking shop assistants were huddled around the storeroom entrance. Best resisted Barker's efforts to usher them all inside. He knew that it would prove a difficult place to conduct interviews. Also, that the body could have been stored among the stock, and he wanted to examine the room before it was disturbed even more.

He asked Barker to have it sealed off then escorted his quartet of assistants back through the tunnel to the ready-furnished drawing room.

'You sit down and wait here,' he said, directing three of them to the armchairs just outside the room.

'Oh, no. They can't do that!' exclaimed the acting department manager, Harold Luke.

'Why not?'

'We're not allowed to sit down at work,' he said. 'Rule three,' he added weakly on seeing Best's expression of disbelief. 'Fine sixpence.'

'Look,' said Best with a slight edge to his voice. It had been a long day. 'The circumstances are exceptional and *I* am in charge here.'

Sensing the man's remaining doubt he added, 'Mr Barker has given his permission.'

He hadn't, of course. Must remember to have a word with him, Best thought.

Eventually, Luke gave a brief nod to the assistants, who sat down but kept looking over their shoulders fearfully.

Best took Harold Luke into the stage-set dining room and told him to sit down on a chair beside a mahogany pedestal table. The gaunt and now trembling man shook his head vehemently. 'This is one of the special displays!'

'Oh, for heaven's sake!' shouted Best.

Luke sat – perching on the edge of the chair, as though by appearing to be uncomfortable and obviously acting under protest his offence might be mitigated. Best sat opposite him and, to calm him, began by asking him to describe an average day in the Beds department. It proved a depressing scenario.

The assistants who lived in and all juniors arrived at 8.30 a.m. – 8.00 a.m. in the summer. Those on the cleaning squad, which dealt with the general areas, came in a quarter of an hour earlier. Those living out were allowed to arrive at 9.00 a.m. These hours, Luke assured him, were far superior to those of many other local shops, as were their conditions.

Certainly, Best knew, they were a lot better than those of London shops.

'The department is cleaned in the morning, then?'

'The sweeping is done straight after closing, the night before. Dusting and taking out of stock is done the following morning.'

'Meal breaks?'

Luke gulped and banged his bony knuckles together, his reddening Adam's apple scraping on his starched collar. He realized what Best wanted to know – whether the department had been left unattended at any time.

'The assistants have twenty-five minutes for dinner. They go in four parties from 12.00 midday to 2.00 p.m. Then they are allowed twenty minutes for tea between 4.00 p.m. and 5.15 p.m.'

'Some of them must linger?'

He looked shocked. 'No!'

Best raised his eyebrows knowingly.

'They can't. A bell is rung when their time is up, so that the room can be got ready for the next party.'

'What if they haven't finished their meal?'

'Oh, they must. No food is to be left on the plate. Rule eighty-seven.'

'Right,' said Best wearily and tried another tack. 'But what about the gap when one party is coming back and the other leaving.'

'No assistant must leave the counter for meals until his partner has returned,' Luke parroted. He fished a small booklet from his inside jacket pocket, held it up, tapped it, and said, 'Rule seventy-six.'

Best nodded. 'The fine being?'

'Sixpence.'

Toilet breaks were similarly orchestrated. Ten minutes only there and back. Fine for loitering two shillings and sixpence.

That should cause some constipation, thought Best. He could see that the strict rules would make it unlikely that any part of the department had been left unsupervised but he didn't know of any rule that wasn't broken. Indeed, to his mind, the very existence of the fines actually demonstrated this.

No, Luke concluded in answer to Best, there had been no sign of anything unusual in the department all day.

Except, thought Best, the presence of the body of a young girl done up as if she was Ophelia.

Six

Freddie, an urchin-like apprentice lad with cowlick of brown hair, gazed up at Best and muttered, 'Doonbythefeulseezfeootendtesters.'

Freddie, who, as his lowly position warranted, came last among the interviewees, was apparently *not* practised in speaking to customers. The fact that he had buck teeth that added a lisp to the strong Geordie accent did not help.

Painfully, Best had established that the lad, who lived in, was always the first to appear in the department – which he started dusting straight away.

'Where do you begin?' Best had enquired.

Freddie had looked puzzled. 'In 'ere.'

'But whereabouts in here?' Best had persisted, which was when he had got the indecipherable answer, 'Doonbythefeulseezfeootendtesters.'

Best glanced up pleadingly at Fairbrough, an assistant he had already interviewed and kept on hand to assist with just such a difficulty.

The Yard inspector had a good ear for languages and accents and was already starting to tune in to the rising tones of the Geordie sentence and the flat 'a's and the 'y' sound before a vowel. But when they rattled a sentence off and ran all their words together to make one he was lost. He knew if he called in Barker they would all be struck dumb.

'Down by the full-size foot end-testers,' Fairbrough translated.

'And an end-tester is?'

'A bed with a curtain canopy rail at the foot.'

'Ah.' Best paused. 'And they are at the left end of the row of beds as you face them from the bottom?'

'Yes.' Best could see the man was wondering why he was interested in such trivial matters. The Scotland Yard crime stories featured in *Illustrated Police News* mentioned no such pedantry.

Slowly, painfully, they established the lad's progress along the row of iron and brass bedsteads. His dusting started at the bottom left of a bed then progressed around in a circle back to where he started. Then it was on to the next bed. Any missed corners would elicit a reprimand and a fine. How on earth did these people have any money left at the end of the week?

'And you saw nothing unusual?'

The lad hesitated. It was clear he had almost as much difficulty in understanding Best as the Scotland Yard man did him.

'Why, no,' he said eventually.

'And you did not see the body in the bed then?'

'Why, no,' the lad said again. 'I would 'ave said so, wouldn't I?' he asked with perfect if irritating logic. 'Anyways,' he paused, 'I couldna see eet even if eet wyas thyere, could I, man?'

Best opened his mouth and looked at him and said, 'Why not?'

Freddie sent Fairbrough a glance which asked, is this man daft or what?

'Cos the curtains wyere pyulled, of course. Did you not know that?'

Best said, 'Of course, of course.' But, in fact, he did not know that. Why hadn't he asked that before? And why hadn't they told him? They expected you to know, that's why. It was obvious.

The lad looked pleased with himself.

Fairbrough explained that there were two each of these particular, more expensive, French testers. Two full-testers – with curtains all round; two half-testers – with curtains only at the top; and two foot end-testers.

They were 'dressed' with curtains supplied by the Furnishings department – to demonstrate how they would look in the home. One of each pair had the curtains drawn back and on the other they remained down and pulled right around the bed, effectively closing it in.

The curtains were removed once a week, shaken and maybe changed for another pattern according to the latest style or the change of season, then put up again – carefully arranged and pleated. After that, they were not touched.

'The bed in which the body was found was the one where they always stay down?'

Fairbrough grimaced with distaste at the thought and nodded. 'Yes.'

'Nobody pulls them back?'

He shook his head. 'No.'

'But the customer did.'

'She was being shown through, and she stopped and—'

Best raised his eyebrows. 'Shown through?'

'Customers must always be accompanied from one department to another, never just pointed.'

'Rule?'

'Six.' Fairbrough paused, obviously unwilling to criticize a customer. But sudden irritation at the woman's foolishness caused his tongue to revert to Geordie and his voice to rise. 'I canna think why the woman did that. Could she not see that the one down by was the same but with them taken back?'

So Phoebe's body had been there all day. Had she remained any longer the smell, if she had been dead since her disappearance yesterday, would have soon told them. But had she?

Clegg appeared at the dining room display entrance wearing an air of satisfaction.

'Finished?' he asked.

'Yes, for now. Was the lady any help?' Best enquired politely.

Clegg shrugged. 'A little.'

He knows that the bed-hanging was down, thought Best, and he is hoping that I don't.

'Was just on my way to report to the DI,' Clegg smiled. 'Tell him what I found out.'

'That the curtain had been down all day?' asked Best.

In fact, it had been bloody obvious that it had been down all day and if I hadn't been so tired or such a bloody fool I would have realized that straight away, Best thought.

'Er . . . yes,' was the crestfallen reply.

It was Best's turn to shrug. 'Pretty obvious that it must have been, wasn't it?'

'Oh, yeah. Yeah,' nodded Clegg.

Don't try to take me on, thought Best with untypical venom. I learned in a hard school.

Had Clegg but known it he had rekindled a small spark in the Scotland Yard detective.

Seven

They heard Sir George Threapleton long before they saw him. His agonized wail echoed towards Best and Clegg as they walked back into the gallery, causing an exchange of glances that, on this occasion, contained a hint of fellow feeling.

The pair approached the rearranged tableaux around the victim's bed quietly and unobtrusively but there was little need for their caution. Lost to all but his grief, Sir George clung to the body, the white roses entangled in his hair.

'My Phoebe! My pet! My little girl!' he wailed.

By his side was an elegant, frock-coated gentleman wearing a redundant stethoscope, which swung forward across his chest as he tried to comfort and restrain the distraught father.

Another man stood stiffly by, apparently at a loss as to what to do next. This must be Captain Sam Joiner Nicholls, the chief constable. McLeod was nowhere to be seen.

They allowed Threapleton a few more moments to cradle his dead child before the chief constable tried to extract him, murmuring, 'We will do everything possible to find out who did this, Sir George. We have asked Scotland Yard to assist us.'

Clegg raised his hand and pointed towards Best, who felt obliged to move forward, announcing, 'Inspector Best of Scotland Yard. I will be working with the Newcastle constabulary to help catch whoever did this dreadful thing.'

As he spoke, he edged nearer and began gently but firmly removing the man's arms from around his daughter's body. Fortunately, the mighty industrial magnate was small of stature and weak with grief. With a nod of his head Best signalled to the doctor to escort him away.

The chief constable moved to assist but Best caught his arm, delaying him, a familiarity which clearly did not please him.

'As soon as you are able, sir,' Best whispered, 'ask Sir George whether the six white roses signify anything to him.'

'I hardly see—' exclaimed the chief.

'I do,' said Best crisply, fixing him in the eye. 'In fact, it's *very* important.'

The chief hesitated. Any hint of obstruction could bring down the wrath of the Watch Committee and Newcastle's worthies.

'Er, well,' murmured the chief constable, glancing anxiously after Threapleton. 'If it's important . . .'

'Yes.' Best took a deep breath and added, 'It is. I understand your difficulty,' he said quietly, 'but if you explain that it is for the sake of the other girls.' Best paused, then with a hint of threat in his voice said, 'We mustn't forget there *are* other girls, must we, sir?'

That was sufficient. A Scotland Yard man was not constrained by local politics and, who knows, might even begin talking to the press.

'Of course. You will have your answer very soon,' the chief promised and hurried off to catch up with Sir George and the doctor.

Best noticed the deputy department manager of Beds, Harold Luke, almost propping himself up against the customer counter in a manner which, Best was convinced, must transgress some disciplinary rule. But Luke seemed transfixed by the sight of a great industrialist brought low in his department.

'How does the stock arrive here?' Best asked him without preamble.

Luke turned dazed eyes upon him. Best repeated the question, this time more sharply. 'I said, how does the stock arrive in this department?'

Luke shook his head, refocused, then pointed his bony hand towards the stock room.

'By hoist, from the basement.'

'During opening hours?'

'Oh no.' He seemed shocked by such an idea.

'So, after hours only,' said Best half to himself. 'Late evening or early morning?'

'Yes. We check the stock after closing at the end of the day and send down a requisite form.'

'Who brings the stock up here? Porters?'

'Yes.' The man's Adam's apple shot out even further from his stringy neck, bobbing up and down convulsively.

'Always the same porters?'

'I don't know. I'm not here.'

'Your goods all come from outside suppliers?'

'Oh no. A lot of it comes from our factories over there.' He pointed out of the window towards a jumble of flat-fronted buildings.

What a curious place this is, thought Best. The street frontage was quite narrow, about the width of three average shops, but, once inside, the establishment expanded and extended ever deeper and wider. Bainbridges of Newcastle certainly appeared to justify its claim to be the 'Emporium of the North'.

An inspection of the bed department stock room revealed little of any use apart from reinforcing Best's impression that this was a remarkably well-ordered, well-run business in which it should prove difficult to hide and move a body without attracting notice.

Nonetheless, a body had been hidden, and moved and placed with the intention of causing the maximum shock. But – oddly, given this fact – only revealed accidentally. Who would have guessed that the woman customer would choose to pull back the curtain like that?

What if she hadn't? The smell would soon have revealed its presence, thought Best grimly.

'That bed,' he asked as they left the stock room and began walking back along the gallery. Luke reluctantly looked where Best was pointing and swallowed. 'The bedclothes – are they exactly the same ones as when it was made up?'

Luke nodded miserably.

'And when were they due to be drawn back and changed?'

'Tonight. After closing.'

Ah, so they would not have had to wait long for the unveiling. That suggested that the perpetrator had knowledge of the department procedure.

'Have you ever seen Miss Threapleton before?'

Luke shook his head miserably. 'Never.' He hesitated, as though surprised by his own certainty. 'Well, not as far as I know.' He stopped again. Clearly a stickler for accuracy, he added, 'I did see a photograph of her – after she went missing.'

Luke's eyes suddenly filled up. Best thought the man might cry. He reached over and patted his hand.

'Can't see how you could possibly be blamed for any of this.'

Luke smiled wanly then managed to bring some of his automatic customer handling expertise into play with a weak, 'Thank you, sir.'

They both knew it didn't work like that. Somebody would have to be blamed and it was always easier to blame the employee than the owner or management. Exactly like in the police.

'I will inform the management that you have been very helpful – and efficient.'

'First time I've been left in charge,' Luke confessed suddenly. 'Mr Brent is ill and . . .'

'You surprise me,' said Best, then added, 'You will let me know if you think of anything which might help? Anything strange you might have noticed or anything odd that happens now. No matter how trivial it seems.'

Luke nodded but Best had the feeling that the man was too lost in his own misery and had stopped listening. Or had he more on his mind?

Guilt, perhaps?

Eight

'Sir George insists that white roses mean nothing to him,' shrugged McLeod before biting firmly into his pork pie. The detectives were holding a conference while partaking of some desperately needed sustenance in the Royal Turk's Head Hotel in Grey Street just a few yards around the corner from Bainbridges.

Indeed, it was actually on the same block, and the rear room opened on to the same inner courtyard. Which meant, Best realized, that access to the Bainbridges delivery area by outsiders would not be difficult. He did not care to speculate on how many more suspects that could add to the equation.

Many of the hotel's other customers were dressed in surprisingly sumptuous finery. The gentleman's *de rigueur* black tails were alleviated by double-breasted white silk waistcoats and ruffled shirts, while the gradual return of the bustle was being signalled in the silk and velvet dresses of the ladies. At 7.15 p.m. precisely the ladies' finery began to be cloaked by the high-fashion seal-skin jackets and sable muffs.

'They're off to the Theatre Royal,' said McLeod, noting Best's surprise. 'It's just across the street. We get all the latest shows from London, you know.' He smiled. 'Just now I believe it's John Cole in *Valjean: Man of the People*. But the pantomime will be a local production.'

Good lord! Christmas is that near, thought Best. The less he thought about that the better.

Phoebe had last been seen alive leaving Bainbridges yesterday afternoon.

'I hate to be obvious, but she did definitely leave the shop, didn't she?' Best asked.

McLeod swallowed a mouthful of ale and nodded. 'Aye. Barker says he put her into a hansom cab.'

'She was alone?' he frowned. Odd, a girl of that age and class being out without a chaperone.

'Her maid had been in the shop with her but Phoebe insisted that she wait in the store to collect a fur bonnet she had bought.'

Best frowned. 'There must be a delivery service.'

'Oh, aye. But Phoebe wanted it immediately and it was taking a wee while to pack so that the fur was protected properly and not crushed.'

'So she was in a hurry to meet someone?'

'Ann Meldrew, that's the maid, said not so far as she knew.'

'But?' said Best, whose antennae were well tuned to the unsaid.

McLeod inclined his greying head, shrugged his shoulders and said dryly, 'Contrary to her claimed sainthood, it seems that the lassie, God rest her poor soul, was a wee bit impatient at the best of times.' He sat back, pushed his plate away and wiped his mouth on his serviette.

'So, while she may have dashed away to meet someone, she could just have been showing the impatience of a rich, indulged child.'

McLeod nodded. 'Absolutely.'

'Barker?'

'An unimpeachable servant of Emerson Muschamp Bainbridge.'

'Who is where at the moment, might I ask?'

'On business in London. He has interests in coal, railways and shipping.'

All of which are centred here, thought Best. 'Family in the business?'

'Oh yes. Tom and George.'

'And where are they?'

'Well, Tom's out saving souls, as is his habit.'

Best raised his eyebrows.

'The family are devout Methodists. Tom especially. He does a lot of missionary work – even has a Gospel car, like a caravan. Means he can carry the message to those who otherwise might be unfortunate enough to miss it through living off the beaten track,' said McLeod with a wry smile.

'Admirable.' Best thought evangelists were impertinent, but he thought McLeod was being a little daring, making his feelings obvious to someone he didn't really know.

'Nonconformism is big around here,' McLeod added.

It usually was in working-class areas.

'Their set are Wesleyan and a lot of them have grown wealthy.'

'And complacent?'

'You might say that.'

Many Methodists did, which was why they had broken away into separate groups such as the Primitive Methodists, Bible Christians and Methodist New Connexion – which obliged those remaining Church to call themselves Wesleyan Methodists.

'Tories to a man.'

'They say that some Wesleyans care more for men's souls than their bodies.'

'Oh, a Presbyterian like me can hardly comment,' said McLeod with a grin.

'You haven't traced the cabbie?'

He shook his head. 'No. Barker didn't know him and he hasn't come forward yet.'

'Did anyone else see Phoebe leave?'

'The doorman and a messenger boy.'

Both of whom could have been persuaded that they had witnessed whatever their formidable chief floor walker wanted them to have seen. And even the worthy Bainbridge family might want to conceal the fact that she was last seen within their emporium. Well, she was back there now with a vengeance.

McLeod read his mind. 'We saw the doorman and the messenger boy separately and warned them of the dire consequences of any deception.' He smiled as he pushed his spectacles back up his nose, his expression more like that of a curious scholar than a tough policeman. 'I think we frightened them out of their wee wits.'

'You don't really need me,' laughed Best just as Clegg

36

arrived. He had been interviewing porters in the basement and was clearly unhappy.

He shook his head in answer to McLeod's unspoken question. 'Nobody saw anything unusual at any time. But,' he shook his head despairingly, 'with all that clartin' about they do down there, who's to know?'

'How many porters?' asked McLeod.

'Twenty.'

'So the suspects could be any one of the twenty? No way of narrowing it down?' asked Best.

'To only twenty!' snapped Clegg contemptuously. 'You must be . . .' He caught McLeod's icy glance and continued less aggressively but was unable to keep a note of triumph from his voice. 'Any one of more than a hundred more like!'

'Over eighty of the assistants live in,' McLeod explained. 'Some of them hardly more than bairns – apprentices.'

Best groaned. 'Of course!' Freddie and his like.

'Mind you,' he added, 'their movements within the building are strictly controlled, particularly at night.'

'I'm sure! Against the rules.' Best pulled out his copy of Bainbridges' Rules and Regulations.

McLeod nodded. 'And we both know what that means.'

'Nothing,' said Best.

McLeod raised his glass, 'Welcome to our guest from the Great Metropolis. Glad to have you here.' He seemed to mean it.

Best saluted in return. 'I hope I will be able to help.'

Clegg said nothing.

They heard the voices speaking in unison long before they reached the staff dining room.

'Evening prayers,' explained McLeod. 'Apprentices are "required" to attend morning and evening prayers and all others who live in are "invited" to take part.'

An invitation they could hardly refuse, thought Best.

'Let us thank our Father,' intoned a gentleman standing on a box facing the assembly, 'for all the many good things He has bestowed upon us.' Good grief, it was Eustace Arnold.

As soon as he had finished the prayers and given a short

address Eustace came over, a broad smile on his face and his hand outstretched.

'Ernest, how wonderful to see you so soon!' He shook Best's hand heartily. 'Obviously you had no need of my assistance with your "business matter" – though I confess to being puzzled as to what can be bringing you here!'

Best sidestepped that question by asking one of his own. 'I had no idea you were a minister.'

'Oh, I'm not, I'm not. Not even a lay preacher. Just someone who helps out the local minister when needed to assist in his efforts to keep these young men on the straight and narrow.'

Little chance they have to get off it in this place, thought Best.

They were being shepherded into the staff library, where rows of chairs had been assembled.

'What a terrible business all this is,' murmured Arnold stroking his long, silky side-whiskers. 'Poor, poor girl. Of course, everyone's agog with it. I would have said a prayer for her but I understand that the staff haven't been told the full facts yet.'

He stood back to allow Best into one of the rear rows.

Best held up his hand apologetically and said, 'I think I'd better join them on the platform,' indicating McLeod and Clegg, who were ploughing ahead.

Arnold frowned and adjusted his pince-nez the better to see Best. 'But I understand that they are policemen . . .'

'So am I,' said Best and blushed. Telling fibs or avoiding the truth was part of his job, but being found out could still embarrass him.

Arnold smiled. 'Well, well. And I was quite certain you were prominent in Manchester goods or were a buyer of glass for some London emporium.'

''Fraid not,' said Best apologetically.

The buzz of excitement had grown loud now that the shop workers had had the chance to discuss the rumoured drama.

It was quickly silenced when a handsome, sober-looking gentleman got to his feet and held up his hand. He was around forty years old and possessed of a straight and noble nose, a fine forehead, a neat curved moustache and a smartly trimmed beard.

'Mr Tom Bainbridge,' murmured Arnold.

Best moved quietly up front and took his place at the end of the long table facing the audience just as Mr Bainbridge began introducing McLeod.

The detective inspector did not mince words. The rumours were true, he announced. Miss Phoebe Threapleton had indeed been found dead in the Beds department. There were gasps from his audience. He had their undivided attention.

The police were here to request help from members of staff who lived in, McLeod explained. Their importance as possible witnesses could not be over-estimated, he assured them. They would return in the morning to speak to those who lived out.

Best was impressed. How clever to make them feel important, these young people, who normally were scarcely allowed to breathe for themselves.

'Should you remember *anything* unusual you must get in touch with us *directly*,' he insisted.

Mr Bainbridge and Mr Barker stiffened at this. 'Don't wait until you can catch the attention of your superintendents or floor walkers. They are busy people, and inexperienced in such matters, thank goodness. Something which may appear trivial to them could prove important to us,' he explained.

He smiled and nodded towards the two men, who had no choice but to look benign and approving. This was a clever man, thought Best.

'For the sake of your business, justice, and the prevention of any similar tragedy, haste is essential,' McLeod added.

How could the hierarchy object to those sentiments?

'I know I have the full backing of the Bainbridge family in this,' he finished, inclining his head respectfully towards Mr Tom, who shifted in his seat, then, outflanked again, slowly nodded back.

'My men will be coming in twice a day and the police station is only around the corner. So rack your brains. Your information will be treated as confidential.'

What now, thought Best.

39

Nine

Anne Meldrew had obviously been weeping. Her large, dark eyes were scarlet rimmed and her face patchy from the attentions of the handkerchief now scrunched up in her left hand.

Nevertheless, she sat erect and dry eyed before Best as she complained, 'I already told Mr McLeod all this yesterday.'

'I know,' agreed Best. 'But, in the light of the latest developments . . .'

She blanched at the word 'developments' but came right out with the words, 'Her being dead, d'you mean?'

'Yes,' said Best. 'In the light of that, I am going over everything again.' He paused then explained. 'You see, sometimes another person can see something which the first one didn't, and sometimes,' he locked eyes with her, 'the witnesses themselves might recall something new.'

'I never witnessed nothing,' Anne Meldrew said bluntly. 'I told him that.'

She was sparky for a servant and obviously felt the need to defend herself. Why?

'Yes, I know,' he said patiently. 'But you *were* one of the last people to see Phoebe alive,' he added in a slightly sharper tone. 'And you were close to her, knew her better than most, and,' he softened his voice and smiled at her, 'we need your help.'

Anne blushed and looked about her. Clearly she was not in the habit of receiving dazzling smiles from such a handsome man, and certainly not one in a position of such authority.

'You're that bloke from Scotland Yard,' she said.

'Yes.'

She thought for a moment then said, 'You're the one what caught Alice Harper and saw her hanged, aren't you?'

Her remark jolted Best as she must have intended. It wasn't really surprising that she knew about the case or his name. Alice Harper and her mistress, the woman she had murdered, came from a small village just outside Newcastle; northern newspapers must have been full of it, and reports of murder trials always featured the names of the detectives.

Being a servant herself she must have been particularly interested. But it was almost three months since Alice was hanged and Best had been hoping that no one up here would make the connection. So far no one had, until now. Someone must have told her. Someone who wanted to make his enquiries more difficult. She was staring at him accusingly. He cleared his throat. No use trying to hide it now.

'Yes, I was involved in that case,' he admitted. 'It was very sad.'

That caught *her* unawares. 'Oh, aye, I suppose so,' she replied.

Her manner was a strange combination of vulnerability and impertinence. He suspected that she might have got the idea that he was a soft Southerner unable to comprehend wily and tough Geordies. Then again, maybe he was being over sensitive. She was scarcely more than a child and had suffered a great shock. What's more, may have been blamed for letting Phoebe go off on her own.

Best wondered whether Anne Meldrew had been crying over Phoebe or because she might lose her job. Or was it fear? Or guilt? He frowned to himself. Surely this wasn't another case of servant/mistress murder?

They went through the business of Phoebe leaving her in the Hats department.

'Did she mention earlier that she might want to leave soon?'

'No.' Anne shook her head. 'Well, not so I'd noticed anyway.'

What did that mean?

'I . . .' She stopped and looked anxious. She had clearly not meant to say that. 'Miss Phoebe talked a lot. But I didn't always listen,' she confessed.

'That's not unusual with servants,' Best assured her. The girl looked surprised.

Indeed, it wasn't. Best knew that masters and mistresses

who deigned to share thoughts with their servants usually only talked about themselves. They little imagined or cared that the servants might have lives of their own despite the fact that they were allowed so little time to enjoy them. More importantly, they might choose to confide in servants at the very moment they were distracted by the practical tasks they were performing. Ladies' maids in particular were the recipients of precious secrets.

'It was mostly about nothing,' Anne explained, then looked guilty at speaking ill of the dead. 'You know,' she burst out, 'she was a canny lass, reely, no badness there. She was just—'

'A bit spoiled?'

'Aha. That's right.' Then she added thoughtfully, 'She missed her mam, you know.'

Best nodded. 'Very sad. Poor girl.'

The atmosphere between them was improving. Anne Meldrew was pleasant – once she relaxed a little.

Like Best, she looked different. Not quite English. But in her case it wasn't Italian blood that diffused the Anglo-Saxon. Her soft brown hair and wide cheekbones spoke of some Slavic influence. Well, Newcastle was a port.

Best realized that Anne's habit of only half listening to her mistress might limit her usefulness as a source of information. But one never knew. So, he soldiered on.

'Was Phoebe having a romance with anyone?' Even to him that sounded stilted and old-fashioned. How did young people speak of such things these days? He wasn't sure.

'Oh, no, hinny!' she laughed. Then, more soberly, 'Well, I don't think so, anyway.'

'Had there ever been anyone?'

'Oh, aha. But that was finished in the back end.'

'What,' said Best patiently, 'is the back end?'

'Autumn, like,' she said as if he should know. The Geordies, he'd noticed, seemed to be under the impression that their local sayings were universal.

'His name?'

'Arthur Meredith. She met him at one of her auntie's At Homes. He was Mrs Hesketh's nephew – at least that's what she called him, but he wasn't really.'

'And they saw each other a lot?'

'Oh, no. Not really.'

'How often?'

'Three times. No, I tell a lie. It was four. Twice at Mrs Hesketh's – she didn't know what was going on, Phoebe reckoned. Then she invited him home to tea once and he called on her da and her once. Her da made him come.'

'That was all?'

'Aha. I think so. It was no good, you see.'

'Why not?'

'He had no money and her da said he was just after hers and stopped her seeing him.'

Or thought he did. Phoebe was a wilful girl by all accounts. I need to know more about 'Da' and about Arthur Meredith, thought Best.

'So,' he concluded, 'nothing more you can tell me?'

'No.' She seemed genuinely sorry that she couldn't help more. Well, that was an improvement.

'You noticed nothing unusual?'

'No.'

'What about her regular calls?'

She shrugged. 'How d'you mean?'

'People she visited often and places she went to.'

'She only went to friends she'd had since she was a bairn.' She stopped. 'Oh, except there was . . . '

'Yes?'

Best tended to sense when a breakthrough and was imminent – and he did now.

'There was one funny thing . . .'

'Which was?'

Tell me, for God's sake, woman, he wanted to shout.

'She started going out every Wednesday afternoon, and when she came back she often seemed a bit het up, like. Sometimes she was all bright eyed and excited but other times a bit weepy.'

'And she never told you where she went?'

She shook her head. 'No. I *was* curious, like, about that, I'll admit. But she never said. Nearly did tell me once mind,' Anne remembered, 'then she stopped herself – just as if she weren't supposed to say. That wasn't like her. She usually had to let it all oot. But not that.' Tears started in her eyes and her face began to crumble. 'I would have listened up then,' she added sadly.

Ten

Best's was not the only vehicle drawing up before the red-brick semi-detached villa that was number seventeen, Neville Avenue.

He paid the cabbie quickly so that he could attach himself to the group of people approaching the stained-glass, panelled door. These were a young couple in deep mourning and two short, stout, middle-aged women, one wearing a mauve ensemble and the other in purple.

The door was opened by a raven-haired, anxious-looking young woman dressed in a simple, pale-brown gown draped around with a darker brown wrap. This ensemble caused her almost to merge into the hall behind her, which was a symphony in browns ranging from pale-cinnamon and tan geometric floor tiles and floral wallpaper to a mahogany hall-stand.

The young woman welcomed the other callers by name.

'Mr and Mrs Ross,' she nodded. 'Mrs George, Miss Young,' then directed them to the room on her right saying, 'Florence is waiting.'

They greeted her as Hermione and apologized for being late.

Best thought quickly. He had kept close behind the two ladies to give the impression that he was with them, and now brazened it out by bowing his head and smiling slightly in acknowledgement and saying, 'Ernest Marchetti.' That had been his mother's name and it just so happened that she had spoken of distant relations going to live in the North East.

Hermione smiled back and was lifting her arm to direct him towards the front parlour when a slight frown creased her brow and she began to bring her arm down.

45

'Do we know you, Mr Marchetti?' she enquired. 'I don't recall . . .'

The urgent ringing of a hand-bell came from the inner sanctum, causing Hermione to glance up quickly at the hall clock, which read 2.55 p.m.

'Goodness me,' she exclaimed and ushered a relieved Best through.

Heavy velveteen curtains kept daylight out of the front parlour. What dim light there was came from one small hanging oil lamp, a few scattered groups of candles in silver holders and the fire flickering in the heavy iron grate.

At the centre of the room was a large, oval table, draped in plush, ruby-red velvet. Around it, on mahogany dining chairs, sat the four people who had entered with Best plus six more, alternating male and female. Best found a space between Miss Young and Mrs George.

At the far end of the table, in lonely state, sat a slight, fair-haired young woman with bunched curls spilling over her fore-head. Her small, pale face wore a pensive expression. This must be Florence.

At the very moment the mantel clock began to chime the hour Hermione closed the door and joined them at the table. As the third stroke died away Florence closed her eyes and bowed her head. Suddenly, Best's right hand was grasped by Miss Young.

He pulled back in surprise and she turned, frowning, to stare at him. Recovering quickly, he smiled an apology, took the proffered hand and at the same time accepted the rather firmer grip of Mrs George to his left.

What with the full mourning worn by the young couple, the mauve and violet half-mourning of these two middle-aged ladies and the preponderance of black-enamelled, mourning brooches and tie-pins, he had already begun to realize what this was all about. The hand-holding confirmed it: this was a seance.

It had not been so difficult to prise the destination of Phoebe's Wednesday outings from Threapleton's coachman, who was only too relieved by Best's assurance that he would not go out of his way to inform Sir George of his complicity.

'Let us say a prayer, said Hermione, 'for the safety of fellow members.' Best realized that she could be referring to Phoebe's safety and that they may not yet know about her death.

Florence began shaking and quivering, her head fell forward and when she lifted it she stared ahead unseeingly. Strange groans and murmurings escaped her lips. Suddenly, her eyes shot open, she looked around wonderingly, then, in a boyish voice, exclaimed, 'Here I am. Young Bertie is here!'

Judging by the indulgent smiles of the sitters young Bertie was a familiar spirit, probably one of the skittish, mischievous variety.

'Who have you got for us then, Bertie?' cajoled Hermione.

'Janey. Janey wants to tell her parents not to fret. Her brother Arthur has arrived and they are having a lovely time!'

At the name Arthur a sob escaped the lips of the young wife and her husband began straining forward as though willing Florence and Arthur to materialize the child itself.

Bertie went on to describe how Janey was starting to walk. Then he brought a light of recognition into the eyes of an elderly gentleman by telling him that Annie had also settled in nicely and that she was anxious to reassure him that she had felt no pain when she died.

This was all familiar territory for Best. As with many people, his first contact with spiritualism had been when he had desperately hoped to get in touch with a loved one – his young wife Emma.

Since then, he had learned a lot about spiritualism through fraud cases. He knew that the practice had begun in the United States back in 1848 after the two Fox sisters, twelve-year-old Katherine and thirteen-year-old Margaret, had heard knockings and rappings in their reputedly haunted farmhouse in upstate New York. The girls had established contact with these 'spirits' with a rapping code, and they went on to become famous.

Subsequently, spirit rapping swept America. Four years later it arrived in England via an accomplished American medium. She made many influential British converts including the famous philanthropist Robert Owen. Even Queen Victoria and her prim and proper prime minister, William Ewart Gladstone, had indulged.

Spirits began speaking through mediums or 'sensitives' and even materializing amidst layers of white muslin. They moved objects about and sometimes played pianos and accordions. The practice was met with disbelief and derision in some quarters – particularly the pages of *Punch* magazine. Despite this the British gradually went spiritualism mad.

Opposition also grew apace and Scotland Yard received an increasing number of complaints of fraud in connection with seances. Indeed, just before Best had come north, the Yard had received warning from the New York police that a couple of allegedly fraudulent mediums, said to have spirited much expensive jewellery from a wealthy woman, were heading their way on a transatlantic ship.

Bertie's voice had now given way to the lighter, softer, more insinuating tones of 'Matilda'. With her arrival came the scent of gardenias and a cool breeze that caused the candle flames to wave and flutter, their flickering movement reflected and scattered by the mantelpiece mirror and glass-domed ornaments.

'Oh, and who have we here!' exclaimed Matilda suddenly. 'I think we have a stranger among us.' She laughed girlishly.

People began glancing at those sitting next to them. Finding them familiar, they looked around further until their eyes came to rest on Ernest Best. He felt naked and exposed but tried to appear unconcerned.

'I have a message for this stranger – for Ernest,' trilled the voice. Then it paused, as though listening. 'What did you say? Oh – Mary Jane says she fell for you,' Matilda exclaimed.

Best became rigid with shock and anger. He felt sick.

'She wants to know if you still love her.' There was glee in Matilda's voice.

Best's right hand tightened like a vice over Miss Young's fingers causing her to cry out with pain.

That brought him to his senses. He was a police officer on deadly serious business.

'Ask her,' he barked back, 'whether Phoebe has arrived yet? If she hasn't, tell her she is on her way!'

At this, ladies screamed and there were gasps and shouts of 'I say!' and 'Good God, man!'

Florence was overcome by shuddering paroxysms and began shaking her head and whimpering with distress.

Hermione rushed to her.

'What are you doing!' she shouted at Best. 'You'll kill her!'

The screams and shouts increased. Pandemonium reigned.

Eleven

Best contemplated the now silent group of people ranged around the table. He was in a quandary. They must be questioned before they had time to consider what they were going to say or to discuss the matter between them.

Ever since he had yelled at them to be quiet and announced himself as a detective inspector from Scotland Yard they had been staring at him as though mesmerized – which was rather apt. Franz Mesmer was one of spiritualism's founding fathers.

Florence had now been persuaded out of her trance. Hermione sat beside her, her right arm around the young medium's shoulder and an accusatory eye levelled at Best.

The sensible thing for him to do would be to send a servant to the nearest police station and ask them to telegraph McLeod and Clegg. Unfortunately, Best suspected that someone was trying to thwart his enquiries. Possibly, someone at police headquarters. He guessed who that someone might be – a man eaten up by jealousy and resentment: Clegg. However, revealing these suspicions to McLeod might make the situation worse.

He made a decision. He would plough straight in. Take advantage of their shock and rapt attention.

'Phoebe is dead,' he announced bluntly. 'Her body was found yesterday evening in Bainbridges.'

Shocked gasps and cries of distress filled the air. Young Mrs Ross let out a bleating sound and pressed her black-edged handkerchief to her quivering lips. But there were no deafening screams. Noises that were too loud and too long might make his words inaudible and they wanted the whole story now.

'I'm sorry it had to come out in that shocking manner,' Best said. 'But my hand was forced.' He glanced coldly at Florence, who averted her eyes. 'I can't give you any more details at present but I offer my sincere condolences for the loss of your friend and appeal for your assistance in solving both the mystery of her disappearance and her death.'

'I can't see how we can help. We scarcely knew her.' An elderly gentleman wearing a monocle spoke up.

Most of the others nodded assent.

'A charming, delightful girl,' said Miss Young, 'but we really do know very little about each other . . .'

'So I see,' said Best dryly.

'It's better that way,' put in Hermione. 'It protects privacy.'

'Nonetheless, you know a good deal more than I do,' he assured them, 'and I want you to pass on every little detail. No matter how trivial it may seem.' He paused. 'I want to get a picture of this unfortunate young woman.'

Good heavens, he was beginning to sound like Cheadle with his 'pictures'.

'I will be speaking to Miss Hermione and Miss Florence first,' he said, 'but it would be helpful if two of the sitters could stay behind so I can speak to them afterwards.' He nodded to his left and right. 'Perhaps you, Miss Young, and you, Mrs George?'

They nodded assent. Good. Middle-aged ladies were much more observant about small details and tended to sense feelings and atmosphere – certainly much better than most men and even younger women.

'If the rest of you would be kind enough to leave your names and addresses,' he pushed over a pad to the ascetic-looking young man opposite him, 'I will call on you as soon as possible.

'I want to speak to Florence first – alone,' he told Miss Young and Mrs George after the others had left the room.

'Oh no, you can't do that!' exclaimed Hermione. 'She is still in a very vulnerable state . . .'

'Oh yes I certainly can!' Best cut her off. 'A young girl is dead! This is a murder inquiry and I have the full backing of the Newcastle Borough Police, their chief constable, the Watch Committee and the judiciary!'

He wasn't at all sure about all that, but it sounded convincing and certainly made the two young women sit up. They might not want the eyes of the law to look too closely into their business.

It was usually only mediums giving public performances that charged an entry fee. Private mediums were considered much more respectable on the grounds that they had no motive for deceit. But they could gain undue influence over gullible sitters – which was where the fraud cases came in.

'I will treat Miss Florence with the utmost sensitivity,' he assured Hermione. He stood up and waited for her to leave.

Reluctantly, she withdrew her arm from her friend's shoulders and also rose. 'Her sanity is in your hands,' she announced dramatically. But there was somewhat less aggression in her voice since Best's mention of police attention. She turned and left the room.

Best sat down again but said nothing. Silent policemen disturbed people. They often felt the need to fill the void or, as in this instance, find out why it had occurred.

Florence did this by gradually raising her head. She found Best sitting opposite her, mildly surveying the parlour.

She drew his attention by dabbing at her eyes, sniffing and then saying, 'Yes?'

'Ah.' He rested his elbows on the table, leaned his chin on his hands and brought his gaze back to her.

'Tell me about yourself first,' he said quietly. 'Like you, I need to get in tune with the spirit of a person. But in my case with living persons.'

She clasped her hands together and began looking about her anxiously as if for assistance. Lost without Hermione it seemed.

'How old are you?' Best enquired helpfully. 'Where do you come from and how did you become a medium?'

He already knew part of the answer. Most of the earlier successful mediums or 'sensitives' had been middle-aged, middle-class women. Their leisurely lives allowed them time and opportunity to indulge in parlour pursuits, and the deaths of some of their many children or siblings gave them added reason to try to make contact with the spirit world.

More recently the pastime had been taken up by young, working-class girls. It was certainly a less tiring and more comfortable option than the only other occupation open to most of them – domestic service.

Some of these girls had become famous – largely due to their daring spirit-phenomena productions. Florence didn't appear to be one of these, but did produce voices and might be planning to start on 'physical manifestations'.

'Well,' she said reluctantly, 'I come from Lower Elswick – just down the road from here you know – by Armstrong's Works.'

Even Best knew that Armstrong's were in the business of supplying artillery to the world.

'Me da had a good job there. He was a mechanic,' she said with some pride. 'An' he believed in education for bairns – even for girls.'

Her pale-blue eyes glanced at him uncertain whether this was what he was after.

He nodded his interest. 'And your mother?'

'Oh, me mam died when I was ten. Six days after our Eddie was born.'

'I'm sorry.'

'Aye.' She nodded absently. Now launched on her tale she was lost in it. 'There were seven of us. All still living,' she added. 'I'm the second eldest.' She paused, looked sad and said, 'It was hard, you know, but we was doing all right. Well, not bad anyway. Then me da had an accident at work and took pneumonia and died. I was fourteen. Me Auntie Rosie took the youngest three, two of the lads joined the merchant navy and us two older girls went into service.'

Enough softening. Time to cut this short a bit.

'And that's where you started as a medium? When you were in service?'

'Aha. Yes.' She paused. 'But I'd done it a bit at home. Me da used to go to Mrs Foster's down the road to try to get in touch with me mam. We tried it out at home and I was quite good at it. Then when I went to work for Mr and Mrs Wright they got interested – it was after their little boy died – and I helped them, like.'

Best smiled. 'And you do seem to be quite good at it too.' There was a slight edge to his voice.

Florence shifted uncomfortably on the cushionless chair. Mediums were not permitted to sit on padded chairs or cushions lest they be affected by the accumulated influences of those who had sat there before them.

'Maybe today wasn't one of my best times,' she said nervously, refusing to meet his eye. 'At least I don't think it was.'

'So,' he hardened his voice, 'who told you about Mary Jane?' But his voice faltered over her name as a vision of her on that terrible day sprang into his mind.

Florence gazed at him wide eyed. 'Mary Jane?'

'Yes!' he almost shouted at her. 'That's right. Mary Jane. You said her spirit was there and . . .'

'No, not me,' she said, backing away from him. 'I was in me trance. I divn't kna what the spirits say – they just speak through me . . . they just take me over. I'm just a vessel.' Her voice rose, 'I divn't kna what they say, do I, man?'

She was panicking and resorting to the practised prattle mediums gave to disbelievers and the spiritualist investigators who dogged their every move. He hadn't meant it to go like this.

'It's not *me* that says it, it's *them* . . .'

Best's anger at her stonewalling continued to rise. He dug his fingernails into his palms in an effort to maintain control. Sensing he might lose his temper altogether at any minute he jumped to his feet. 'I'll be back,' he snapped. 'By which time I suggest you come up with a more satisfactory answer. I am not a spiritualist investigator – I just want to know the truth. And that is, who told you about Mary Jane!'

Twelve

Hermione appeared to have sensed Best's suppressed anger and to be attempting to cooperate whilst maintaining a slight air of injured pride. He, in turn, was frustrated that she had had time to think about what she would say to him. Curses on Clegg.

Hence, she revealed that Phoebe had been coming to them for about eight weeks – but she could not remember who had introduced the girl. She assured Best that they kept to the rules of the *Spiritualists' Almanac* for meetings:

1) Regular starting times
2) Always in the same room, which was neither too hot nor too cold
3) With the same group of sitters
4) They should be seated if possible alternately according to opposites: male/female, light and dark haired, active and quiet personalities.
5) The medium's back was always to the north and she was never seated on a padded chair or cushion.

All this so as not to disturb the spirits, who could so easily be upset by change or a lack of harmony. But, she reiterated, they did not know very much about the sitters who attended – in case the medium was accused of foreknowledge about whom they might wish to contact. That was reasonable.

'And who,' Best cut in, 'was Phoebe trying to reach?'

'Her mother.'

'And her mother came through?'

'Several times.'

What a surprise.

'It was a great comfort to her,' Hermione added defensively.

'I'm sure it was,' Best said dryly. 'And what did her mother say?'

Hermione gave the matter some thought, then said, 'Well, as far as I can remember, the things a mother would – initially – such as advising her to take care of herself and saying that she was pleased that Phoebe was being good and such a comfort to her pa.'

'Does Florence produce any physical manifestations?' he asked, cutting across her bow again.

She hesitated then said, 'Sometimes the spirits will decide to materialize – if they are in the right mood and the atmosphere is particularly conducive. They won't appear,' she warned, 'if they sense any antagonism.'

Very wise of them, thought Best.

'There must be harmony.'

Those amber-hued eyes were really quite hypnotic, Best thought. Surprising that it wasn't she who was the medium.

'And did Phoebe's mother materialize?'

Again, Hermione paused to give the matter some careful thought. 'No,' she said finally, nodding her head as she considered, 'not that I recall.'

'Had Phoebe been expecting her to?'

'I think she was hoping that she would,' Hermione said carefully. 'I get the feeling that her mother's spirit had indicated that she might.'

Best gritted his teeth. Questioning these women was like wading through molasses. All responsibility for anything dubious could be blamed on the spirits. Useful, he thought. He could do with a spirit or two to blame when his cases went wrong and he had to parry Cheadle's questions.

It seemed clear to him that they had given Phoebe the impression that she might see her mother – and this was why she had kept returning. Only to have her hopes raised up – then dashed. Which may be why, as Anne Meldrew claimed, she sometimes returned home happy and sometimes very tearful.

'You do keep records of your proceedings?'

He knew that the 'rules' advised circles to have a 'recorder', but even if they did the thoroughness of the notes taken varied considerably.

'Of course.'

'I will need them.'

She looked aghast. 'I *couldn't*! They are confidential.'

'Oh yes you could,' he insisted. 'And you will. Even if I have to get a warrant.'

There was a short silence. Eventually, she turned those luminous eyes on him again, brushed back her soft cloud of dark hair, and said softly, 'Very well, Mr Best. For Phoebe's sake.'

He terminated their interview swiftly and stood up. Doing that could be disturbing, particularly if an interviewee had planned to finish with some information that reflected well on them.

Hermione, however, did not appear disturbed and managed to insert such a comment anyway. Looking up at him with those almost feline eyes she murmured, 'You realize that we have been thoroughly investigated by the Newcastle Society and that they found our seances to be well run and Florence's mediumship exemplary. There was no hint of fraud.'

'Who suggested fraud?' said Best.

Miss Elspeth Young sat forward attentively on the edge of her mahogany dining chair. Though pleasantly plump she had delicate little hands and a certain air of fragility about her. The hands fluttered about her ceaselessly; now tucking stray strands of silvery hair under her fur- and feather-trimmed hat, now plucking at the cord frogging and satin-covered buttons on her mauve wool dress.

'We were so upset to hear about poor Phoebe,' she told Best, 'we just can't get over it.'

He believed her. There was a genuine sorrow in her voice.

'She was so young, and so pretty.' A tear started into Miss Young's eye. 'Did she suffer?' she asked suddenly. She didn't wait for a reply. 'I do hope she didn't suffer.'

Mrs Beatrice George, with her severe half-spectacles and more sober half-mourning attire, provided a still presence beside the ever-mobile Miss Young, but she nodded her agreement and announced firmly, 'Anything we can do to help, we shall.'

Best usually separated interviewees, but not only was time pressing he thought that it might be more profitable to talk to these two together. They would be more relaxed with him as a duo as well as being likely to jog each other's memories in the manner of long-married couples and very old friends.

He soon established that, like them, Phoebe had attended the meetings regularly, always arriving early and going straight into the seance room as recommended in the almanac rules. Early arrival and consorting with the others helped foster the magnetic force. Phoebe had conversed with them pleasantly about the weather and about the latest fashions from Paris and London. She, of course, was more concerned and informed about the latter than they were, but they had done their best to show an interest.

'Did she seem happy?' Best asked.

They looked at each other.

Mrs George was the first to speak. 'Well, she varied. Sometimes, yes. Other times she did seem, well, rather anxious.'

'Missing her mother, of course,' put in Miss Young, pulling gently at an earring as she spoke. 'That's why she wanted to talk about the latest hats and such like with us.'

'We understood that her mother had been something of a beauty,' Mrs George added with only a slight hint of disapproval.

'We tried to hold our own,' smiled Miss Young, lightly touching and stroking the fur trim on her own hat, 'and the dear girl was patient with our ignorance.'

That was nice of her, thought Best dryly.

He was quietly edging on to his chief point of interest. Had there been any romantic interest at the seances? This was a tricky subject. The spiritualist movement had long suffered from accusations that improprieties were conducted beneath its cloak. Illicit affairs carried on at regular, apparently innocent, meetings. Spiritualism's reputation had not been helped by the fact that some of the early American mediums had espoused the causes of women's rights and even free love.

Some of that taint had been shaken off. Nonetheless, it *was* a fact that seances could indeed provide an ideal setting for secret assignations and also that the semi-darkness and intimate aura of the mixed-sex proceedings could add a frisson of excitement to a budding affair. But he had to be careful of the suggestion that such goings-on were occurring here. The ladies might take umbrage and cease to cooperate.

He approached the matter obliquely. The rules advised that if possible they always sit in the same place, next to the same persons. So, who were Phoebe's regular neighbours?

'Oh, Mr Alexander,' said Mrs George instantly, 'and Mr Springer.'

'And which ones are they?'

'Mr Alexander is the gentleman with the monocle who sat opposite you today,' said Mrs George.

Ah, not exactly love's young dream.

'And Mr Springer?'

'He was not here today,' said Miss Young, 'which is unusual. Isn't it, Beattie?'

'Fairly.' Beattie George nodded carefully.

'Tell me about him,' said Best, trying to appear only mildly interested. 'Is the young man in business?'

'Oh no,' laughed Miss Young. 'Mr Springer is a gentleman – and no longer young. In fact, almost elderly. Alternates you see.'

'Anyone else missing – not here – today?' said Best hiding his disappointment.

They thought a little then spoke in unison, giving emphasis to the second syllable, 'Only Mr Quarrell.'

'Oh, now *he* will be *very* upset about Miss Phoebe,' Miss Young exclaimed, bringing her hands together and clasping them to her plump bosom.

'He is a young man?'

'Well, no. Quite middle-aged,' said Miss Young.

Best sighed inwardly. So, no romance there either.

'Oh, I don't know,' corrected Mrs George. 'I would say he is only about forty.'

'Well, that's middle-aged, my dear, don't you think?' exclaimed Miss Young, pushing strands of hair under her hat. 'Well, early middle-age, at least.'

Clearly Mrs George was the older of the two. Which would make Mr Quarrell seem younger to her.

'Why would Mr Quarrell be *particularly* upset?' Best enquired calmly while crossing his fingers under the table.

Mrs George fixed her gaze on him over her half-spectacles and said, 'Because it was he who introduced her to our circle, wasn't it, young man?'

Thirteen

'It turns out,' said Best, 'that Mr Quarrell is an investigator for this Newcastle Society.'

'Not surprised,' said McLeod before pausing to take a swig of his ale. 'It's very big around here, you know.' He made a face. 'Don't know why I drink this stuff. It's too strong for me on an empty stomach.'

He looked tired and drawn. His superior officer, Detective Superintendent Tunnah, was still away, handling an appeal case, and doubtless the town worthies were coming down even harder on McLeod now that city status was looming.

'So, what's it all about, this Newcastle Society?'

'Well, the members of the Newcastle Spiritual Evidence Society are all very respectable and influential.' He wiped the froth from his mouth. 'They were responsible for the rise of Miss Wood and Miss Fairlamb – the society helped them become the darlings of Newcastle.'

Miss C. E. Wood and Miss Annie Fairlamb were the most famous exponents of spirit materialization outside London. Best had heard that their performances were sensational.

'There was a falling out for a wee while,' McLeod went on. 'I'm no sure why. But Miss Wood at least seems to have returned to the fold now.'

'Hermione and Florence were eager to claim connection with the society.'

McLeod shrugged. 'Oh well, they would be. The Newcastle Society can make or break a medium. They can give them respectability – a great asset.'

'I'm going to see them,' said Best. 'Do you want to come?'

McLeod shook his head. 'No. I'm off to see Mr Threapleton,' he sighed.

'Oh, I don't envy you.'

Technically speaking, Best was in overall charge of the investigation. But as McLeod was an experienced detective and had the local knowledge he was happy for the man to make his own moves. There was no way of Best keeping in touch with every development as it occurred. They couldn't send a telegram to Best every time something new came up. Too distracting and time wasting. Regular meetings to exchange information were the only solution.

'Would you no like to take Clegg with you when he's done with Arthur Meredith?'

Best hesitated just a little too long before saying hurriedly, 'Oh, I think his time would be better spent interviewing some of the other seance sitters.' He took out his list of addresses. 'I've made one or two notes about the most important questions to ask.'

McLeod took the list and the note but kept his eyes on Best.

'You are getting cooperation from our laddies, aren't you?'

'Oh yes. Yes,' nodded Best, before looking up to acknowledge the arrival of his plate of roast beef and potatoes. One thing he had learned over years on such intense cases was eat when and where you can. You never knew when the next opportunity would arise. 'They're all very friendly and helpful.'

'But?'

The man was no fool.

Best reached for the salt and pepper and grimaced. 'But,' he conceded as he sprinkled his food, 'this business of people already knowing who I am. The Mary Jane spirit and that maid, Anne Meldrew, asking me about the Maud and Alice case.' He picked up his knife and fork and sliced firmly into the beef. 'It's almost as if,' he added as he loaded his fork with exaggerated care, 'someone was going around ahead of me giving ammunition to suspects and witnesses.'

McLeod shook his head worriedly, 'You're no saying you think it might be one of us?'

'I don't know.'

'Oh, dear. It's not good,' McLeod admitted. 'Look, I'll give them all a talking to . . .'

'No.'

That was just what Best *didn't* want.

'Don't worry,' McLeod assured him, 'there will be no hint that we suspect that any cats have *already* been let out of the bag. Just a warning that nothing should be – or heads will roll.'

'All right,' Best nodded.

'I'll insist that it's in *our interests* to cooperate,' he emphasized, then sighed.

Best leaned over and patted his arm. 'Don't worry. We're going to solve this one.'

He wished he really felt so sure. At the moment he was totally confused.

McLeod nodded acknowledgement. 'I hope so.'

'Of course,' Best pointed out comfortingly, 'I do realize that it would be easy for anyone – even the murderer – to find out about me.'

McLeod brightened a little. 'Aye, that's true. The Maud and Alice case was headlines here for quite a wee while you know – local lasses coming to grief in big bad London – and even your own tragedy was in the national papers.'

'Your own tragedy', that was a nice way of putting it. The tragedy that now makes my life not really worth living, thought Best.

Clegg could see how a young girl might be drawn to this man. Arthur Meredith was darkly handsome and had an incisive and commanding manner unusual in one so young. Clegg could just imagine the young barrister haranguing police witnesses in court.

When he was told that the detective sergeant was on further enquiries regarding Phoebe Meredith he grudgingly allowed the sergeant into his bachelor flat. 'I've already told you everything I know,' he sighed, 'and that is very little I assure you. I haven't seen the young woman for months and, in any case, our acquaintance, as I am sure you already know, was brief.'

It rankled Clegg that he called her 'the young woman' in that dismissive way.

As he led him into the drawing room Meredith took his watch out of his embossed silk waistcoat. 'This will have to be brief,' he insisted. 'I have an important dinner engagement.'

'As brief as I can, sir,' said Clegg, who was not about to be bullied by a young lawyer outside court.

The drawing room was handsomely if sparingly furnished. Could it be that Meredith's taste went against the current fashion, now reaching epidemic proportions, for cramming every corner with knick-knacks? Or had he really little money of his own? If so, he was clearly not yet sufficiently successful to indulge himself enough even to impress the fine friends who would judge a man on such matters.

'What exactly is it you wish to know, officer?' he asked crisply as soon as they had sat down.

'Well first I have to tell you something,' said Clegg. 'Something that has not yet been released to the newspapers.'

'Yes, yes, man.' Meredith glanced impatiently at the mantel clock.

Right, if that was how he wanted it. 'Yesterday evening in Bainbridge Company showrooms we found the body of Phoebe Threapleton.'

Meredith's mouth dropped open and his face blanched a chalk white. 'What do you mean, the body!' he exclaimed.

'Miss Threapleton is dead,' said Clegg, 'Murdered, we think,' he added bluntly.

'Oh, my God! Phoebe! Oh no!' His hand went to his mouth. Clegg thought he might faint. 'It can't be true!' He began to sob. 'Tell me it's not true!'

'I'm afraid it is, sir,' said Clegg.

'How did she die?'

'We don't know for sure yet. We should have the surgeon's report soon.'

One thing was clear. No matter how unpleasant were his personal traits, this news had been a terrible shock to Mr Meredith.

'I'm very sorry,' said Clegg, handing the man his handkerchief. 'Look,' he said when it seemed the tears were unlikely to abate for a while, 'I must ask you some more questions, but I will give you time to recover first.'

Meredith didn't seem to hear him so Clegg got up and quietly left the room.

'We must discuss the other girls,' said Best.

McLeod nodded.

Best felt guilty that he had not brought them up before. It was not, as some may have imagined, because those young women did not have wealthy and influential fathers. Just that it had been urgent that they act quickly in Phoebe's case before the trail went cold.

'I have the list and a few details about them.' Best retrieved a crumpled report from his pocket. 'But, of course, that doesn't tell me much.'

The list read:

> Mary Donovan, aged fifteen, barmaid at the Ridley Arms Hotel, Sandhill.
> Kate Thomson, aged fifteen, seamstress, of Elswick East Terrace.
> Amelia Cook, aged sixteen, of Brandling Village.

What Best needed to know was whether there was any connection between the girls or any similarities in their circumstances. But he kept being dragged back to Phoebe.

'Before we go over them – one thing,' said Best as he pushed his plate away and wiped his mouth. 'This Bainbridge business. D'you think one of their employees might hate them enough that they would leave the body in their shop to try to ruin them?'

McLeod blew out his cheeks and shook his head. 'Shouldna think so. They're held to be quite good employers, you know. For that trade anyway.'

Best recalled all of the irksome, pitiless rules and fines. But it was common knowledge that shop workers' conditions were worse than those of domestic servants. Even mill workers and miners had unions these days, but there had been an uproar when some shop workers formed an early closing association and suggestions had been made that chairs should be provided behind the counter for the assistants as well as in front for the customers. Even *Punch* had taken up their cause with passion in recent times, with poems such as *Rest: The Plea of the London Shop-girl.*

Arthur Meredith sat staring at the glass of whisky in his hand that Clegg had taken the liberty of pouring from the lawyer's crystal decanter.

It was all a bit of a wasted effort. Even when he was finally persuaded to speak through his sobs, Arthur Meredith's answers were unchanged. He still insisted that he had not seen Phoebe for many weeks and that, indeed, they had only enjoyed a brief acquaintance.

Why, then, was the man so upset? Surely even a blazing passion, when not replenished and without hope of success, would have died by now?

'She was the love of my life,' he admitted eventually, 'and I lived in hope.' He sat up a little straighter and took a gulp of the whisky. 'I've been doing well at the bar, lately,' he spread his hands helplessly, 'and I just hoped that Sir George would relent.'

'What about Phoebe? Did she agree?'

He nodded miserably. 'She said to leave it for a while, let her father realize that no one else would do for her. That there was no one as good as me around.' He raised a wan smile. 'Then he would relent.'

'And if he didn't?'

'She would pine and he would become desperate. That was her plan.'

Somehow Clegg couldn't see a clever man like Meredith being enamoured of an apparently shallow girl like Phoebe – young, innocent and, by all accounts, wilfully selfish in some respects. But he realized that there was often no reason to these things. Himself, he preferred a woman with a bit of sense.

Fourteen

Many ancient English towns had walls. Few had so much need of them as Newcastle-upon-Tyne.

Ever since the Roman Emperor Hadrian had decided to bridge the River Tyne and terminate his amazing cross-country defensive wall at this spot it had been a frontier station in the battle to keep out the marauding Scots. He named the resulting settlement Pons Aelius.

When a Norman castle was sited there in 1177, again to keep out the Scots but also to help subdue the natives, the name was changed to Newcastle.

As they tend to do, the names of the various town gates lived on. Florence and Hermione resided just off Westgate Road, and it was to Newgate Street, now in the centre of town rather than guarding its edges, that Best went on a chilly evening in search of the very active Newcastle-upon-Tyne Spiritual Evidence Society.

This was a less elegant part of town, where decaying buildings were plastered with advertisements for Andrews Liver Salts, Nestlé's Milk and Lipton's Tea. Even the wall abutting the churchyard of the town's most ancient place of worship, St Andrew's, was so defaced. Guarding its north side were the crumbling remains of the town's Roman wall and New Gate.

South of the church in Newgate Street were many narrow, arched entrances and doorways. These led off into murky courtyards lined with an assortment of warehouses, workshops and the dwelling houses of the poor, plus the occasional handsome old residence.

It was in one of the latter, in Weir's Court, that Best eventually located the Newcastle Spiritual Evidence Society.

By now, he had learned that the society had been founded

67

several years earlier by three respectable local citizens: corn merchant, Mr John Mould; florist and seeds-man, Mr William Armstrong and civic dignitary and old Chartist, Mr T. P. Barkas.

They had made it their business not only to foster spiritualist circles in their own homes but also to promote high-quality test seances at the society's premises. In doing so, they had achieved fame both inside spiritualist circles and beyond. Only London and Manchester could compete with the prestigious Newcastle Society.

Judging by their current programme displayed in the hall, the society remained active. There was no doubt either that Miss C. E. Wood had been accepted back into the fold. Three of her Form Manifestation seances were listed alongside that week's talks and classes such as Spiritualists Improvement and the Development of Circles for Members and Friends. The notices also carried the strict warning that no strangers would be admitted without an introduction from a member.

It seemed clear to Clegg that Henry O'Brien, now sitting upright in a hard wooden chair opposite him, was his own man.

Although of a more lowly social status than the other members of the circle, who were lower middle class, Henry had a certain bluff assurance about him. This was based, Clegg guessed, on the respect his skilled work afforded him. Henry O'Brien was a senior mechanic at Armstrong's Ordnance Works. It was on such practical men, engineers and mechanics, that the North East had built much of its industrial prosperity.

Clegg would not have thought him to be a gullible person, nor one given to fanciful thoughts. Rather one who kept his own counsel and made his own decisions. What, then, was O'Brien, the clear-headed mechanic, doing at a seance?

Then again, reasoned Clegg, many apparently sensible working men were enthusiastic spiritualists and it was very popular among the miners. Of course, with their accident rate, they had more reason than most for wanting to be reassured about the hereafter. Since their terrible disaster, Seaham Harbour's most popular medium had been obliged to turn people away in droves.

Nonetheless, Clegg found it hard to imagine this strong, dignified, manly man pushing a glass about on a wooden planchet to spell out a message or asking questions of a ghostly white muslin-draped figure that flitted about the room chucking men under the chin.

'I was hoping to reach my son and his family,' O'Brien said simply.

'Oh.' Clegg nodded. With such a loss, he, too, might seize such hope.

'Mr Quarrell is not here,' said Mr Amos Dunne, the Deputy Hon. Secretary of the Newcastle Spiritual Evidence Society, a tall and stiff-backed man with a misplaced confidence in his own dignity.

'Is he coming this evening?' asked Best.

'I doubt it. We are usually made aware of his intended arrival beforehand,' said Dunne pompously.

Quarrell was a man of standing then.

'But he *is* a member?'

'Oh yes. Certainly,' Dunne admitted stiffly, adding, 'You understand that I would not normally divulge such private information regarding our members, but Mr Quarrell's connection is so well known . . .' His tone suggested that Best should have realized that. 'Mr Quarrell *is* an investigator of some renown.'

'Well, if he doesn't come, I'll need his address,' Best said bluntly.

Dunne gawped at him in horror. 'I couldn't possibly . . .'

'Oh yes you could, Mr Dunne,' Best snapped. 'I insist.'

Dunne glared at him and opened his mouth to protest further.

'What's more,' continued Best in the steamroller mode which he reserved exclusively for the pompous, 'I am certain that Mr Morse, your Secretary, *and* Mr Quarrell would be only too eager to assist us in a murder inquiry. Aren't you?'

Dunne's eyes widened. 'Murder!'

'Yes, we believe so. Miss Phoebe Threapleton's body was found yesterday.'

'Oh my God!' He looked truly shocked. 'The poor girl!'

'You knew her?'

'Yes!' He stopped, gulped, then added hurriedly, 'Only in passing, you understand.'

'Passing where?' Best enquired dryly.

'Oh, here. She came here. But only once or twice.'

'When?'

'Oh, I don't know. Er . . . Four or five weeks ago.'

'As whose guest?'

'I'm not sure.'

'You have a register?'

'Of course?'

'Please check it.'

The dazed man began moving towards his office.

'Just a minute.' Best stopped him. 'Her father is not a member by any chance?'

'Sir George Threapleton? Oh no.'

Dunne unlocked his office door, went over to his desk, sat down and stared at Best unseeingly.

'Your register,' Best reminded him coldly.

He started. 'Oh, yes.' He reached in his waistcoat pocket for the keys. 'You must understand, this has been a terrible shock.'

I'm relying on that, thought Best. But he still couldn't understand why the Deputy Hon. Secretary seemed quite so stunned if he had only met the girl 'in passing' once or twice.

O'Brien's pale-blue eyes looked thoughtful. 'To be telling the truth,' he said, the remnants of an Irish accent still discernible, 'I have but little recollection of this young woman. But then I am not a regular at that circle.'

'Oh.' Clegg frowned. 'But I thought you had to be – so that the spirits could get used to you.'

He had been trying to keep the disdain and irritation he felt about such nonsense out of his voice, but O'Brien tuned into it and smiled slightly.

'Well, I'm thinking that this "regularity" is really so that the sitters get used to each other, which makes for a more harmonious atmosphere. Well, so they tell me, anyway. This, in turn, is conducive to the arrival of the spirits.' He shoved his hand through his coarse wavy hair. 'But they make an exception for me. What with my work an' all, I can't always get to my usual Friday evening meeting, so sometimes I go to this Wednesday afternoon one instead.'

Clegg already felt this business of questioning the spiritualist circle was ridiculous and now it was confirmed as a waste of time. The man didn't even *know* Phoebe.

'So you never got to know her? Even though you had met her on occasion?'

O'Brien shrugged. 'Well, you'll be seeing how it is. First of all you speak to those you already know, that being the easiest thing. And me always being on the late side and this Miss Phoebe only having been there a few times.' He hesitated. 'But, come to think of it, I do remember seeing a pretty young thing already settled near the top end of the table and thinking to myself, what's a young girl like her doing among all us older folk. I suppose that was all.'

That was odd. 'But you knew she had been only a few times?'

'Of course. Wasn't it the talk of the circle, when they couldn't find her?'

Clegg had the feeling that something was not quite right here, but for the life of him he couldn't quite make out what it was.

From Dunne's reluctantly produced registers Best had established that Phoebe had attended three of the Newcastle Society's manifestations as a guest, not of Mr Quarrell, however, but of Mrs Hesketh.

'Her aunt,' said Best.

'That's right,' said Dunne looking surprised.

It had been Mrs Hesketh who had introduced Phoebe to Arthur Meredith, the young barrister.

Quarrell had not yet arrived at the society's rooms, but while he waited Best intended to extract all the information he could from the shocked Deputy Secretary.

'In your opinion,' asked Best, 'why do you think Mr Quarrell would have introduced Phoebe to Florence's circle?'

Dunne hesitated but Best had him in his thrall. He had realized that the man liked the sound of his own voice and that, if pandered to by having his opinion solicited, his caution would be overcome.

'Oh, well, I imagine he may have thought it more suitable for a young girl.'

Ah, thought Best. So what was it about the society's seances that might be *unsuitable*, he wondered, but enquired innocently, 'In what way?'

'Er . . . well . . .'

Dunne seemed to regret his previous statement but he could scarcely back down without making it seem worse.

'Well, it would be a quieter and more tranquil setting. More homely for a delicate young girl.' His glance wandered about the moulded ceiling as though in search of a better explanation.

Suddenly he hit on it, sat up, looked directly at Best and said in his official voice, 'You must understand, Mr Best, that our seances are held under rigorous control. It is essential for our reputation as an investigative society that we, well, investigate,' he finished lamely. But it was obvious he now felt on safer ground, toeing the official line. 'We have to take appropriate steps to ensure that our manifestations are genuine.'

He took a deep breath and sat up even straighter in the Secretary's high-backed chair. 'This of course means that sometimes the events are not as relaxed as those in more domestic settings.' His voice had risen again but he made an effort to lower it as he explained, 'Some mediums even complain that we frighten their spirits away . . .' He shook his head and gave a slight, indulgent, smile.

Well, I did ask, thought Best. He let him go on. Nervous ramblings sometimes produced tiny gems of information.

'So, to ensure success in an atmosphere suitable to a fragile young girl, he may have thought . . .' He stopped and shrugged. 'But I confess that I have no real way of knowing Mr Quarrell's intentions. I have merely been speculating.'

'And very helpfully, sir,' said Best, and meant it.

Fifteen

Much of the ever-expanding population of Newcastle lived in Elswick's steep terraces. These ran down towards their employers, Armstrong's Engineering Works, who produced everything from steam engines to ships' guns, shot, shells and torpedoes. The factories were strung alongside the Tyne, blocking off almost a mile of riverside.

Byker, almost Elswick's twin, lay on the opposite, eastern side of the town. Here, also, had been built hundreds of the minimal-space 'Tyneside flats' to house the workers in the local shipyards, pits and factories.

The east and west of the town centre were thus given over to industry and working-class housing. As Armstrong's workers spread north, Upper Elswick was also fast becoming undesirable to the well-to-do.

Thus the only places for anyone with pretensions to gentility to live were the few tall and elegant terraces between the town's two northern parks – Castle Leazes and the Town Moor – and the lovely suburb of Jesmond.

Jesmond straddled the north-east edge of Newcastle and boasted handsome villas, an increasing number of desirable terraces and a long, leafy dene. Through this wooded valley ran the Ouseburn on its way towards the River Tyne.

It was at Jesmond that Sir George Threapleton chose to build his spacious villa. Like its nearest neighbours, Middleton Hall was set amidst sweeping green lawns, lofty trees and landscaped gardens.

The house itself was white, square and castellated. The windows were lancet-shaped and the doorways framed by pointed arches. The whole resembled a squat, icing-sugar castle.

Anne Meldrew had obviously not yet been 'let go', as it was she who opened the door to McLeod, took his hat and coat and showed him into the light, oak-panelled library. There, on a high-backed Gothic revival chair, like some medieval baron, sat a bereft Sir George.

The cheerful fire flickering in the heavily moulded cast-iron grate seemed almost to mock his hunched figure, as did the jewelled shafts of light filtering into the room through the stained glass panels in the carved oak mantelpiece.

The man looked ten years older than when McLeod had seen him two days earlier. His wavy silver hair was now dishevelled and his once-fine moustache stained and bedraggled.

The inspector had been dreading this visit. What could one say to a widower who had now lost his only, beloved, child? Particularly if one had little progress to report in the search for her killer.

McLeod had decided that all he could do was to prevaricate. Pretend that he was following some promising lines of enquiry. Not for the first time he was relieved that he would not be ultimately responsible for the outcome of this case. That would be down to Best, poor fellow. In some people's eyes, if Scotland Yard couldn't solve it, nobody could.

As it happened, prevarication was unnecessary. Sir George had sunk so deep into despondency he seemed unable to climb out. Justice and revenge must have little point, McLeod realized, if your reason for living had gone. The anger would probably come later. At the moment, the man could only just tolerate a series of questions from the inspector.

As McLeod had expected, Sir George's replies were of little use to him. The man had only the vaguest idea of how Phoebe had spent her time. She had received callers, attended her aunt's At Homes, shopped in Newcastle, joined outings to the Theatre Royal when something suitable was being performed and attended balls and musical evenings held by their neighbours and friends.

As they spoke Anne Meldrew entered the room to attend to the fire, which didn't need much tending. They both watched her trim figure and neat movements as she kneeled to her task. She was a pleasant sight, the fire lighting up the edges of the wide, snowy wings of her apron and little white cap and collar.

'But who was closest to Phoebe?' McLeod asked.

Sir George stirred in his chair. 'Oh, her cousins and various friends. Anne – Miss Meldrew – will give you details.'

At the mention of her name she looked up, a sympathetic expression in her dark eyes. Was it a rather too intimate glance from a servant to a master? These *were* unusual circumstances and, McLeod reasoned, he understood from Best that Miss Meldrew's personality was also quite an unusual one for someone in her position.

'We can talk before I leave,' he said.

'Of course,' she replied, without adding a 'sir'.

What about her present position? Wasn't it rather unusual for a lady's maid to quickly metamorphose into a parlour maid? A lady's maid's skills in hairdressing and as a seamstress were a far cry from cleaning, hearth-blacking and fire-tending.

Their standing also differed from that of a parlour maid. It was expected that they would be brighter and more refined than the housemaids, so that their presence would not jar on the mistress with whom they spent so much time.

Miss Meldrew had been kept on but apparently demoted. However, this did mean that she spent more time in the presence of the master. Perhaps he found her a comfort because she had been so close to his daughter. That was understandable. Wasn't it?

'Any luck?' asked Best.

Clegg shrugged. 'None of them knew anything but what the spirits had told them.'

Best held his tongue. He did not like Clegg's dismissive attitude to the evidence of the members of Florence's circle – an attitude that might cause him to miss clues. On the other hand, he could have discovered something vital but be deliberately keeping it to himself so as to thwart the nasty Scotland Yard detective.

'It's that boyfriend,' Clegg announced firmly. 'You watch.'

Well, that's a nice easy guess, thought Best. It very often did turn out to be 'that boyfriend' or husband. But in this case he didn't quite see how – yet. He'd better get a good lead soon. Time was flying, giving the murderer the opportunity to cover his tracks.

So far they had had no luck in tracing the cabbie who had picked Phoebe up from Bainbridges, and the post-mortem had not been much help. The surgeons were baffled but tentatively suggested suffocation as the cause of death.

There were no wounds but there were some strange lines of faint bruising across her body. The medical men were hedging their reports about with ifs and buts. Probably waiting until we find the killer and get a confession, thought Best bitterly.

They were in the Newcastle police headquarters, only a stone's throw from Bainbridges. This was certainly a conveniently compact city, Best thought, and this is one of the most impressive police headquarters I have ever seen.

The massive building, which stood on the corner of Worsnick Street and Pilgrim Street, housed both the police station and court and resembled nothing so much as a well-established Parisian hotel. Overlooking the court entrance were colossal stone figures representing Truth, Justice, Peace and Mercy. The whole façade was studded about with medallions and scrolls while the roof supported an amazing array of ornamentation surmounted by a large tower topped with a diadem and a weather vane.

Would the new Scotland Yard, ever being promised to replace the chaos of the old, live up to this, even if, as had been suggested, they took over the half-built Grand Opera House on the Embankment?

'Before we come back to the boyfriend and others,' Best said, 'perhaps we need to look again at any connections between Phoebe and the other missing girls.'

He said 'we might' and 'look again' as a sop to McLeod and Clegg in case they hadn't got around to doing this yet.

McLeod nodded, uncommitted. He was still raw from his meeting with Sir George and preoccupied by the post-mortem he had attended. The decaying body of this young girl had made him feel quite sick, and the sight of Best tucking into sausages and mash was not helping.

'I admit I can't see what the connection would be,' Best admitted doggedly, as he speared another pork sausage, 'and I need you to guide me here.' He knew that the other girls were of a lower class, two of them much lower. 'This Jesmond, where Phoebe lived. Is it only the wealthy who live there?'

McLeod and Clegg nodded.

'Aye. More or less, these days,' agreed McLeod.

'Well, then, the only possible connection I can see is that they may have attended the same events or been to the same places, but that seems unlikely.'

'The only connection I can come up with,' said McLeod, now pulling himself back to the present, 'is that one of the lassies worked at Bainbridges.'

Best's fork stopped halfway to his mouth.

'What!' he yelled, thumping the table so hard with his right hand that the salt cellar fell over and his ginger ale jumped out of its glass. 'You never told me that!' This time he was unable to keep the anger out of his voice.

'Oh, aye. But the lassie wasna working *there* when she disappeared,' said McLeod casually. 'She'd been gone three months.'

'Even so,' Best said tightly, 'it might have helped to know that!'

McLeod and Clegg exchanged surreptitious glances but Best didn't care. He was sick of tiptoeing around them. Let them be careful of him for a change!

Sixteen

Mary Donovan's parents were among the thousands of poor Irish people drawn to Newcastle in search of work during the town's rapid mid-century industrial expansion. However, the building of worker housing had not kept pace with industrial growth and most of them, including Michael and Bridie Donovan, had ended up crowded into the reeking slums of Sandgate just above Newcastle's Quayside.

But this couple were determined to better themselves for their children's sake. During the week they had worked hard scraping a living, he labouring, she cleaning. On Sundays, after church, they picked out the better trousers and dresses from among the wretched rags spread on the ground in Paddy's Market.

Some were to clothe themselves, others, when duly washed and pressed, to set up a stall of their own in the Bigg Market in the centre of town. A fruit and vegetable stall in the open air Green Market by St Andrew's Church was the next step.

At first this was tended by Bridie alone, braving even the coldest North-Eastern winter days outdoors. Then, when they were able to upgrade to the indoor Grainger Market just up the road from Bainbridges, both Donovans gave up other work and their business began to thrive.

It was to the Grainger Market that Best went on a morning so bitterly cold and windy that despite his high-buttoned Chesterfield overcoat and the thick scarf and gloves loaned him by McLeod, he kept his shoulders hunched and his head down. Ye Gods this was a freezing place.

The arched entrances to the market, in a row of Grainger Street shops, were modest, which left the newcomer unprepared for the spectacle within. The height, light and spaciousness of the interior quite startled Best, but the protection from those razor sharp north-east winds pleased him even more. He loosened the scarf from about his ears and gazed around.

He was standing in a long, paved avenue of handsome, stone-built butcher's shops. So much meat! More than he had even seen in one place apart from at the London docks!

An archway in this avenue led him to another avenue, then another. Meat again. Sides of beef and lamb and plump poultry interspersed with fat strings of black pudding and dangling sheets of glistening tripe. Other shops sold pots and pans; books and magazines; clothes and ornaments. The Grainger Market was huge and Best took his time looking around while he warmed up. Even his brain felt frozen after the short walk from the Royal Exchange Family and Commercial Hotel, where he was staying. As he thawed he enjoyed the lively scene while girding his loins to face the Donovans.

Their daughter Mary had done well to get a job as a barmaid at the Ridley Arms Hotel. In an area so rife with prostitution and crime it may not have been perhaps the best of places for a young girl, but she had pleaded that she had grown up nearby, knew the dangers, and that the landlord would keep a good eye on her. Besides which, the hotel catered for local businessmen and people from the Guildhall, not roughs.

Nonetheless, one evening three months after starting work at the Ridley Arms Mary had failed to return home.

Another avenue and another arch led Best to the market's final aisle, which was three times as wide as the rest and soared to twice their height. At least forty feet, Best thought. The beautiful trellised glass roof allowed floods of light to bathe the colourful fruit, vegetable and flower stalls along the centre and spark off some of the bright baubles that set off Christmas trees already garlanded with holly and mistletoe. What a place!

A softly rounded woman with tumbling, raven-black curls finished placing russet-skinned apples in pale-green tissue paper, then stood back to check the stall. This must be Bridie Donovan – she was so like the girl in the photograph Best had seen of Mary. The same deep-set eyes, rosebud mouth and tentative expression.

As he stopped she looked up.

'Mrs Donovan?'

'Yes.'

There was a sudden fear in her eyes. She knew who he was.

'I'm Detective Inspector Best from Scotland Yard.'

She stared at him.

'Yes?'

She thought he had bad news.

'I expect,' he said quickly, 'that you've heard that I've been invited to assist the local police with their enquiry about the missing girls?'

She nodded; her mouth moved but nothing came out. The short but muscular young man who had been humping and stacking crates emerged from behind the counter and moved quickly towards them.

'Well, I'm talking to all those concerned in the hope that my fresh eye might spot something that may have been missed.'

The young man was now standing directly behind his mother, his hands on her shoulders. He glared stonily at Best. This would be Robbie, Mary's brother.

'Or that you may have remembered something since the police last spoke to you,' concluded Best.

'Suddenly important is it, now that a rich man's daughter is dead?' Robbie spat out. 'Taken your time to get around to us, haven't you? You've been up here three days.'

His mother glanced up at him. 'Stop it, Robbie, that'll not help any.'

'I do understand your frustration,' Best conceded, 'but I had to concentrate on Miss Threapleton's murder otherwise important clues might be lost. Clues which might help trace Mary.'

'Huh! Expect me to believe that? I think . . .'

'I don't care what you think, young man,' Best snapped. 'I'm here to talk to your parents now and don't think we should waste our time bickering!'

The lad flushed and opened his mouth. Suddenly there were a lot of people waiting to be served, or pretending they were as they strained to overhear what was being said.

'Serve the customers, m'dear,' said his mother quietly and patted his hand.

He went off, simmering. Best and Bridie exchanged rueful half-smiles.

'Excuse the boy,' she said. 'He's hot headed but he loves his sister.'

In fact, Best would have liked to speak to Robbie, alone. Young people share secrets to which their parents are not always privy and even they may not realize their significance.

'We can be going over to the café,' said Bridie. 'It'll be nice and quiet there just now.'

'Is your husband here?'

She shook her head. 'No. He's gone out to look for Mary. He's doing that every day whenever he can.'

Just as well. Wives, too, were often privy to secrets about daughters, which husbands did not know about, particularly when the husbands were strict. His own mother had been the keeper of many a tale and they of hers. In common with many households, 'Don't tell your father' was a familiar cry.

'She is a very pretty girl,' murmured Bridie Donovan and looked fearful.

'Like her mother,' said Best gently and meant it. She really was still a very attractive woman. Her simple black high-necked dress and white pinafore complemented her true Irish beauty. The skin on those soft, rounded cheeks was almost flawless, but the shadows beneath her aquamarine eyes were evidence of sleepless nights.

As with many of the Irish Best had met as a boy in London's East End and among his police colleagues, Bridie had a natural friendliness while at the same time retaining an air of remoteness. Almost as though the affability were a cloak. Perhaps this was because they didn't trust the English. He wondered if they were very different among themselves or when back home in Ireland.

'Mary was never flighty,' Bridie was insisting. 'All that attention was never turning her head.' She paused in her efforts to persuade Best that her daughter was not the sort of girl to run off and leave her family on a whim – which might have been the suggestion from the police when she first went missing. 'She always kept to her books at school . . . so we

81

paid to keep here there and . . .' she tailed off and contemplated the table's oilcloth cover sadly.

'Her job,' said Best, 'down by the Quayside?'

Bridie glanced up quickly, clearly alive to the suggestion that allowing a very pretty, very young girl to work in such a place was foolish to say the least. 'The Ridley Arms is a respectable place,' she insisted. 'Isn't it used by magistrates and lawyers from the Guildhall, the managers of the banks and officials from Trinity House and the Customs House and all.' She paused to push a black curl under her white cap then rushed on, eager to get it all in. 'Even the men who stay there are all respectable businessmen.'

Best nodded. 'I see.'

'You should, you should,' she said, becoming agitated. 'Just because it's down by the docks doesn't mean it's rough. We would never have let her go to anywhere like that!'

'I'm sure you wouldn't.'

She was starting to cry. Best leaned over and patted her hand. Bridie was doubtless aware that respectable businessmen could be as much a threat to a pretty young woman as any rough, but also that in the hard working world you couldn't protect your children from everything.

'You know the landlord?'

'Oh, of course! Of course!' Her lovely eyes flashed as she dabbed at the tears with her apron front. 'Joe Brannigan is an old friend and promised to look after her. See she came to no harm.' She paused again, had a thought. 'It wasn't *only* because she was so fair to look at that he wanted her there you know. She was good at figures and had a fine hand – which he doesn't.'

Best realized her 'is' and 'has' when talking about Mary had turned to 'was' and 'had'. She already knew that she had lost her daughter for ever.

'It's not all sin down there because of the boats,' she insisted. 'You should go down and see.'

I will, thought Best, I will, but he leaned over and grasped her hand tightly. 'I'll do my very best Mrs Donovan,' he said. 'You don't deserve this,' he added as her tears brimmed over and spilled down her soft cheeks.

Seventeen

Best strode down the fine sweeping curve of Grey Street towards the lower town and Quayside. His progress was overseen by Earl Grey, the parliamentary reformer so beloved in the North East, from his lofty position on top of a column at the head of the street.

'You should go up there when all this is over,' McLeod had said. 'The finest views in Newcastle and only a hundred and sixty-four steps to get there!'

In fact, Best was getting the feeling that it would never be all over. What had happened to that old optimism of his? Gone for ever with Mary Jane, that's what.

But these surroundings lifted him a little.

To his left was the splendid Theatre Royal, which, with its majestic portico supported by six Corinthian pillars, resembled a Greek temple. South of that, a parade of elegant shops – their windows glowing in the low winter sun.

For once he felt quite cosily warm, partly from the sunshine and partly the briskness of his gait. He could even feel his fingers and toes quite well.

He had no illusions that this situation would last. It was always colder by the water, as he had learned on his many ship-searching tasks on the Thames. But who knows, he comforted himself, the fact that the river ran through what was almost a ravine might mean that it would be sheltered from the icier winds that whipped down the North East coast from the Arctic.

They were hardy folk these Northerners. Best had noticed Clegg's sly half-smile when he had seen Best's pink ears and blue cheeks.

But for the moment the world looked brighter. Best strode

on down into Dean Street, where the grand stone-clad Grey Street gave way to a motley array of brick-built and plaster-faced buildings of varying heights, ages and stature.

Damn! He halted in his tracks. He'd forgotten to ask Bridie about Bainbridges and whether Mary had any connection with the store. Well, that would please Clegg – if he let on about it. Usually he was all for sharing knowledge with colleagues, even when it meant admitting blunders, but was of the growing opinion that Clegg would have to be the exception to this rule.

Lower still and Best entered The Side. Here most pedestrians were shabbier and the children dirtier. But what was most striking was the gigantic bridge which rode high above them, skimming the tops of the tallest buildings, its arch forming a huge frame for the street below, so that entering The Side was almost like stepping on stage. An extraordinary theatrical effect that greatly appealed to Best's love of the dramatic and unusual.

As he passed under the great arch a northbound train began puffing its way overhead, showering sparks and soot on to people below as it went.

'Wasn't she just like my own daughter,' exclaimed Joe Brannigan, shaking his head mournfully.

Past tense, Best noticed. But maybe that was just his manner of speaking. The landlord of the Ridley Arms did appear to be truly upset. Not that that counted for much.

One of the things that had most surprised Best when he had first joined the police was just how widespread was the talent for telling plausible lies and for pretending to be what you are not. He had been caught out several times before experience had caused him to become more sceptical.

Joe Brannigan was a big man in every way: monumentally tall with the shoulders of a brick heaver and hands like spades. He had the look of someone made for the outdoors but who rarely managed to get there. His large square fleshy face was framed by damp wavy black hair and his dark eyes were like plump raisins emerging from pale dough. He also seemed like a jolly nice fellow.

It had indeed proved to be even colder down by the water

but, by now, Best had cast off his top layer of scarf and gloves and was warming his hands over the fire in a cosy stone alcove. As the feeling began to creep back through the rest of him he removed his overcoat and hat.

He realized that his outwear had attracted some attention when he came in. Obviously, the high hard-crowned bowler with the wide curled brim was not as yet daily wear in Newcastle – despite the worthy efforts of Bainbridge & Co. to keep the locals up to date with London fashions.

Cheadle was partly right in his opinion that a detective's appearance should not attract attention, but Best always countered that you couldn't blend in everywhere and that a good appearance could be a useful asset, so went on dressing just as he pleased.

In this case, the hotel's expensively attired clientele, being mostly older men of some standing, probably dressed for dignity rather than fashion. They certainly fitted in well with this staid background of mahogany and brass.

While he was speaking to Joe Brannigan Best noticed that a fair and pretty slip of a young barmaid kept glancing in his direction – as if to attract his notice. With his dark good looks he was accustomed to female attention but there was an urgency in her glances that suggested other motives.

'Is it all right if I have a word with the bar staff as they become free?' Best asked casually after he had established that Joe Brannigan could be of little help with new information. Mary Donovan had simply left after work one evening and never been seen again.

'Oh, they'll not be knowing anything,' Joe assured him sadly as he rolled his black side whiskers between his fingers until, incongruously, they began to look like sausages.

Best shrugged. 'You're probably right, I'm sure, but,' he adopted a conspiratorial tone, 'you understand my position. Coming in from the outside, I have to be seen to be thorough . . .'

He could easily have demanded access but instead chose to speak as one outsider to another. Driven from their homes first by the potato famine and lately by land evictions the Irish made up about a tenth of Newcastle's population.

They were held in low esteem locally, often being blamed for the filth in which they were obliged to live in the town's direst slums. As for jobs, they were given only the lowest: unskilled labourers, shop assistants and cleaners. In some areas even mining was considered something you had to be born to – locally.

Evoking this comradely feeling proved to be a good idea. Joe responded warmly.

'Oh, of course. Of course. Whatever you want – if only it helps find the poor wee girl.'

He also promised to pass on any titbit of information to Best alone. One ally made at least, thought Best. I could do with some.

Sadie Wilson, the barmaid who had been sending signals to Best, proved to be a nervy young woman. She had scarcely begun speaking to him when her shoulders gave an involuntary jerk and her head a compulsive little shudder.

Was this twitchiness usual with her? Or was she frightened of something? Not me, I hope, thought Best. Otherwise I'm not going to get very far. He assumed his most sympathetic and fatherly expression.

She was, indeed, little more than a child. Very fair and thin with particularly bright eyes and a flush to her cheeks, which, he hoped, did not signal incipient tuberculosis as it had with his wife, Emma. He knew the disease was rife in the lower town slums which, he'd been told, also saw more than its fair share of outbreaks of cholera, typhus and smallpox.

'There was a man,' Sadie insisted breathlessly, 'that Mary talked to – once or twice.'

Best tried to hide his disappointment. A public house full of male customers – it would be surprising if she hadn't chatted to some of them.

'Did she say anything about him? This man that she talked to?'

'No! Oh no,' insisted a surprised Sadie, shaking her head into a small spasm. 'It was as if she wanted to keep it secret. She used to look around to see if anyone was watching.'

Someone was. Sadie.

'Where did she speak to him? In here?' They were in the plushly cushioned and draped lounge bar.

She nodded. He could see that she sensed his doubts. 'Once he passed something over to her – a note,' she added hurriedly. 'I saw her reading it later on when she thought no one could see. She could read and write you know – ever so well.'

And were you jealous of her, wondered Best? This, by all accounts, unusually pretty girl, so well thought of by the land-lord?

'Oh, and once I saw her talking to the man down by the Aberdeen Wharf.'

Ah, the plot was thickening.

'Did she seem afraid of him?'

'Oh no. Excited more like. She seemed pleased about some-thing. She was smiling.'

'So, she had a boyfriend.'

Sadie shook her head into another paroxysm. 'Oh no! He wasn't a *young* man, or handsome or anything!'

What he was, it transpired, was middle-aged with side-whiskers and a close-trimmed moustache and wearing a black tailcoat and grey striped or checked trousers. Like most of the men here, thought Best.

'You told the police about this?'

'No. Well, they never asked me!' Her shoulders jerked and shuddered and her head went into spasm. 'I was off when they came. Anyway,' she added, 'I've just thought of it – now that you asked if we'd noticed anything at all.'

She glanced up towards the bar door, as if sensing someone's presence. A handsome, well-muscled young man was watching them.

'Who is that?' asked Best.

'That's John, the landlord's son,' she answered and blushed.

Curious that Joe had not mentioned him.

'What's he like?'

Sadie blushed again. 'All right.'

'Is he interested in any particular girl?'

'No.'

She wouldn't meet his eye. He decided not to pursue the matter or the handsome John at this stage. Unfortunately, Sadie did not know the name of the mysterious stranger and, indeed, had not seen him lately.

Was he imaginary? Made up to make her seem more interesting and important? It had been known, particularly with fanciful young girls.

Her attacks of the spasms ceased, he noticed, as their conversation wound down. Obviously they were brought on by excitement. There had been no sign of them when she had broken off to serve a customer. Just as well or she'd be throwing beer and whisky around all over the place.

He gave her his card. 'I'm staying at the Royal Exchange Hotel and working from the Worswick Street Police Station. The minute you see this man, send me a message.'

She looked doubtful. He realized why and dug some coins out of his pocket. 'Pay them with this. And tell them they'll get more if they *hurry*! Don't fail me. Lives may depend on it!'

That sent Sadie off into a juddering fit. If she hadn't been frightened before she certainly was now. And maybe that was a good thing.

Eighteen

The Aberdeen Wharf, where Sadie had seen Mary Donovan speaking to the strange man, was just to the east of the ingenious new Swing Bridge, which turned on a central pivot to let water traffic through.

Looming high above both was Robert Stephenson's monumental High Level Bridge, which swept from the upper reaches of Newcastle to the twin town of Gateshead.

At Aberdeen Wharf, snorting steam cranes and sweating dock labourers were unloading the cargo of the steamship the *Countess of Aberdeen*. Some of her goods were being transferred into a long quayside shed while others were merely piled, higgledy-piggledy, on the dockside – an incongruous sight just opposite the dignified and stately Guildhall.

A steady stream of horses and carts trundled to and from the stacks of barrels, crates and sacks, like ants invading a sugar heap. Gradually they whittled away at it, carrying their booty, off up to their nests in the upper town.

It was amazing how much such a small craft could hold, thought Best, especially when it also carried passengers to and from the Granite City.

Nobody among this heaving, sweating humanity, or the load-checkers with their clipboards, remotely resembled Sadie's mystery gentleman, but just in case this venue was significant Best obtained a leaflet listing the sailings and fares.

Somehow, he sensed that the Aberdeen Wharf was not significant in itself. But he had been wrong before. He would at least warn the Aberdeen police to look out for the missing girls and make some enquiries about the company who ran this weekly service.

A damp, brownish-grey and chilly fog was settling along

the river. Best beat his arms about his chest to try to restore circulation. With luck, the mystery man would reappear at the pub. All would be solved and he could go home to where the weather was kinder.

The fog grew denser as Best wandered further eastwards along the Quayside. Sailing-ship masts and stubby steam funnels became ghostly fingers, looming in and out of sight, beckoning him on. In the background was the huffing and snorting of numerous steam cranes.

Suddenly, he heard shouting. A workman was running towards him waving his arms, then, on drawing level, he gave Best a violent shove – out of the way of the dockside train that was puffing towards him. In his preoccupation he'd been walking along the centre of the railway track!

He moved over to the pavement in front of houses, pubs, inns and the Customs House. Between them were one or two mean-looking alleys, or Chares as they called them. The Hull, Leith and London Wharves hove into view. Beyond them, across the river and now and then peeping through the murk, was a forest of blackened chimneys, factories and warehouses. This was the industrial North all right.

As he drew alongside the railway engine shed the clamour grew. This was obviously the real business end of the quay where tall ships, some with strange-sounding names, were berthed.

What he saw then halted him in his tracks: the hoardings marking the Antwerp, Hamburg and Rotterdam Wharves.

It was the sight of the Antwerp Wharf that riveted him. What a fool! Of course! Why hadn't he thought of that!

He wandered on, his mind racing, until he reached the outlet of the Ouseburn. So lovely on its journey through elegant Jesmond, it was hugged by no leafy dene now. Indeed, the Ouse was a singularly appropriate name for these waters. Here, they were black and stinking from their passage between slaughterhouses, potteries, coal wharves and the direst of slums. It was like a scene from hell.

On the opposite bank of this now unlovely stream stood the River Police Station and, next door, the Dead House. How very apt.

He decided not to cross the stone bridge to investigate further.

His mind was now focused on one word, Antwerp.

'Abduction to the Continent for the purposes of prostitution,' announced Best.

Clegg choked on his beer and shot a conspiratorial glance at McLeod, who deliberately failed to respond.

'We divn't have those sort of goings on around here, man,' said Clegg, wiping his mouth in a pretend attempt to conceal a smirk. 'That's one of them fanciful rumours put about by that London woman.'

Time to show this man who is boss, thought Best, but countered mildly, 'I think you'll find that that London woman actually hails from these parts and that the "rumours" turned out to be only too true.'

McLeod grinned sympathetically. 'And a wee bit embarrassing for the Yard, if I'm no mistaken?'

'Extremely,' admitted Best.

The matter had first come to light when the captain of a Boulogne-bound steamer had noticed that a party of drunken English girls, accompanied by 'foreigners of a repulsive aspect', appeared to be perfectly respectable young women when sober again. He was so concerned that he had had them followed – to a house of ill-repute.

At the same time, the claims made by anti-Contagious Diseases Act campaigner Mrs Josephine Butler that very young English girls were being spirited out of the country and kept captive in Brussels brothels had become so persistent that the Belgians invited Scotland Yard over to investigate.

Detective Inspectors Greenham and Williams were shown around and given every assistance by Lenaers, Chief of Brussels Morals Police, his Deputy, Lemoine, and Commissaire Schroeder. They had returned to report that the accusations were all false.

Unfortunately for Greenham and Williams, shortly after their three-week jaunt one of the Belgian detectives who had helped escort them developed a conscience and reported the dreadful truth to Josephine Butler.

This was that brothel owners had been warned of the visit and police themselves had removed young English girls and children from their premises. They could scarcely remove a girl who had complained to Josephine's fellow campaigners, Alfred Dyer and Alexis Splinguard but she was well beaten and informed that if she did not tell the British detectives that her first statement was all lies her life would be forfeited.

In addition, the Belgian detective told Josephine Butler that Deputy Chief Lemoine himself owned two large brothels and Schroeder's son was superintendent in chief of immigration and so had been able to ensure that the girls were imported without a hitch.

Despite many warnings that it was unseemly for her to do so, Josephine published this information in CD Act abolitionist newspaper *Shield*. It attracted little notice in England but was widely reprinted on the Continent and inspired a storm of controversy and threats of libel action.

Soon, however, the campaigners rescued an English girl, Adeline Tanner, who had a horrific tale to tell. Evidence was now sent to the Home Office, who in turn consulted Inspector Greenham, who said, do nothing. There is no problem. However, more enquiries were made and pressure applied and, eventually, something was done. At that very moment, twelve men and women were about to go on trial in Brussels for enticing English girls into prostitution.

McLeod sucked his teeth thoughtfully. 'But do you no think they'll be being more careful just now?'

'Maybe,' Best nodded. 'Switching their port of departure to Newcastle could be part of that strategy. They may even have shifted their operations to another Belgian city – Ghent or even Antwerp itself. When Greenham was coming they moved English girls to other cities – and where there is money to be made people like that don't usually give up.'

Clegg was clearly simmering.

'Well, *I* divn't see why they would need to bother clartin' about collecting innocent young girls from here when Antwerp will be drowning in whores just like down on our docks.'

Best gave him a withering glance. 'Some men prefer very young and innocent virgins, but the age of consent over there

92

is much older than ours and penalties are severe for inducing young women into prostitution. It's safer for them to import our girls, who don't speak the language, and lock them away.' Best paused then added acidly, 'I'd have thought you'd have known that.'

Strangely, instead of being upset by Clegg's attitude it seemed to be bringing him back to life. The petty opposition was sparking his anger and he hadn't felt much of that for quite a while. Indeed, he hadn't felt much of anything.

'Remind me when the girls went missing?' he said as he spread the Tyne Steam Ship, Newcastle to Antwerp sailing programme on the desk between them.

They found that the journey took thirty hours aboard the *Dragoon* steamship, which sailed every Saturday, sometimes in the mornings, sometimes in the afternoons. Single fares were first class: twenty-two shillings and sixpence; second class: eleven shillings and sixpence.

McLeod peered back and forth from his list to the programme while Clegg looked over his shoulder.

'They don't match,' announced Clegg triumphantly.

'Of course they don't match *exactly*,' Best snapped. 'I didn't expect them to! But Mary Donovan, who went missing on a Friday evening, could easily have left on the six a.m. the following morning!'

He exchanged glances with McLeod, not attempting to hide his displeasure.

The inspector looked ruefully apologetic and hurriedly put in, 'Aye, he's right.'

Clegg blushed. 'But there's quite a big gap between the disappearance of Kate Thomson and the next sailing,' he said in a tone that tried to sound as though he was attempting to be helpful not obstructive.

'Quite right. Very astute,' said Best.

Clegg stared angrily out of the window on to Market Street.

'But abduction or white slave traffic or girl farming or what- ever they call it is, well, certainly a possibility,' agreed McLeod.

'Only just that at the moment, of course,' admitted Best. 'One of many.' He picked up the sailing programme. 'When the *Dragoon* gets back again let's have a Customs welcoming party on the lookout for contraband. We can tag along out of interest and meanwhile throw a few unexpected questions at the crew.'

'Good idea,' said Clegg.

'Thank you, Sergeant,' said Best quite kindly. He hated working in a bad atmosphere and felt that once Clegg got over his antagonism they could rub along together well enough. McLeod had insisted the man was really a nice bloke and a good copper.

'I'd like you to go and see Mr Threapleton,' Best said to Clegg. 'Find out a bit more about him and his daughter and what the gossip is below stairs. Your fresh eye might turn up something new.'

Clegg nodded. Best was giving him the opportunity to save face and showing confidence in him. Mr Threapleton was a man of some substance and had been interviewed by McLeod in the first instance.

'And, Cameron, if you'd do the same with Meredith?' he asked McLeod. 'As for me, I'll being dashing back to the market.' He sighed. 'And I have a confession to make about that.'

Both men looked surprised.

'I forgot to follow up what you said about the Bainbridge connection with them – very sloppy of me. So, I'll have to retrace my steps.'

They greeted this statement with bemused expressions, uncertain how to react, but grinned when Best shrugged and hung his head sheepishly.

'About this abduction business,' Clegg put in, again in a more reasonable and helpful voice and this time managing to sound a little more sincere. 'What could that have to do with Phoebe's murder?'

Best stared at him in silence for a moment then exclaimed, 'To tell the truth I haven't the faintest idea!' Then he laughed.

Both men joined in, McLeod guffawing and slapping the table and Clegg grinning widely and chortling. All three men were soon unable to stop.

That was better, thought Best. Quite apart from lightening

the atmosphere between them it provided a welcome antidote to all the strain and worry they were under.

Now all they had to do was solve these awful crimes.

Nineteen

To Clegg's surprise Sir George Threapleton was not mono-syllabic, as McLeod had warned. On the contrary, he seemed eager to talk. In fact, there was no stopping him. Could it be that as well as the effects of the whisky he was imbibing he was happier talking to a fellow Geordie rather than another of these outsiders? Outsiders who always seemed to get all the best chances.

Not that Sir George had been completely without advantages himself. This was obvious in his speech, which had the soft Northern cadences but used little of the local vernacular.

The son of a Church of England minister he had been educated at a minor public school, but he was at pains to point out to people that that was the only advantage he had received. There had been no money. None at all.

To Clegg the education and the relatively comfortable childhood seemed enough. He'd had to take advantage of the force's elementary classes to help him with his reading and writing. But at least the man was a proper Geordie.

His talk was mostly of his darling Phoebe, perfect in every way, and so like her darling beautiful mother, Sophie. He pointed to their photographs encased in a solid silver frame decorated with climbing roses.

There was no doubt that the mother had been the real beauty. Her face a perfect oval, her sloe eyes soulful and her dark curls piled on her head and spilling down the side of her lovely neck. The picture showed her resplendent in a dark satin ball gown with a low square décolletage edged by white lace.

The flaxen-haired Phoebe, however, was sweetly pretty in

pleated muslin with pearls and had a pleasing air of mischief about her.

Clegg made suitably admiring comments and gave his condolences, meanwhile wondering if the difference in ages between Sir George and his wife was as wide as it appeared or whether it just seemed so because the photograph was an early one. He was also wondering how he was going to broach the topic he had been instructed to investigate – Sir George's business interests and personal affairs and any areas of contention, as Best had put it.

Much of the former was, of course, common knowledge. Or could be gleaned from magazines and newspaper reports that surrounded the man's business dealings and had turned into a torrent on Phoebe's disappearance.

He knew, for example, that Sir George was part owner of the Blackwall Colliery and owned two more in Durham, where the coal was softer, the digging easier, the miners' union less militant, and therefore the wages lower.

He also owned three colliers, which shipped coal to Latvia, and various other merchant craft. What Clegg needed to learn was whether there was any bad feeling associated with any of these enterprises. He wasn't accustomed to interviewing such an eminent man and was uncertain how to go about it.

Clegg decided to be straightforward. Seizing a pause in the eulogizing of mother and daughter he said, 'About your business interests, Sir George. Have you made any enemies?'

This question emerged even more bluntly than intended. Sir George stared at him for a moment, passing his soft white hand over his lushly silver hair and bringing it down to touch and pat his silver-grey cravat before exclaiming, 'Of course, young man! Of course!' He almost smiled. 'It's business!'

Clegg smiled back, relieved. 'Why I'm asking . . .'

'Oh, I know why you're asking!' The fire that made the man so successful re-ignited for a moment. 'You want to know whether anyone hated me enough to do this terrible thing to my daughter!'

Clegg nodded, embarrassed.

'Who's to know! Who's to know!' exclaimed Sir George. 'I've always been fair in my dealings. Tried to be a good

Christian. Given money to charity. Endowed buildings . . .' There were tears in his voice now.

He stared off into the fire, which he had insisted on sitting over even though it didn't appear to warm him. Clegg, who had been obliged to sit beside him, was cooking, and painfully aware that his sweat-beaded brow and flushed cheeks did not help him appear calm and in control.

'People do sometimes take offence for no reason,' Clegg offered with what he thought was admirable tact.

Sir George nodded. 'You're right, my boy. You're right.' He was slipping off into a reverie now. Clegg recognized the signs.

'If you could think of any particular cases?' Clegg asked, in what he hoped was a firm enough voice to bring him back.

Sir George didn't seem to hear.

'Wasn't there that Gold Guardian insurance case about a year ago?'

That had him sitting back up again, his right hand tugging angrily at his silver beard. 'What nonsense that was! What impertinence!'

Well, he was angry enough about it and he had won, so it stood to reason that the other party must be angrier still.

'But they lost, didn't they!' he exclaimed, almost with glee. 'They lost!'

Clegg nodded. If he remembered rightly there had been a great loss of life involved as well.

'Who knows what *they* would be wicked enough to do in revenge! I don't!'

Clegg scribbled in his notebook and said, 'If your secretary could list any possibilities?' He hesitated. 'Any difficult business dealings . . .'

Sir George waved his hand vaguely. 'Have a word on your way out.' He took another gulp from his whisky glass, spilling some on his glistening cravat but not noticing.

Clegg cleared his throat. He still had to broach the other difficult matter before he was dismissed.

Sir George glanced up at him. 'You want to know whether there have been any personal fallings out, don't you!' he exclaimed in the commanding voice which had silenced many a boardroom. 'Well, there *haven't*.'

Clegg didn't say anything, just waited. Often the best policy.

'Apart from that stupid young man who pursued my daughter – what was his name . . .?'

'Meredith.'

'Meredith – such impertinence.'

'If you divn't mind my asking, sir,' said Clegg quite firmly now, 'what was it you didn't like about the lad?'

'He was after my daughter's money!'

He banged his whisky glass down causing drops to jump out over the carved oak side table. 'The man had none of his own and he imagined he was going to get hers!'

And, of course, if they had wed he would have got it in full, since the Married Woman's Property Act had been so transformed by the House of Lords that instead of giving married women possession of their inherited wealth, as was intended, it only allowed them the right to any money they had earned personally – and the likelihood of Phoebe earning anything at all was nil.

Until the current supporters of an amendment got their way heiresses would still be at the mercy of fortune-seekers. Clegg wasn't in favour of these silly women, like that Mrs Butler, fighting for their 'rights', but as a policeman he had seen wealthy women badly treated over their money and he didn't like that. But surely Sir George was astute enough to have tied hers up in trusts?

Maybe there was more to it than that. Could it be that the old industrialist wanted a suitor of higher social standing? An aristocrat even? That was the ambition of many who had clawed their way up into the middle classes. But heirs among the landed gentry were few and far between in the thinly popu- lated counties of this part of the country and most of them were spoken for.

Sir George began to cry and now seemed totally oblivious of Clegg's presence as he stared into what tawny liquid remained in his glass.

The detective sergeant rose to his feet. A discreet departure seemed sensible. He was obviously not going to get anything more from the old man. As he turned away, his eye was drawn once again to the photographs of mother and daughter. He stopped, picked them up and stared at them, frowning. There was something . . . What was it . . .?

A loud sob from Sir George caused him to lay them down again and make a hurried exit, still frowning. Still perplexed. But it would come to him.

Best sat in a dimly lit room at the hub of a semicircle of about twenty people. Two more people, 'scientific gentlemen' he was informed, were standing in a corner about ten feet away examining a floor-to-ceiling wooden cabinet.

'He is Mr Blackburn,' whispered Quarrell with some awe, pointing to the middle-aged man testing the strength of the attachment of some gauze netting to the cabinet's wooden frame, prodding and pulling at every join. 'Mr Blackburn is a prominent Manchester industrialist,' Quarrell confided, 'and a great supporter of our aims.'

Which are? Best wondered.

On eventually meeting Quarrell Best had immediately been invited to join the audience at the imminent seance. Since it was evident that he was going to be unable to speak to the man at length until it was all over, he agreed. Besides, he was hoping he might learn something useful about the society's famous investigative methods.

The scientific gentlemen were evidently satisfied with the arrangements. They turned and nodded towards Mr J. Morse and Mr John Mould, Secretary and Chairman respectively of the Newcastle Spiritual Evidence Society.

A few minutes later the room door opened and a small, dark-haired young woman entered. She moved silently towards the corner and entered the cabinet. The scientific gentlemen moved forward again, inserted screws into the cabinet frame and tightened them. Again, they expressed themselves satisfied, drew a green baize curtain across in front of the cabinet, and moved back to take their places at either end of the semicircle.

For a few moments there was silence, then quiet and harmonious conversation began as was required to encourage the spirits to materialize.

The main topic proved to be the case of the alleged spiritualist frauds of Mrs Fletcher, presently arraigned at Bow

Street Magistrates Court, from where further sensational evidence was emerging daily. The case against her was that she and her husband, who had somehow evaded capture, had 'spirited away' much jewellery and a small fortune from an elderly lady whom they had persuaded that they could put in touch with her dead mother.

Best was surprised by the light laughter following the expression 'spirited away' but the general consensus was how awful it was that such frauds brought disgrace to a worthy enterprise and encouraged further scepticism regarding spiritualism. Much gratitude was expressed that their society was so rigorous in its investigations that it saved them from such embarrassments.

'The risks of seances by public mediums,' one plump lady pointed out, and received agreement from all sides.

After a while, Mr Mould murmured that the content of this conversation might be proving disturbing to their mediums and their spirits and suggested gently, 'Perhaps we should move on to happier subjects?'

The plump lady obliged by starting to sing softly, 'In the sweet by-and-by, we shall meet on that beautiful shore.'

Others nodded their approval at this most suitable Moody and Sankey hymn and gradually joined in.

Best was becoming impatient. What am I doing at this sing-song? He fidgeted. When was something going to happen? Should he be here? Wasting his time chasing spirits of the dead when he ought to be out discovering how some of them had passed on?

Twenty

Meredith may have been utterly devastated by Phoebe's death, as Clegg had claimed, but if this were still the case it wasn't evident. He had certainly regained his lawyerly hauteur. But McLeod had been patronized by better men than him and had found that he often saw the mighty fallen.

He had the feeling that there had been something not quite right about the relationship between Phoebe and this darkly handsome young man who went to such pains to assert his authority. He was determined to find out what it was.

'I want to know,' he announced with some firmness, '*everything* about your relationship with Phoebe Threapleton.'

Meredith stared at him and enquired haughtily, 'Am I charged with something, Inspector?'

'No. Not as yet.'

'Then I am not obliged to answer. It is none of your business.'

'Oh yes it is,' countered McLeod coldly. 'If necessary I will charge you with obstructing the police in the execution of their duty.'

He paused to let this sink in before adding quietly, 'But I think the mere suggestion that you refused to cooperate would not help your career – given the seriousness of the case and the eminence of those involved.'

Meredith's lips tightened petulantly and his dark eyes glared. He'll remember this and get his own back on me in the witness box, thought McLeod.

'Well, if you really want to know, this business has been bad for *my* business already!' Meredith admitted sulkily. He suddenly looked the young man he really was and McLeod began to feel just a little sorry for him. 'It's been bad enough losing Phoebe!' Tears started into Meredith's eyes and he tried to brush them away.

Tears for her or for himself?

'Why don't we just go through everything from the beginning,' McLeod said gently. 'In my experience, laddie, the sooner things are out in the open, the sooner people forget about them.'

'Very well,' he sighed. 'We met at one of my Auntie Hettie's At Homes.'

'That's Mrs Hesketh, of The Grange at Heaton?'

'Yes.'

'She was also Phoebe's auntie?'

He left the obvious conclusion hanging in the air.

'Yes.'

McLeod said nothing.

'Of course she isn't really *my* auntie,' Meredith admitted eventually.

'No?'

God, was he going to have to drag everything out of Meredith like an opposing counsel?

'No. She knew my mother and was always part of my childhood so I just called her auntie.'

McLeod was puzzled. 'But you'd never met Phoebe at her house before?'

He shook his head. 'I never went to her house before. She always came to us.'

'Because?'

This was becoming tiresome.

'Because,' Meredith leaned forward and confided softly, 'we were not of the same class. Aunt Hettie came to us bringing charity – on behalf of the chapel.'

Ah. Things were becoming a little clearer now.

'But she did invite you to her At Home?'

'No. Not really. I was there professionally. Her husband was having a little difficulty with a business partner. I was there when the guests began arriving. Besides,' he added dryly, 'by then, I was becoming a little more socially acceptable and she was short of male guests that day.'

Good heavens. Such is fate.

What McLeod couldn't understand was why Meredith had allowed himself to be warned off so easily. He knew that Phoebe was the apple of her father's eye, all the man had, in fact. His remaining link with his darling beloved dead wife. Surely Meredith had realized that if he had held on Sir George would have had to capitulate? He would have hated having a distraught, unhappy daughter around the house, loathing him for denying her what he had enjoyed – marriage to the love of his life.

In any case, Meredith was becoming quite presentable. Not wealthy, perhaps, but with the prospect of a good career and some status ahead of him. With some clever investment in the railways and mines, he should prosper. True, the market was difficult at the moment but with a father-in-law who had so many contacts and such business savvy . . .

That puzzle had preoccupied McLeod while en route on the tram.

'Did you see Phoebe more often than you first admitted?' was his next question.

The young lawyer pondered this question for a moment then, eventually, said, 'Yes. I saw her about once a week for three months after that dreadful day when I was "invited" to Middleton Hall for tea.'

This was the summons from Sir George that Best had told him about. So, the last contact was in fact only a short while before Phoebe's death.

'Two weeks,' said Meredith, reading his mind. The man must be quite a good criminal mouthpiece.

'And what was the situation between you and Phoebe when you last met?'

'We realized that it was hopeless. She swore she had tried everything to persuade her father but to no avail. I couldn't understand it. Why would a father deny his daughter's happiness?'

Jealousy? wondered McLeod. Was the relationship more than that of father and daughter, at least in his eyes? He'd seen it before often enough, particularly when the mother was no longer alive. Then there was the money.

'Did you and the lassie no think about running away together?'

'With what, Inspector?' said Meredith, spreading his elegantly tapered hands. 'If we eloped I'd be finished professionally and I could hardly expect a girl brought up to every luxury to live with me in a hovel.'

That was a bit dramatic. Times might be hard but there were plenty of honest jobs for an educated man that could afford him at least a modest living. But it had obviously been too high a price for Meredith.

'I refused to consider it.'

'Phoebe asked you to?'

He nodded. 'Oh yes. But then she didn't know what it meant. She had never been poor.' He averted his head and made pretence of consulting the watch that he had fumbled out of his waistcoat pocket.

Maybe I am doing this man an injustice, thought McLeod. He'd seen crocodile tears aplenty and these did not seem to qualify. It seemed that this man had truly loved his fair Phoebe.

The singing ceased and a hush fell over the room as a small square of a white filmy substance drifted to the floor outside the green baize curtains.

The square began undulating, elongating and widening as it did so. Even Best, who had seen a few of these performances, was transfixed. Gradually, the substance extended upwards and outwards and began assuming the form of a small human figure that became more and more solid, and human, and female, as it grew.

There was a collective intake of breath when the form ceased undulating, became very still for a moment, then came towards the watching group, its voluminous white raiment flowing and fluttering as it moved.

Mr Morse took the spirit's hand and led it to several members of the audience, with each of whom it shook hands. It held on longest to that of a tubby gentleman with puce cheeks, saying to him, in a soft Geordie voice, 'Hello, Winkle, it's good to see you. I hope you've been good and taken Rascal for a walk.'

At this the man gasped and clutched at his chest. Oh, please, no, thought Best. Not a heart attack to disrupt the proceedings now that they had finally begun.

Fortunately, the man recovered his breath, sat down and reached in his pocket. Not for smelling salts but a large white handkerchief with which he dabbed at his wet eyes with one hand while stretching out the other towards the spirit, which, by now, had moved on.

Though clearly not meant to be included in the hand-shaking ceremony Best assumed a suitably bemused expression and reached for the hand himself. It proved to be small, warm and as solid as any human appendage.

Then she was gone, drifting back towards the curtains, and then simply melting away. Amazing! Best was impressed.

Suddenly, another female form appeared, taller this time and faster and more vigorous in her movements. She headed straight for Best, whom she seized by the arm and led towards the curtains, which she opened before directing his hand towards the latch and screws fastening the door. They were in place and tightly and firmly fixed. Although again impressed he was not surprised. These were high quality performances.

Other sitters were taken on the tour of inspection then escorted back to their seats. This form dissolved and was replaced by a tiny, child-size figure that was talkative and tactile. It moved about, speaking to people in a high-pitched, piping voice, giving them messages about lost children and causing many a gasp of delight and sob of pleasure.

Well, if it made people happy, thought Best. It seems pretty harmless.

This vision, too, melted away and silence reigned for a moment until a tall, ghostly figure opened the curtains and undid the cabinet fastenings. A spirit with a screwdriver! This is something new, thought Best.

Inside, the seated figure of Miss C. E. Wood was revealed, apparently in deep trance. Her face was turned away from the audience. Someone came forward and placed a white handkerchief on her head, which made her position more clearly visible in the dim light.

Suddenly a shadowy form appeared and tried to get around

the back of Miss Wood and out of the box. It failed, struggled then disappeared.

'The power must be exhausted,' murmured Quarrell. 'You'll have to come back again if you want to see our star, Pocahontas, or Pocky, as we call her.'

Not on your life, thought Best. But he did want to find out more about this curious business.

Twenty-one

'The secretary gave me a list of dealings where there had been some bad feeling,' said Clegg, 'but it was very short.' McLeod nodded absently. He was shuffling detective officers' reports, inquest findings and the usual welter of correspondence the police received from the public in such cases.

'Well, I suppose we can get more information elsewhere.' He picked out the photograph of Phoebe's body and placed it alongside the one of her in real life. 'But it will be a bit of a business following it all up. Especially since we're not financial experts.'

Clegg's glance kept returning to the photograph of Phoebe when still alive.

'How did you get on with that Meredith lad?'

McLeod smiled at the thought of how the snooty young lawyer would react to being described as a 'lad'.

'Well, he was bloody minded to start with, of course.'

'Lawyers.'

They exchanged a glance of fellow feeling.

'But he eventually admitted to more meetings with Phoebe than he had initially.' McLeod shrugged. 'They didn't seem to amount to much, however. He swears they ended it two weeks before she died.'

McLeod's glance also wandered to the lively picture of the young girl. 'I have to say he did seem genuinely fond of the lassie,' he said, recalling Meredith's bereft face. 'One thing I did forget to ask him – and now it's bothering me.'

'Oh, aye?' Clegg fingered the photograph. Something kept trying to jump into the forefront of his mind but just as he was about to grasp it it shot away again. What was it? What was it?

'If he was so poor, who paid for his education for him to become a barrister?'

'Love child?'

'Seems like.'

'There's something *familiar*,' said Clegg holding up the photograph.

McLeod glanced at it again. Stopped, put his head to one side and took in the short straight nose with the slightly flaring nostrils and curved eyebrows like frames to a pretty picture.

'Good God!' he exclaimed, jumping to his feet.

Clegg stared at him.

'Get a cab. Get a cab!' yelled McLeod. 'I'll leave a note for Best.'

At first the house appeared to be empty, but insistent and continued loud knocking and ringing eventually brought a somewhat dishevelled and red-faced domestic to the door.

'He's gone,' she said bluntly in answer to the request to see the master of the house.

'Where? To his chambers?' Instinctively McLeod knew that was not so, even before he received the answer.

'Why no, man. To Copenhagen.'

'Copenhagen!'

'Aha, that's right.'

'What for?'

'Divn't ask me, hinny.' She paused. 'For Christmas, I expect.'

'Or escape,' muttered Clegg.

'To the Malmo Wharf and fast,' McLeod shouted to the waiting cabman, 'and stop the next free cab you see. I have a message that needs delivering.'

As they climbed in he turned to Clegg. 'You stop off at the other European wharves and check out the sailings.' As the cab dashed along he wrote furiously, his pencil jumping on and off the page. 'I'll send this note to Best and tell him to take some men to the Central Station to check the trains just in case his destination isn't Denmark after all.'

The screw steamer *Georg* was clearly making preparations for departure. The crew were bustling around on deck checking that everything that needed to be battened down was, and that any object that didn't need to be on deck was stowed away below before they ventured out into the hostile reaches of the North Sea. The engine chugged into life and began to settle into a steady throb, sending smoke and the raw Newcastle-coal fumes swirling into the evening air.

The crew were obviously not pleased to see McLeod storming up the gangplank in a manner that looked as if he meant business.

He held up his badge of office and snapped, 'Passengers?' at the second mate.

'First or second class?'

'Oh, first, I'm sure. Name is Meredith.'

The man pointed aft. 'Second left.'

Meredith was astonished when McLeod interrupted his quiet smoke and glass of brandy.

'Good heavens!' he exclaimed. 'What's all this drama about, Inspector? I hope you're not intending to stop me visiting friends for Christmas?' He laughed.

McLeod was in no mood for jocular niceties. 'You and Phoebe were kin,' he said bluntly.

Meredith became very still but kept his eyes fixed on McLeod. Then he shrugged and made a rueful face. 'Don't tell me you are arresting me for that?'

'I didn't say I was arresting you.'

'Looks like it. Arriving with all the cavalry like this, stopping the boat! It'll be all over the *Newcastle Daily Chronicle*, I can tell you!'

'I could easily make a good case against you for withholding information pertinent to a murder inquiry,' said McLeod dryly.

'It's not pertinent. I haven't done anything.'

In truth McLeod had no idea what was pertinent and what wasn't any more. Nor what this new information did or didn't mean, and Meredith was obviously not going to offer him much assistance in sorting it out. He sighed. He was sick of all this stupid nonsense.

'Don't you *care* whether we catch Phoebe's killer?' he snapped.

110

That hit home. Meredith closed his eyes, tears rimming his dark lashes.

'Even if you haven't *done anything*, causing confusion like this and wasting our time sorting it out is making damn sure that we don't.'

'That's not fair.'

'Oh yes it is!' McLeod shouted. '*Tell me what was going on!*'

'She was my sister,' Meredith admitted and sighed. He sat down by his bunk and stared up at the framed picture of Copenhagen's Tivoli Gardens on the wall above. 'Well, my half-sister anyway.'

McLeod nodded. So, Meredith *was* a love child. Sir George's love child – or bastard. 'And Sir George warned you off?'

Meredith pursed his lips and nodded slowly.

'And you knew he was your father and you still . . .?'

'He wasn't,' Clegg put in quietly.

McLeod stared at him, perplexed. 'But . . .'

'They both had the same mother, Sir George's wife, Sophie.'

McLeod was astonished. 'Good grief!'

Meredith nodded. 'Well done, Sergeant, and no, Inspector, I was bad news, very bad. Sir George knew I wasn't his. Don't ask me how. But he was prepared to keep and forgive the beautiful Sophie but not,' he added bitterly, 'prepared to accept her bastard child as his heir.'

'You were farmed out for adoption?'

Meredith nodded and smiled. 'While the world was informed of the sad news that Sophie's baby had died shortly after its birth. A common occurrence.' He paused then murmured ironically, 'Money can purchase many things, including silence.'

'You knew all this and you still paid court to Phoebe?'

Meredith's eyes grew angry at the suggestion.

'No!' he shook his head emphatically. 'I didn't know. I told you, it was pure mischance that we ever even met.'

McLeod's and Clegg's digestion of this news was interrupted by frantic knocking at the cabin door, which opened to reveal the agitated captain and the pilot.

'We must leave now,' he insisted, 'or we'll miss the tides and hit the bad weather brewing up in the Arctic!' He turned to the pilot for confirmation and he nodded hard.

'Aye, man, there's a wicked north-easter blowing up!'

'Just give us a moment,' McLeod told them and shut the door.

'Well, Inspector,' said Meredith. 'Now you know the dreadful truth. I fell in love with my half-sister – or kin as you would have it – which is scarcely a crime – and was naturally warned off by her father. Now, may I carry on with my festive journey?'

McLeod pondered for a moment, digesting the new information and trying to make some sense of it. He was right. No crime. No reason why the grieving suitor should not seek solace in a trip to friends abroad. But once he left, would he come back? Was there more to this than met the eye? There were still too many unanswered questions, which he hadn't even had time to formulate never mind ask.

'No,' he said finally and firmly. 'You can't go.'

Meredith raised his eyebrows sardonically. 'You're arresting me then?' he asked incredulously. 'Are you certain you want to do that?'

There was more than a hint of a threat in his voice.

'No,' said McLeod again. 'I'm not arresting you. You have kindly offered to remain to help us clear up some mysteries regarding Phoebe. And we,' said McLeod, making sure there was a heavier hint of a threat in his voice, 'are *very grateful* for your cooperation, which we find typical of such a responsible citizen and fledgling member of the bar.'

Meredith glanced up at McLeod, almost in admiration. He'd been outwitted and could see he was being offered a bargain of sorts if he agreed to stay. No arrest or detention for questioning, nor any revelations regarding his family connection with Phoebe. For the moment, anyway.

'Very well, Inspector,' he sighed, and inclined his head in salute. 'I must confess I have been feeling a little off-colour and have decided that I can't face a sea journey just now and would, after all, rather spend Christmas at home with my loved ones.'

The way he intoned the words 'my loved ones' gave the impression that that was the last thing they were.

Best grinned at Clegg, patted him on the arm, and said, 'Well done! But how on earth did you guess?'

The two inspectors gazed at him expectantly. Clegg savoured the moment. He would like to have said good native thinking from a proper Geordie, but admitted, 'Well, there was something worrity about them pictures of Phoebe and her mother but I just couldna think what it was.' He scratched his head recalling his frustration.

'All I knew was that there was *something* that reminded me of *somebody*. Start off, I thought mebbe it was just that I'd seen Phoebe's body and was harkin' back to that.' He shook his head wonderingly. 'Then,' he paused and wagged his right forefinger, 'when I saw Meredith sitting there and noticed that nose and them prissy lips of his, I suddenly knew! Just like his mother.'

Best held up a photograph of Sophie Threapleton and exclaimed in admiration. 'Well, *I'd* never have got it. It's not as if the likeness is *that* striking. The mother was very dark and the daughter very fair and, of course, being of a different sex to Meredith makes it even more difficult . . . Brilliant observation. I think that deserves a promotion recommendation, don't you, Cameron?'

McLeod nodded enthusiastically. 'Absolutely. Absolutely.'

Clegg was pleased. Maybe Best wasn't such a bad bloke after all. Couldn't be easy coming in to a strange place and taking over . . .

'Well,' Best glanced at McLeod, 'I don't know what you think, Cameron, but since Bertie here has made such a breakthrough I think he should be allowed to follow this strand through?'

McLeod nodded. 'Aye, of course.'

He was pleased that his colleague had shown this Scotland Yard man that the Newcastle Borough Police were not bigoted provincial idiots and relieved that the atmosphere between them was improving.

'We can leave it up to you in which order you follow up

Meredith's story,' Best continued. 'Obviously, talk to his adoptive parents — that should be interesting!' They exchanged speculative grimaces. 'Then Sir George, of course, and some of the servants, but most of all this Aunt Hettie woman. She seems a bit of a kingpin in all this, wouldn't you say, Cameron?'

McLeod nodded. 'Aye. I would. Kept an eye on the lad and kept the mother informed, I'd guess. Which does beg the wee question . . .'

'Why did she let them meet?' said Clegg, who now felt he'd earned a more important place in these exchanges.

'It's all very strange,' nodded Best, then spread his hands and grinned, 'and the solution to this particular mystery is all in your capable hands . . .'

Clegg grinned back.

'Aha. An' as wor lass says, "I'll do it all wiv or wivout me marrows!"'

Best turned bewildered eyes on McLeod, who obligingly interpreted. 'And, as his wife says, "I'll do it with or without my friends."'

They all looked at each other and laughed.

'I'm damned sure you will,' agreed Best. 'Damned sure.'

Twenty-two

On his way to the Grainger Market Best saw all the signs of fast-approaching Yuletide festivities.

Bookshops were crammed with the latest children's Christmas annuals and toyshops piled high with model trains and velocipedes. For the girls, at least the more privileged little girls, there were beautifully boxed, sumptuously dressed dolls wearing miniature versions of the latest Paris fashions – their additional items of clothing laid out in their very own travelling trunks.

Even the greengrocers joined in, with announcements about the imminent arrival of 'Oranges for Christmas' from faraway Valencia and Seville.

The notion of Christmas was a particularly depressing one for Best, reawakening, as it did, so many poignant memories. He recalled Emma's delight in the festivities during the early days of their marriage, then her efforts to show enjoyment while exhausted by her illness and fading away before his eyes. That was when he stopped believing in God.

Then there were the Christmases with Mary Jane, when she was still a child, acting as a customer at the new toy sweet shop he had just bought her. Later, after she had blossomed into womanhood, they celebrated their engagement on Christmas Eve. Was that really only a year ago?

He was a curse on all the women he became involved with, Best decided. He pulled himself up. At least, he chastised himself, you might try to make some amends by sending a present to Mary Jane's mother. The woman who so steadfastly refused to blame you for what was so clearly your fault.

A length of dress material. That would be suitable he thought when he saw the sumptuous display in the windows of Bainbridge & Co. The woman scarcely had a needle out of her hands. Recently she had been given a Singer sewing machine by her husband in an effort to occupy her hands and mind and revive some of her spirit.

But what material? He entered the shop and gazed around at the dazzling array of silks, satins and velvets. Something luxurious that she could not normally afford would be nice. But it would have to be practical so she could wear it at simple family events such as she might attend.

He spotted a fall of duchesse satin that was claimed to be 'extraordinary value at 4/11 a yard'. Its folds glowed and shone just like those on the ladies' gowns in Old Master paintings. Pity that it would have to be black. That luminous violet would set off her dark eyes and hair, but it was too early for that yet. He reached out to touch the material.

'Beautiful, isn't it, sir,' said a familiar voice from behind him, 'and quite the vogue just now . . .'

Best's head shot round, his mouth fell open and he stared in astonishment at the young man now before him.

Smith! It was Detective Sergeant John George Smith, one of the Metropolitan Police's finest, got up in the frock coat and high stiff white collar of a shop assistant, a tape measure draped around his neck.

'Better stop staring at me like that, sir,' Smith suggested quietly, 'or some people might start thinking that you know me.'

Slowly Best turned his attention back to the dress material. Usually, he was adept at not noticing colleagues when they emerged in surprising places. But this! This was so unexpected! And so *pleasing*. He tried to stop his mouth stretching into a grin, turning it instead into a smile of approval for the goods. 'What in God's name are you doing here?' he muttered as he peered more closely at the slippery satin.

'Making enquiries,' Smith murmured.

Best laughed out loud.

Suddenly, the department manager loomed behind Smith's back. Best said nothing but quickly scratched the left side of his nose with his right hand.

'Have you considered these lovely sateens, sir?' asked Smith, his right hand extending towards a colourful cascade of shiny material.

Best shook his head. 'Sadly, it has to be black.'

'Ah, I understand, sir.'

'I'll have three yards of the black duchesse satin,' said Best, 'if you think that will be enough for a gown.'

'From your description of the lady, sir, I would say that would be perfect. And if I may recommend a little matching lace or frogging to complete the ensemble?' He began ushering Best towards the Lace and Fancy department and away from the Silks and Velvets and that department's hovering manager.

'We must meet,' hissed Best as he contemplated a froth of black lace flounces and shimmering lengths of crystal- and jet-beaded nets.

'Lockhart's Cocoa Rooms in Clayton Street at six thirty p.m.,' said Smith quietly as he held up the jewel-encrusted nets, moving them so that they glittered and glowed under the brilliant light from the chandeliers. 'It's not five minutes away,' he explained, now proffering a black bead drop trimming for inspection.

'Fine,' said Best, thinking, has the man gone mad? Cocoa Rooms!

He smiled, wrote out the name and address of the recipient of the gift, which Smith already knew by heart. 'Include some of these,' – he pointed to the lace and net – 'to appropriate length. I'll leave how much to your good judgement.'

Might as well give this novice salesman a good order.

Smith nodded, took note of the price tags, totted up the amount, gave Best the total and escorted him to the till. As Best recalled, it was essential that customers were 'shown through'.

George and Tilly Meredith were adamant.

'We never knew who Arthur's mother was,' Tilly insisted, 'and we never asked!'

George patted Tilly's hand. 'We were that pleased to get a wee bairn we didn't really care.'

Clegg nodded. 'I can understand that.'

117

Yes, they had been a bit curious at first, they admitted eventually, but that soon faded when the bairn grew and flourished and became truly theirs.

'We had him right after he was born, do you see,' said Tilly, her motherly currant-bun face creasing with pleasure as she recalled the happy moment, 'so he wasn't ever really anyone else's.'

George laughed. 'And a right wizened, pathetic little thing he was!'

Tilly shot him a reproving look and Clegg was sure that this was just the sort of confidence that Meredith would not appreciate. He had not been pleased when told that George and Tilly were to be interviewed.

'They know *nothing*,' he had insisted. 'What a waste of police time. You'd be better employed catching some of those poachers who plague the estates or the thieves who raid the cargoes down on the docks.'

George and Tilly proved to be members of Newcastle's lower middle class. He was the owner of a small chain of jewellery shops, which was how he had heard about a healthy baby boy being available for adoption. Aunt Hettie was one of his customers, and while visiting her to show the latest hair ornaments and tiaras from Paris for a ball she was to attend they had got to talking about children and then their lack of any.

This didn't quite chime with Charles Meredith's version, where Aunt Hettie had been the bringer of charity to him and his parents. While not wealthy, his parents did not seem to be in need of charity.

'I expect it was one of her servant girls that had got into trouble,' murmured Clegg and smiled.

'Well, that's what we thought at first,' said Tilly, lowering her voice and assuming a confidence sharing air, 'but when . . .'

She stopped suddenly as George shook his head and frowned warningly.

'Not a servant girl?' Clegg shrugged as though it was of no consequence. 'That makes a change.' He smiled.

George straightened up in his Queen Anne armchair and said in what was probably his businessman's voice, calm and very reasonable, 'As we said, we never really knew.' He shrugged. 'And it didn't really matter.'

He paused then, appeared to be making a decision. 'I must say, Mrs Hesketh always took a very kind interest in him and it was through her and her charities that we were able to give him such a good education. We intended to give him one as good as we could, of course, but with her help we were able to make it better.'

'University, in the end,' said Tilly proudly, as she fingered her glowing amber necklace, an excellent advertisement for her husband's trade.

'He was very clever at school,' admitted George.

'Not surprising,' agreed Tilly, and received another, almost imperceptible, warning glance, 'considering how hard he worked,' she added hurriedly.

Best was twenty minutes early at the Cocoa Rooms. He found a snug alcove in the far corner out of sight of prying eyes and looked around.

These places had certainly improved since his childhood, he noticed, particularly since they were now mostly run by business people like the Lockharts instead of the temperance movements.

Thank goodness they didn't just serve cocoa. There was also coffee and tea – but, well, why not. Cocoa was nice and warming and it, too, had improved. It no longer tasted like fatty gruel.

He placed his order, took out his cigarettes and unfolded copies of two Newcastle newspapers and the *Daily Chronicle*.

Time to catch up on the local and national news.

He soon learned that Gateshead, Newcastle's twin town across the Tyne, had decided to invest in a public library, while the authorities at the fishing port of North Shields at the mouth of the Tyne had been delighted with the success of their temporary home for fallen women and wished to make it permanent.

Shipbuilding yards were proposed for upstream Scotswood, now feasible since Tyne-widening and clearance and the replacement of the little old stone bridge with the new Swing Bridge.

Mr Joseph Swan had demonstrated his electric street lighting in Mosley Street in the middle of Newcastle, and a well-supported meeting of the Consett Parnell Defence Fund had taken place.

The steady trickle of fatal mining and shipping accidents continued and there had been a Fatal Poaching Affray at Yetholm up by the Scottish border. Poachers had attacked and kicked and beaten a police constable, who had later died when lockjaw set in. The coroner criticized the gamekeeper, also present, who had protected himself with a shotgun but failed to do the same for the constable.

Another policeman dying to protect the rich man's property and, in this case, just rabbits!

When it came to the national news, there had been another confrontation with the natives in Afghanistan, a revolt in the Transvaal and the Irish situation was worsening. Nothing changes, thought Best.

Oh, but what was this in the *Daily Chronicle*?

ENTRAPPING OF ENGLISH GIRLS ABROAD
Results of the Trial (By Submarine Telegraph). From our own correspondent

All twelve accused had been found guilty, he read, and received sentences of up to six years imprisonment.

There was also a leader on the subject. Oddly, this blamed the importation of young English girls partly on 'the exceeding difficulty of them finding remunerative employment at home'.

When it came to the difficulties with the authorities faced by those attempting to stop this trade the leader writer declared that 'at one time there was a strong suspicion that the latter connived at the traffic but the trial tends to exonerate the police from complicity in these nefarious activities'.

Oh, really. Well, well. They had got away with it. Would that make his efforts to trace the girls harder or easier? Easier, in some ways, he decided, as everyone would be more nervous. On the other hand, that could also mean that they would try harder to conceal girls already there.

As 6.30 came and went, Best began popping his head around

the transom every now and then so as not to miss Smith's arrival. It was a long time in coming.

'Sorry I'm late,' he said as he puffed into view at 7.15 p.m. 'I was held up with a customer and then I still had my stock to clear away. Wouldn't have got here now but someone helped me out.'

'Busy lad,' murmured Best. 'What's it like to have to work for a living?'

Smith shook his head wearily. 'Terrible. Such a long day, being watched all the time – and as for all those rules! I'll never complain about Cheadle again. The man's a saint!'

They both laughed.

'Yes you will!' said Best.

Smith took a gulp of his tea and held up his cup to salute Best.

My, but it was good to see him. The lad did look tired though.

'Right, tell me everything,' said Best.

Twenty-three

Detective Sergeant Clegg sat at a plain, oak desk under the severe gaze of the Empress of India. The bejewelled monarch was somehow managing to stare down at him, as he struggled with his report on the interview with George and Tilly Meredith, while at the same time gazing off into the distance towards her faraway dominions. All right for her, thought Clegg, she doesn't have to sit in the CID room writing reports to be read by the better educated.

He realized that he had failed to get George and Tilly to admit that they knew the identity of Arthur's real mother. Indeed, he wasn't even sure that they did know. But he was certain that they were aware that she wasn't a servant girl with whom the master had had his wicked way but a lady of more substance.

And if they knew, it was virtually certain that darling Arthur had also known beforehand. Given the younger man's lawyerly skills and delusions of grandeur surely he would have probed further into the mystery of his real parenthood. The answers were not so hard to find.

But why did he deny it? To hide the fact that he had deliberately courted Phoebe? That would certainly have revealed him to be dishonest at least, and calculatingly cold-hearted and – what else?

And what was it all about? Why would he court her knowing she was his half-sister and therefore that they could not marry? What was the point?

Clegg struggled to find the right words to convey these thoughts. He wished McLeod and Best were there so he could just tell them what happened and they could discuss it and maybe appreciate the fact that he had made another, if minor, discovery. They were probably enjoying a friendly pint together somewhere while he was getting the feeling that he had been shunted off into this Meredith business, which they didn't really consider to be that important.

The front-office clerk put his head around the office door.

'There's a Miss Sadie Wilson wanting to see that Inspector Best.'

'He's not here.'

'Oh, right,' said the clerk and began closing the door.

Clegg stopped him. 'What's it about?'

'I divn't kna, man. She never said. But,' he added mischievously, 'she was certain it was *him* she wanted to speak to.' He paused, then, seeing Clegg was not responding, added, 'She is very het up about *something*, though, man. Keeps saying it's urgent.'

Clegg threw down his pen, blotted his half-written report and threw it into the top drawer of the desk. 'I'll come down.'

Words were spilling forth from John George Smith in a most unusual manner.

His normal delivery was measured and thoughtful, picking out the right words, particularly when among more educated people such as some of the other Yard detectives. But he had just been released, albeit temporarily, from his shop assistant's bonds and the wearing task of pretending to be someone other than he was.

Then there was his delight on seeing Best again. The combination had unlocked his tongue with a vengeance.

'I can't understand what people are saying half the time!' he exclaimed. 'They're worse than foreigners!'

Best got a word in here and there to prompt him and he went on to explain how he had ended up on the shop floor at Bainbridge & Co. – and why. Though delighted to see the man Best was angry at the manner of his coming and furious that he had not been warned. What was Cheadle up to!

He had promised Best he would send Smith up when he was available, but not without informing him and the local police. That was another thing. If they found out, it would set his efforts to make friends with them back into the Stone Age.

'McLeod and Clegg are good men,' he exclaimed, 'and efficient police officers! They shouldn't be treated like this!'

'Well, you know,' said Smith carefully, 'it's partly your fault that I was sent up without telling anyone.'

'What!'

It transpired that, after Best had left, people of some importance in the North East had approached the Home Secretary emphasizing how important was the solving of this crime to a town approaching the status of a city and pointing out that they were anxious not to frighten off investors with a crime-ridden image. Foreign money was pouring in for armaments and the country was in need of foreign money. Consequently, the Home Secretary had put pressure on the commissioner, who, in turn, had put pressure on the Yard.

'It was the suggestion in your report of possible abduction to the Continent for prostitution that had them sending me up,' Smith sighed. 'They were worried that the local police might be involved.'

Best groaned. Oh, that was typical. Just because the police were accused of being involved before – and foreign police at that . . .

'It was only one possibility!' Best fumed. 'Out of many!'

All of which didn't help Best with his quandary. Should he just tell McLeod and Clegg about Smith's arrival? Trouble was, he still wasn't quite sure about Clegg's loyalty. He might see this as an opportunity to undermine Best.

'Oh, I'm so sick of all this!'

Smith watched Best's furious expression anxiously until Best reached across, smiled, patted his arm and said, 'It's good to see you, John George.'

'You too,' said Smith and grinned back. He loved this man.

When they had first met he had been taken aback by this arm touching and even, sometimes, the hugging of his shoulders. Not to mention the man's flashing smile and impeccably stylish dress. But he'd soon been carried along by Best's enthusiasm and ebullient personality and realized that some of his vivacity must be down to having an Italian mother.

Since then, the two men had shared many exciting, anxious and interesting times.

Smith thought it terrible that they should even think of sending Best up here so soon after that terrible tragedy of his. The man might be driven to do away with himself! But now here he was, thinner, paler and more tired, a shadow of the vibrant man he had been – but still alive and even, in his anger, showing the odd spark or two of his old spirit.

'Are you trying to make me take the pledge,' Best said glancing around the Cocoa Rooms.

Smith grinned. 'Thought we would be less likely to bump into policemen here.'

He was right there. McLeod had told him how drunkenness on duty at Christmas was once such a big problem that when the present chief constable took over he decided to take radical steps to stop it by granting two days' extra leave to those who could conduct themselves properly over the festivities. Those who could not were severely punished. Problem solved.

'I suppose you have your knowledge of ladies' clothes to thank for all this?' said Best.

Smith grinned ruefully and nodded. He was used to Best teasing him about his experience, gained from a childhood spent hung about with ladies' clothing when his mother had to take in washing. But it had proved useful in more than one enquiry.

'They sent me to some Knightsbridge shops so I could learn a bit about selling and find out what the latest Paris fashions are.'

Best shook his head wonderingly.

'Don't the other assistants wonder what is going on? This Londoner suddenly coming among them?'

'Mebbe a bit, at first,' he admitted. 'But they was told that I was engaged to Ethel, a Geordie girl, and needed a job up here – so that quite pleased them really.'

The handsome Smith's blond-haired and blue-eyed boyish charm pleased a lot of people, particularly the ladies.

'But did not please Betsy, I'll be bound!'

Smith laughed. 'Oh, she don't know about my "engagement".'

'So, who is playing the part of this lady friend?'

Smith shook his head. 'Nobody. Ethel's in service and is

working out her notice. By the time that's up, I'll be gone!' He laughed again and added, 'I hope.'

A sudden feeling of dread gripped Best. He couldn't bear to lose anyone else. He leaned over and squeezed Smith's arm again. 'You will be careful in that place, won't you! I get the feeling that vicious forces are at work here.'

Twenty-four

The clerk had not been wrong. Sadie Wilson certainly did seem het up about something.

'It's him!' she exclaimed after Clegg had eventually persuaded her that he was a suitable substitute for Best.

'Who?'

'The man that Mary Donovan used to speak to sometimes.'

'Oh.' That wasn't very exciting. The girl worked in a hotel. She must have spoken to dozens of men and some must be regulars, so she would speak to them more than once. Clegg was starting to wish that he had not become involved but got on with his report.

'Inspector Best said I was to come and get him as soon as the man came.' Sadie's head jerked compulsively as she watched him. She began turning around as if to leave and have him follow, her shoulders shuddering into a spasm. 'He's there *now*, in the pub,' she insisted anxiously.

Oh well, if Best thought it was that important he had better go with her and let Best see, again, that he wasn't a Northern clodhopper.

'All right,' he said, 'I'll come down.'

It was of course downhill all the way towards the river and little Sadie had almost to run to keep up with him. Realizing he would need some more information if he was to beard this man he slowed down as elegant Grey Street became the less impressive Dean Street before curving into The Side.

A breathless Sadie explained about how Mary Donovan had talked to the man now and then but had not told the others anything about him and, indeed, had almost seemed to want to keep him secret.

'She used to look around to see if anyone was watching,'

Sadie puffed, holding her thin fist to her puny chest in an effort to catch her breath.

Of course someone was watching, thought Clegg. Someone always is.

'Once he passed her a note,' she added, looking up at him in the hope of gaining an interested reaction.

He nodded encouragingly but, again, was not impressed. An older man taking an interest and passing a note to a pretty young barmaid. Nothing unusual in that. But of course, he reminded himself, this barmaid was missing.

'Was she upset by this?'

'Oh no, she seemed excited. But she kept what it said to herself.'

So Mary Donovan could read.

'I saw them once talking down by the Aberdeen Wharf,' she said in a final effort to impress him.

Ah, that did make a difference. Them being in contact outside the pub. Quite a lot of difference. But then, if he was guilty of anything, this mysterious man, he surely wouldn't come back and show himself again, would he?

Smith had not been in situ at Bainbridge & Co. long enough to acquire much inside information. But he had discovered that there had been an acrimonious dismissal at the store a couple of months earlier. A man named Benton, who worked among the printed and plain cottons in the Manchester Goods department, had been got rid of. Some assistants claimed it was because he was radical and had become interested in this new Shop Hours Labour League.

'They want earlier closing hours and a half-day off on Saturdays. And Benton went on about all these bloody rules and regulations and not being allowed sufficient time to eat our meals properly. Said they shouldn't have to stop and dash off when bells rang "like animals in a zoo".'

'So what does the firm say?'

'That it was nothing to do with him being an agitator just that he was lazy and didn't do the job properly.'

'Did the other assistants support him?'

'Well, there's a lot of grumbling, particularly from the

128

apprentices about all those rules and having to stay on their feet all day. That gets exhausting, I can tell you. Feel your legs are going to buckle any minute.'

'A strong lad like you – trained on the beat!'

'Yes. But at least you could walk around then and,' he grinned, 'find one or two bolt holes.'

'So, we have some unrest but probably not enough to warrant murder?'

'Not that I've discovered so far. A lot of the older assistants live out anyway, so they're not so bothered. And they know it's much harder in some of the other shops. Some of *them* don't close until eight or ten at night. Midnight on Saturdays. Bainbridges say they would give them a half-day on Saturdays but the other shops refuse to go along with it and they'd lose trade to them.'

'Then they'd all be out of a job.'

'That's right.' He paused and took a long swig of his tea. 'By the way,' he added, 'they say that that Luke bloke is quite active in the Early Closing Association.'

'Harold Luke, Deputy Manager, Beds? Now there you do surprise me. I thought the man was afraid of his own shadow.'

'Mebbe that's just since the other bloke got the sack.'

'Well, have a closer look at him, will you?'

'I'll try. It's not easy.' He looked glum. 'And it's very boring.'

'Any good place to hide a body?' asked Best, changing tack to distract him. His boyish look was fading a little, Best was sad to see, and being replaced with the slightly more staid and solid aspect of the older family man.

'Dozens! The place is full of them! All those stock rooms, offices, factories and warehouses and then there's that carpet-measuring room they're excavating in the basement.'

'Ah, that sounds promising!' Best said enthusiastically – as much to cheer the young man as to greet the news. 'Do you think we could we get down there?'

'I'll investigate.' Smith smiled suddenly. 'Do you know,' he said with the air of a small boy revealing a big secret, 'that Bainbridges were the first shop to do away with abatement *and* that they tolerate tabbies?'

Best grinned at the welcome reappearance of the more

youthful Smith. He knew that no abatement meant fixed prices and no haggling.

'Tabbies?' he enquired indulgently.

'Women who are just looking and might not necessarily want to buy. Other places get their shop walkers to chase them away, but Mr Bainbridge says that "even those of inferior status should receive politeness and, indeed, they are most sensibly affected by it".'

'How admirable of Mr Bainbridge. And of you. I do like to see a loyal and enthusiastic employee.'

Smith glanced up at the Cocoa Rooms clock and groaned. 'Got to go now or I won't get my supper. Even worse, I'll be late for prayers.'

'Heaven forbid.'

'He's gone,' said the barman. Sadie had asked the man to keep an eye on the mysterious stranger – without making it too obvious.

'Went when I was serving that lot over there.' He indicated a group of shabbily dressed Scandinavians. Sadie had warned Clegg that the clientele was not so select in the evenings when all the businessmen had gone home. But this group looked harmless enough, just getting a little comfort before setting off on the next leg of their long journey to the promised land: America.

'Don't you know who this bloke is?'

'No. Not got a notion.' The barman wiped his hands carefully on a towel and shook his head. 'I've only just started here, you know.'

Clegg stood up to leave but was stopped as the barman raised his hand and waved his right forefinger. 'Hold on a minute, though,' he said. 'I did hear him say summit about having some more business to do tonight – along at Gilroy's Vaults by the Leith Wharf.'

Clearly this was a man who liked to hold back information for the best effect.

'Thanks,' said Clegg. 'Very helpful.'

He and Sadie set off eastwards towards the Leith Wharf. Clegg's heavy tread rang out in the quiet air counterpointed by the tap-tap-tap of Sadie's little boots.

The lights on the High Level Bridge glinted between the masts and funnels of the clustered ships and reflected in long wavering lines in the Tyne's now black waters. Beyond, here and there, was the distant glow of iron works and industrial chimneys spitting out sparks.

Funny time for this man to be doing business if he was a proper businessman – as he had been described.

Once, all the 'fitters', who were the middlemen between the colliery owners and the shippers and the ships' brokers, had actually lived down on the Quayside and done business at all hours. These days they all worked office hours then escaped to houses in the suburbs or beside the sea, leaving the Quayside almost deserted at night.

The only signs of life came from the pubs. There weren't many of those, either, in the first stretch of the echoing waterside, lined by monumental banks and offices built after the Great Fire and Explosion of 1854 had destroyed the medieval houses and shops along here.

Broad Chare, which was by no means wide, now marked the boundary between the end of the solidly respectable business buildings and the beginning of factories, semi-derelict houses and warehouses.

It was darker and quieter still here, although more frequently enlivened by occasional raucous noises and shafts of light thrown from the pubs on to the lonely pavement and cobblestones.

A huge grain warehouse loomed ahead, its high bridges crossing to waterside towers for the unencumbered passage of its goods. Just before it, among a cluster of old two-storey buildings, sat a pantiled and timber-framed ships' chandlers, and their destination, Gilroy's Spirit Vaults.

The road began bearing left, taking them slightly away from the river. To their right were the kegs and barrels of the Tyne Brewery and various sacks and boxes spilling around the waterside sheds of the London Wharf. The lights had been turned off here and only a glimmer from the street lamp reached the edge of the piled goods.

Judging by the distant thumping and creak of steam cranes and dim lights, loading was still going on. But the further lights threw the nearer space into darker and more sinister blackness. It was from here that two male figures emerged and headed towards them.

Their sudden appearance even gave Clegg a bit of a shock, and Sadie grabbed his arm, nodded towards the one in front and whispered, 'That's *him.*'

The man she indicated was obviously the more gentlemanly of the two. As he came forward into the dim street lights he seemed vaguely familiar, but the shadow of his top hat obscured his face. Then he was near enough.

'Oh, it's *you!*' exclaimed Clegg, relieved.

Twenty-five

'You must remember that we *are* investigators,' said Quarrell in response to Best's bemused expression. 'And these are test seances.'

Best had been wondering what was so hypnotic about this tall, black-haired man with the heavy eyebrows over intense dark eyes. Then he realized that no matter what the man said, whether fiercely felt, light-hearted or mundane, his face remained immobile and his head perfectly still. The effect was oddly mesmeric.

I'm an investigator too, thought Best, as he perused the Newcastle Society's test paraphernalia, but I've never seen anything quite like this apart from in some of Soho's more dubious premises.

As well as the wire cage in which they locked mediums before their attempts at spirit materialization there were tapes and threads with which to bind their hands and feet and wax to seal the knots as well as leather straps for similar purposes.

Once affixed, the long ends of these binders were passed outside the cabinet then tied to a chair or handed to sitters so that any attempt by the medium to free herself would be detected in her movement.

'The mediums may be searched before they perform, of course,' said Quarrell, then added rather disparagingly, 'but we would *never* use a galvanometer. We think that could be dangerous.'

It was common knowledge that the famous medium Florence Cook (who had been the star of the Dalston Spiritualist Society in London's East End when, at the tender age of seventeen, she had been the first medium in Britain to produce a full materialization) had once been obliged to complete an electric circuit so that any attempts to escape her bonds would show up on the galvanometer. Best suspected that Quarrell's reservations about galvanometers might be more related to inter-society rivalry than safety concerns.

As though to prove him right, Quarrell exclaimed, 'But we do have this!' Even this ultra-controlled person could scarcely conceal his delight as he whipped back a curtain to reveal a weighing machine.

Best raised his eyebrows and tightened his lips to repress a laugh.

'This splendid machine was presented to us by our esteemed supporter Mr Charles Blackburn, the Manchester industrialist,' Quarrell explained.

Best couldn't think of any response other than, 'How bizarre!' but knew that would be scarcely politic if he wanted to keep the information flowing. He wasn't quite sure where it was leading him, if anywhere, but was convinced that the answer to many of his questions might lie here.

Quarrell, not a man to adapt his behaviour to his company, was unaffected by Best's silence.

'The cabinet containing the medium is mounted on the machine,' he pointed out. 'Any fluctuations in weight during manifestations are recorded here.' He indicated a band of paper wrapped around a vertical metal drum with a pencil held horizontally against it. 'The pencil moves up and down and the cylinder is also in motion, therefore zigzag lines appear on the graph.'

'Impressive. You certainly are very thorough,' Best murmured, managing to inject a note of admiration into his voice.

'You do realize what it means!' exclaimed Quarrell seriously.

Best chose his words carefully. 'That those who accuse the medium of masquerading as a spirit may be proved wrong if there is no fluctuation in the weight.'

'Ye-s,' Quarrell said uncertainly, 'in principle. But it's a little more complex than that.'

He paused, reached into his Gladstone bag and drew out some magazines. 'This one,' he tapped a copy of an October edition of *The Spiritualist*, 'gives a fairly thorough account of the procedure. There are reports of our activities in the others that should give you an idea of our standing in the psychic community.'

'Splendid,' said Best, taking them. Just as well he had stopped going to church otherwise he'd be forever confessing all the lies he was obliged to tell.

How, he wondered, did the mediums feel about being subjected to all this tying up, weighing and constant testing? It was rumoured that some suffered nervous breakdowns from the strain and even ended up in mental asylums.

'Don't the mediums object to all this?' he asked casually.

Quarrell shook his head firmly while managing to move it infinitesimally. 'They are professionals. We make their reputations for them and protect them from the hurly-burly of public mediumship. In any case, most,' he added dismissively, 'are simple, working-class girls, who without us would probably be scrubbing floors somewhere. So they are grateful,' he added smugly.

Or should be, was the message.

He must learn more about this falling-out of Miss Wood and Miss Annie Fairlamb.

The more Quarrell cooperated with him the more suspicious he became about the whole situation, although he could see that he wasn't being quite fair. Was it rather because he felt it was not in Quarrell's nature to be so obliging?

'Was Phoebe witness to these more stringent tests?' Best enquired suddenly. 'The tying-up and so forth?'

Momentarily, the question threw Quarrell.

Recovering quickly he said quite emphatically, 'Oh, no. Of course not. That wouldn't be at all suitable for well-bred young ladies to observe.'

But it was all right for a lot of middle-aged, middle-class men to bind up young working-class girls, thought Best.

He frowned as another question occurred to him. 'Did either of the other three missing girls ever attend the society's seances?'

Quarrell gazed at him wonderingly.

'Good heavens, no. This is a private association, only

members and invited guests are allowed in. I very much doubt whether these three girls would be among them.'

'But you don't know for certain?' persisted Best.

Quarrell straightened up to his full, dignified height. 'Well, no, not absolutely.' His shrug was almost imperceptible. 'Of course it's vaguely possible that a member brought one of their servants along to keep them company or assist them.'

'I need to look at the books again,' Best said firmly.

Best lay on his bed leafing through *The Spiritualist* and *Medium and Daybreak*. He was attempting, first of all, to obtain an overall view of their content. It had been a long day and this was scarcely bedtime reading.

Among the reports of various meetings and investigations of the well-known societies he was bemused to notice advertisements for servants who were also spiritualists.

Why was that? An increasing number of households held their own seances. Were these spiritualist servants required to act as mediums for families that did not contain a 'sensitive' of their own and, if so, was it their role to introduce them to the pastime – as Florence had done with hers? Or was it merely to be sure that the servant would not run off screaming at the sight of a muslin-wrapped figure floating about the house?

Among the short news items was one announcing that Mr Joseph Skipsey, the Northumbrian seer and poet, who did spiritualist work among the miners, was to receive a state pension for his literary services. Another described how some Northern miners had seen spirits and even goblins at the coal face.

There were efforts to equate spiritualism with Christianity, particularly Methodism. Among Primitive Methodists, one correspondent pointed out, speaking in tongues was a common occurrence. Another compared spiritualist materialization with visions of the Virgin Mary seen by the faithful – and even the resurrection. Reasonable enough, Best supposed, although he knew that the very idea would have horrified his mother.

Having taken his overall view and deciding to forgo the pleasures of the poem entitled *The Drowned Sailor and his Spirit Mother*, Best settled down to read the first of several reports on the activities of the Newcastle Society. After only the first few words he drifted into sleep and dreamed not of drowned sailors or goblins down coal mines but of someone falling and he being unable to save them.

Detective Inspector McLeod was not pleased. He had called in at the Worswick Street Police Station on his way to Best's hotel to pick up Clegg's latest report on the progress of his enquiries. He found none.

Here he was, trying to keep up to date with what was happening not to mention protect the force's reputation and keep the peace between Clegg and Best and the man goes and lets him down like this. He knew that McLeod was a stickler for efficiency and keeping adequate notes and reports on each subsequent development.

Now, with no report, the Meredith aspect was drifting out of his control and he didn't like it. And when the aspect concerned someone as influential as Sir George his instinct told him that trouble could develop.

'I know we gave him the task of investigating the Meredith and Threapleton connection,' he complained to Best while the latter finished his breakfast among the commercial travellers, 'but he really ought to keep in better touch.'

Oddly, Best was sanguine.

'Oh, you know what it's like,' he shrugged, 'trying to trace people, finding they're not there, having to go back, meaning to do your report as soon as you get the chance.'

McLeod was surprised. It was common knowledge that it had been this inability to keep track of detectives when they were out on cases that had allowed wrongdoing to develop among the Yard's detective branch. This had resulted in the spectacular fraud case in 1878 that had seen several of them jailed. But Best was right, it was hellish difficult to keep in touch with detectives once they were out on a case.

He was also surprised by Best's defence of Clegg. It seemed a truce had been called.

'To be honest,' admitted Best as he liberally buttered his toast and spread it with honey, 'I'm not sure there is much to gain in pursuing Meredith after all. Now, this spiritualism.

There's something going on there.'

'Well, it's an odd business, isn't it.'

'Yes, but this one seems odder than most,' Best laughed and instantly looked ten years younger. He had clearly benefited from a good night's sleep and, maybe, this diversion from his own personal tragedy. 'I intend to arm myself with a little more information,' he indicated Quarrell's magazines, 'then go off and make a few more enquiries in that direction. Would you have a word with the parents of the two other girls and see if they had any connection with the Newcastle Society – or spiritualism in any way?'

McLeod nodded. 'All right.' He didn't put much faith in that possibility himself, but with the dearth of any other lead at the moment . . .

'Some other connections might emerge now,' Best suggested with a new optimism. 'With Mary Donovan, of course, or something else we haven't even envisaged.' He savoured his coffee. 'Maybe we could meet here again this evening and discuss it along with their files.' He smiled. 'By then, I expect Clegg will have reported back.'

'He'd better have,' said McLeod.

Twenty-six

M r Charles Blackburn, the wealthy Manchester industri-alist, might have been a hard-headed businessman but he was clearly bowled over by a spirit that had materialized at one of Miss C. E. Wood's performances at the Newcastle Society premises. It certainly sounded extraordinary.

The American Indian princess Pocahontas, or, as he referred to her, Pocky, had on this occasion appeared as a three-foot-high child with baby feet, bow legs and a child's face. She had allowed Blackburn to touch her body to check she was not an adult woman on her knees and then the spirit had climbed on his back. Its weight, he estimated, was about twenty pounds.

Shortly afterwards a full human female form appeared and stroked Mr Blackburn's face and fetched him a glass of water before turning her attentions to the rest of the audience.

'Then she said she must go,' Mr Blackburn wrote in a letter to his daughter that he had kindly allowed the readers of *The Spiritualist* to share. 'She gradually vanished before our eyes just as she came. In say eight or ten minutes other forms kept appearing, and it was a glorious sight.'

In an October issue of *The Spiritualist*, Mr John Mould announced that Mr Blackburn had presented the Newcastle Spiritualist Evidence Society with a very valuable weighing machine and described its use.

Before entering the cabinet, he explained, Miss Wood had sat on the machine and been found to weigh seven stone, three pounds. When, after about an hour, she produced a spirit it, too, had been invited to mount the scales. However, the room's dim lighting made reading the register difficult, so this spirit, and later 'forms', were asked to retire behind the curtain each

139

time Mr Mould and Mr Walton, the circle manager, lit a taper to check the reading.

They established that the first spirit form had weighed five stone, three pounds. Mould and Walton asked it for a weight reduction and it returned 'diminished in bulk' and weighed in at two stone, seven pounds. A request for a further reduction resulted in 'diminished volume' and a weight of only one stone, three-and-a-half pounds.

Suddenly, a much more fully developed figure had appeared and registered six stone, ten pounds. Then a 'very portly form' presented itself and was found to weigh seven stone, twelve-and-a-half pounds. Finally, Miss Wood's 'familiar' materialized at two stone before Miss Wood herself returned to the scales, this time to weigh only six stone, twelve pounds.

Well, this might mean something to them, thought Best, but it certainly confuses me. What does it all signify? More to the point, what did it prove? Particularly baffling was the fact that even Miss Wood's weight was inconsistent.

Several other reports on the activities of the Newcastle Society featured in the spiritualist magazines. All of the accounts were written by Mr John Mould, although none of them mentioned that he was a leading member of the society, merely giving his name and address at the bottom as with any other correspondent.

Best found this curious. How could the man's reports be judged unbiased given who he was, and why did he not reveal his status? Was it that the readers would be considered familiar enough with his involvement and that the society's investigative role was sufficiently well thought of to block any doubts?

In his reports he mentioned Mr Charles Blackburn as an observer characteristically independent of thought and expression and alleged that there was no enquirer more anxious than Mr Blackburn to obtain bona fide phenomena. No surprise that the man had reported enthusiastically on one of their seances.

However, Best had to admit that one of Mr Mould's reports did not attempt to hide some of the strain the mediums felt and also illustrated that their performances did not always proceed smoothly.

Indeed, he confessed that two of Miss Wood's spirits had

become annoyed when asked to undertake several tests before an audience – such as standing up against two of them to judge her relative height. It allowed the first measuring but on the second declared it did not care for such comparisons and retired behind the curtain.

Another, 'a little form which usually appears at these seances', was asked to allow the cabinet door to be checked by Mr Matthews to establish that it was still fastened, even being asked by Mr Mould to 'withdraw from our view' without going behind the curtain to do so.

The 'little form' had not been pleased and angrily harangued him. She cried and sobbed that she didn't feel like doing these things and that he had aggrieved the spirit. However, she had eventually not only allowed the cabinet to be checked, but then 'appeared to become invisible, much in the same way that the disappearance of a snowflake impresses the observer'.

Of course, this reluctance may have been deliberate – in the manner of jugglers who drop a baton to show the action is not easy, then succeed to rapturous and relieved applause.

Best sighed, put the magazines to one side, glanced fearfully out of the window at the forbidding sky, got to his feet and armed himself to face the great northern outdoors with overcoat, scarf, gloves and hat. He had an appointment.

There was nothing unusual about the photograph. Kate Thomson posed alongside one of those ornately, even crudely, carved wood tables that seemed to be manufactured solely for the purpose of gracing photographic studios. On the table, a tall and rather sickly looking plant leaned towards the girl, and in her hands she held the usual small basket of flowers deemed necessary for photographs of young girls.

Older women, like men, were allowed to lean, although not too nonchalantly, or stand alongside the carved table or stand that held the flower basket. Young women, it seemed, must carry it, possibly for the assumed purpose of strewing the flowers in the path of an unsuspecting young man.

There was little unusual about Kate Thomson either. A young girl who appeared to be hovering uncertainly on the brink of womanhood. Eagerness, hope and doubt jostled for dominance around her even features. Her slightly open mouth offered a trace of a smile and the olive-shaped eyes dared to be a little direct in their gaze.

'She's a very pretty girl,' said McLeod gently.

'All I've got,' said Mrs Thomson, fighting to hold back tears. 'She looks a bit older now. That was taken last year in a booth at the Hoppin's.'

The Hoppings was a huge, week-long fair held every June on the Town Moor. It was a highlight in the North-Eastern calendar.

There was nothing unusual in Kate's pose either, apart from being a little direct for a young lady, but what had surprised McLeod, or at least McLeod's wife, Sarah, when he showed it to her, were the girl's clothes.

Sarah thought they were very up-to-the-minute and well made for a working-class girl from Newcastle. She'd pointed out the tunic style of the dress and its deep horizontal ruching circling the top of the skirt. Also the square white ruched bib trimmed with lace at the neck and, particularly, her neat little round hat. Like that of a page boy it perched prettily on Kate's Princess Alexandra froth of little flat curls. On top of the hat was what appeared to be a concoction of ribbons and a silk flower.

'She made her own clothes,' explained Mrs Thomson, whose short, barrel-like figure threatened any moment to burst from its cage of tight, black bombazine. 'Mostly from leftovers at work.'

'She was a seamstress?'

It was not usual for businesses to be so generous.

Mrs Thomson nodded, causing her round little chin to disappear into her neck. 'Aha. They let her use the patterns as well. It was getten all that that helped make her look so bonny,' she added with some pride.

They were standing either side of the counter of Mrs Thomson's sweet shop, which had been crammed into the front room of an ordinary little terraced house. A shelf extending into the room had been built from the bottom of the window frame, and upright panels reached up from it to provide a box-like structure that served as a shop window.

Lining the shelves behind Mrs Thomson as she stood at the tiny counter were bottles and jars of jewel-bright boiled sweets, tawny humbugs, gaudily striped sugar sticks, pastilles and toffees. Teetering on top of each other on either side of the counter and on the floor were cartons of sugar mice, liquorice sticks and chocolate.

Mrs Thomson only just had room to move about serving her customers and that task was only made possible by the fact that she knew the exact location of all her stock.

'That lad she was gannin with,' asked McLeod, adapting his speech a little to make the situation seem as normal and casual as possible as he leaned forwards between an open tin of sherbet and a jar of lollipops, 'you said they'd fallen out?'

'Aha. That's right.'

'Why was that?'

'Did he not tell you?'

The singsong Geordie with its rising cadence, which often made quite ordinary statements sound like queries, rose twice as high when a real question was asked.

'Oh, aye, he did.'

Kate's boyfriend, Billie Lang, had seemed a surly young man, but they had been unable to dispute his claim that he had not seen her for a week before she disappeared.

'But what did *she* say about it?'

'Nothing, really.' She shoved a straying hairpin back into her tight, wispy bun. 'But meself, I reckon he was jealous. Didn't like the way other lads looked at her – her being so well got up and all.'

She stopped abruptly as two little boys came in wanting a pennyworth of black bullets, the local minty boiled sweet, and a farthing poke of sherbet.

She'd insisted on staying open to catch the trade from the homecoming school children and promised to shut for half an hour after that so that they could talk in peace. But McLeod had been unable to wait that long so had taken his chances.

He stood to one side while she deftly twisted a piece of paper into a little poke, spooned sherbet inside then weighed up a few black bullets and poured them into another paper poke.

143

McLeod had always had this nagging feeling that these missing girls might all be missing for different reasons and therefore might not belong in the same file at all.

Religion didn't provide a link. Church attendances and events were some of the best boy-girl meeting places and, when not at work, people from each religion tended to stick together. But Mary Donovan was Roman Catholic, Kate Thomson Church of England, and Amelia Cook's parents were Methodists.

'One thing, hinny,' said Mrs Thomson after the two lads had left.

'Yes?'

'She did tell me that Billie said she was getting above herself with all these nice clothes and trying to learn to talk better.'

Well, thought McLeod, that at least meant she was similar to Mary Donovan, who could also read and write well and was trying to better herself with a good job.

'Why did she want to do that? Learn to talk better?'

'Well, hinny, she was mixing with some of them fancy ladies, wasn't she?'

He frowned. 'But she was a seamstress.'

'Oh, aha. That's right. But she had such a nice way with her and was got up so in the fashion that she often was asked to help when they went to see ladies who were being measured and fitted an all.'

Ah. That opened up the possibilities. Had one of them tried to recruit her as a medium? Or had the son of the house, or the father come to that, taken a fancy to her?

'She's always worked for Perkins?'

Mrs Thomson opened her mouth and seemed about to say something. Then she closed it again, took a deep breath and, refusing to meet his eye, said firmly, 'Yes. Since school.'

'You're sure?'

'Of course I am, man. I'm her mother aren't I.'

There was no disputing that. But why, then, the hesitation? McLeod wondered, as a posse of clamouring children invaded the shop. He would not push her now. The set line of her little mouth told him that would be futile. He would have to pursue the matter elsewhere, or come back. He caught her eye above the hubbub of excited bairns, tipped his hat and left.

Twenty-seven

They were sitting in the same room beside the same red-plush-covered table, but this time the heavy curtains had been drawn back and wintry sunlight filtered through the windows, making the room appear much more cheerful and normal.

Glass-domed ornaments and silver candlesticks twinkled subtly in the pale sunshine as did the tiny jet butterflies that nestled in Hermione's soft cloud of raven hair. Indeed, as she moved her head these butterflies almost seemed to fly. Best found them quite hypnotic, as was she, he had to admit, although he wasn't quite sure why.

He had attempted to disarm Hermione by neither referring to Phoebe's visits to their circle, nor by demanding to be told how Florence had learned about him and his tragedy. All he wanted, he had assured her, was her assistance in understanding more about spiritualism in general and the Newcastle Society in particular.

She frowned suspiciously, 'Shouldn't you be asking them to explain themselves?'

'Oh I have, I have,' he insisted. 'I'm merely searching for a wider view.'

'I see.' A slightly cynical, knowing smile plucked at the corners of her mouth.

'Between you and me,' he murmured in his most confidential manner, 'I got the impression that, worthy as they are, they may be a little inclined to exaggerate their achievements.'

At that, Hermione guffawed but said nothing, merely continuing to hold his eye to indicate that she knew exactly what he was doing.

'Don't you agree?' he persisted softly.

She sat up straighter in her high-backed chair, pulled her amber velvet shawl around her shoulders and murmured, 'I couldn't possibly comment on the activities of other spiritualists.'

Best took advantage of the undeniable spark between them by sighing, 'I really do need your help. I'm not after anything scurrilous, you understand, just some confidential impressions to help me decide whether I'm on the right track.'

'Right track for what?'

'In the process of attempting to discover what happened to poor Phoebe.'

That remark contained a small warning that if she didn't comply the investigation may veer in her direction again. He had stressed the word 'confidential'.

'But, if . . .' He made as though to rise. She stayed him with her hand.

'Tell me something,' he asked as he settled back down, 'why is it that you're not a medium? I would have seen you as the "sensitive" rather than Florence.' He held her eye shamelessly, a little flattery never hurt. Another sin. But he was being sincere in this case. More or less.

'Oh, I am, I am,' she insisted and even blushed a little. Again her eyes indicated that she was not taken in – but acknowledged that he was a very attractive man. 'Florence and I work alternately. We support each other – just as Miss Wood and Annie Fairlamb used to.'

Used to.

She clearly expected him to pursue that troubled relationship. But he didn't. She wasn't to know that 'confuse people' was one of his mottoes.

'Tell me about Mr Mould?' he enquired instead, acting on another principle, that of getting people talking with the easy questions first.

She shook her head in surprise and the butterflies danced. 'He's founder member of the Newcastle Society.'

'Well, how can they be unbiased when he's the one who writes the reports of their activities for the spiritualist magazines?'

Hermione threw her head back and laughed out loud. 'They're not. Of course they're not!' She had a lovely throat.

He had her now. He knew instinctively that she would tell him everything. He waited, smiling.

'They never mention the critical reports about them.'

'Such as?'

'Well, earlier this year the *Northern Daily Express* wrote a very funny and sarcastic article about one of their meetings. Mr Barkas, another founder member, was very exercised about it and wrote a furious reply with a description of the event that was quite at odds with theirs.' She paused then added soberly, 'Of course, we are all open to such criticism, but they do rather ask for it with all their tub thumping – then we all pay the penalty.'

Her amber eyes clouded and he wanted to comfort her. Good grief, he thought, get a grip on yourself, man!

'Why did Miss Wood and Annie Fairlamb fall out with the society?'

She glanced skywards. 'Oh, we've had many versions of that sad story.' She took a deep breath. 'The two ladies gave joint seances for a while but they began to disagree between themselves – and then with the society. *They* claimed that they were being underpaid, defrauded in fact. Miss Wood left the society's protection also saying they weren't being properly protected from the unruly elements in the audiences when they gave public seances for the society and that they were being harassed to death with so many tests. Annie Fairlamb followed shortly after.

'Do you know,' she said, adopting a mischievously gossipy tone, 'they say that one of her male spirits, "Sam" he's called, struck a male sitter who was feeling him to see if he was solid. Then he really clouted William Armstrong. He's one of the society's leading officials – another founder member.' She laughed and her jet earrings danced along with her butterflies.

'Annie *was* getting a little out of control but that may just have been because of the way she was being treated. Some people claimed to have heard slapping from behind the curtain before Sam came on. The society said it was all the fault of this man friend of hers, who was giving her ideas. She's married to him now and does private seances in their home.'

'Very interesting,' said Best. As he had suspected, the

147

spiritualist world, just like any other, was alive with gossip. It was just a matter of tapping into it.

'This Mr Blackburn,' he said, switching again.

'Yes?' She smiled a feline smile.

'What do you know about him?'

'I hear he is a very *kind* man.'

'In what way?'

She raised her eyebrows. 'You should ask Florence Cook about that.'

'Why don't *you* tell me,' he smiled his most winning smile, 'the connection between Florence Cook and Mr Blackburn's kindness?'

'Well, he was one of her early supporters – after she first made her sensational debut at Dalston. Gave her money and presents and took her on outings. As did many wealthy men. He even,' she paused, 'escorted her to Paris. For the good of her health, you understand.'

'Of course,' said Best.

'Nowadays, it seems that it is the health of her younger sister, Kate, which concerns him more. She is a medium too.'

Twenty-eight

Where was Clegg? McLeod had searched his desk again for signs of a report from the sergeant, but still hadn't found one. This really was too much. The man was upset because Scotland Yard had been called in on their big case, but such behaviour could only help show that that decision had been the right one.

Neither was there any sign of Clegg's name under today's date in the department's attendance register – or yesterday's! What was the man *thinking* of? It was, in fact, out of character – the sergeant was usually punctilious about such matters.

Perhaps Clegg's enquiries prevented him from coming in. He could have been out late chasing up a clue then out again early to follow it up. If so, he should have telegraphed the office. McLeod had given him carte blanche on that section of the case but he needed to know where the man was, at least some of the time, and how it was progressing. If he was being petulant about Best he was in trouble. Real trouble.

McLeod sat down heavily and wearily at his desk, feeling vaguely uneasy. Could something have happened to the man? An accident or, worse, an assault? No, this part of the enquiry – Meredith, Sir George – could scarcely be described as dangerous.

Was he ill? That must be it. Clegg was sick. He'd been having some trouble with his chest and the weather was very damp and foggy just now.

McLeod called through to the outer office for the branch's newest recruit, DC Clark, who looked all of twelve years old and made the DI feel ancient. He kept expecting the lad to empty his pockets of bits of string, a wooden spinning top and a furred clump of black bullets.

'Yes, sir,' Clark said, almost instantly appearing at attention before him, proudly wearing his new tie, bought as soon as he had saved up enough of his 6d a day detective's clothing allowance.

'Clegg hasn't signed the entry book for two days.' McLeod wrote out the address and handed it to Clark. 'Go to his home and see if he is sick.'

He watched Clark's eager figure dash out then settled down to re-read the notes on the disappearance of the fourth missing girl, Amelia Cook.

Judging by the detective officers' reports, sixteen-year-old Amelia Cook was the least likely of the girls to go missing.

Unlike Phoebe she had not led a lively life in elevated social circles or attended questionable seances. Nor had she gone out to work in a dubious area like Mary Donovan or gained entrance by the back door to many wealthy homes as had Kate Thomson.

There was no jealous boyfriend such as Kate had, nor a reluctant consort like Phoebe's. Indeed, there appeared to be no young man in her life – or none who had been noted either by her family or the servants.

The tone of some of the reports implied that, while it couldn't be said that the other girls had exactly brought trouble on themselves, they were certainly more vulnerable than the amiable, home-loving Amelia.

She was the ideal, good, loving daughter quite content to rarely stray outside her comfortable home in Brandling Village on the northern edge of the town, and certainly never to do so alone. The only social events she had attended were connected either with her family or the chapel.

Then, one morning four weeks ago, she had failed to appear at breakfast. Her bed had not been slept in. Her clothes were still in her wardrobe, apart from the dress she had been wearing the previous evening, but she had not been seen since. Nobody had the least idea of what could have happened to her.

McLeod closed the file. There may be some similarities between these girls – but he had yet to find them. Instead, they seemed to him to be almost wilfully dissimilar.

In the light of the recent developments he would visit Amelia Cook's parents again. Who knows, they might be prominent in the village's spiritualist circles. That line of enquiry certainly seemed to be Best's favourite at the moment and, since McLeod had no other . . .

Might the Cooks have some social connection with the Threapletons? Hardly likely. The Cooks were lower middle class. McLeod was unsure of the exact niceties of the social divides hereabouts, but he guessed they were too wide in this instance. But Mr Cook was a bank manager. Business, now that was a possible meeting ground.

'He's not there,' announced a breathless and bright-cheeked DC Clark, rubbing his hands together to restore the feeling. 'Hasn't been home for two nights. Mrs Clegg says she thought he must be so busy that he was sleeping back at the station – like he did in that Mitchell case.'

McLeod stared at him. Oh God. What now? Where was he?

He turned to the office clerk and barked, 'When did you last see Sergeant Clegg?'

'The night before last,' the clerk replied nervously. 'I was just away off home and he was still sitting there, at his desk.'

'Just sitting?'

'Aha. He was biting his nails about writing out a report. You know how he does?'

It was true. Clegg always found report writing a trial. But he *had* been writing one. So it *must* be somewhere.

'What report?'

The clerk shook his head anxiously and pleaded, 'I divn't kna, man. Just that he was muttering to himself a lot.'

McLeod crossed to the sergeant's desk. Scattered about its surface was a pottery ink well, some well-used blotting paper, a dip pen with a chewed end and a part-filled-out expenses form. He opened the top right-hand drawer, where he found a pad of lined paper with half a page of writing on it and notes scribbled in the margins around it.

The three completed paragraphs in Clegg's blot-strewn schoolboy handwriting gave McLeod some idea of what had transpired at the interview with Meredith's adoptive parents.

The cryptic notes, presumably meant to be included in the continuation, said: *Telling the truth? Really not know who mother was? Clever man, lawyer. Must have! Must have!* Then, underlined in red, *See him again, next!*

'Come on,' said McLeod as a watery-eyed Best entered thankfully, casting off gloves, hat and scarf as he went. 'Better put those back on.'

'Where are we going?'

'To see this damned man Meredith. Something's not right!'

In fact, he suspected, something might be terribly wrong.

'Don't be ridiculous, I have no idea where your bloody sergeant is!' Meredith exploded. 'Are you mad!'

'We are not suggesting you have,' said Best mildly, patting the air with his hands in a calming manner.

McLeod, anxious about his colleague, had, uncharacteristically, gone in all unprepared – which was no way to get results from a slippery man like Meredith.

The young lawyer had clearly not been pleased to see them, settling down as he was with a post-dinner glass of his best port and a copy of the *Newcastle Daily Journal*.

'Obviously we are worried about the man,' Best continued, 'but, come to think of it,' he tapped his forehead and grimaced, 'I think I probably know where he is.'

McLeod looked startled and was about to say something, but was halted by Best's warning glance.

'But, now that we *are* here,' Best continued in a relentlessly no-nonsense voice, 'there are just one or two points we wish to clear up.'

Meredith met his eye but said nothing. So, he did have something to hide, Best thought. Right, I'll take a chance and go straight to the point.

'We have evidence that convinces us that indeed you *did* know who your real mother was all along.'

Meredith failed to respond, but Best could tell by his eyes that his brain was racing. McLeod showed no surprise at Best's blatant lie.

'You can, if you wish, sir, drag all this business out even more with further enquiries and interviews – down at the police station, of course. Or you can come clean now and save us any further waste of time. I am assuming,' said Best crisply, 'that you would not want to waste further police time on what is ultimately probably only a trivial matter. Would you, Mr Meredith?'

The air was heavy with the threats that Best did not trouble to hide. He was tired, worried about Clegg and not in the mood to mince words with this pompous young man in middle-aged guise.

Meredith still stared. Then, suddenly, he sat up straight, took a deep breath and said, 'Yes, I did know. I got it out of Aunt Hester and swore I would not tell anyone that she had told me.'

'Your source is safe with us,' Best said sardonically. 'For the moment at least.' He paused. 'So, knowing this you deliberately wooed Phoebe?' He could not keep the contempt from his voice.

Meredith had the grace to blush. Fixing his eyes on his half-drunk glass of port he said, 'Yes. Knowing that, I deliberately wooed Phoebe.'

'Why, for God's sake!'

The cruelty of it made Best angry. He was sick of cruelty. What was the matter with people these days?

'Revenge,' Meredith replied bitterly. 'Pique.' He cast about for justification. 'I don't know what. I felt robbed.' He rocked a little in his chair, suddenly looking much younger and small-boy hurt and sorry for himself.

'You weren't exactly dealt the worst of cards with your adoptive parents,' Best snapped. 'They are kind. Love you. Did their best for you.'

Meredith nodded. 'True. Well, I paid the price for my folly, didn't I? I fell in love with the girl – with my lovely half-sister.'

'And then what?' asked Best coldly.

Meredith gave a long sigh. 'I realized I must end it. So I did.'

'And Sir George?'

'He never knew.' Meredith paused and his lips tightened. 'Should have, the old bastard. Hurt him in the way he hurt me.'

'Oh, don't worry,' Best assured him, 'he's been hurt all right.'

Twenty-nine

It took a moment or two for Best to recognize the Joe Brannigan standing on the other side of the police station counter rather than behind the bar of the Ridley Arms. Not only was the landlord out of his usual context, but he was dressed in a pea jacket and cap rather than the familiar shirt with buttons straining to contain his vast chest and stomach.

The man's large, fleshy face was earnest as he exclaimed to Best, 'Now Sadie's gone!'

'Who is Sadie?' asked McLeod, glancing from Brannigan to Best and back again.

'A barmaid,' said Best. 'I spoke to her when I went down the Quayside to follow up on Mary Donovan.'

'She's not been seen since that night she came up here to get you.'

Best shook his head, puzzled. 'I never saw her.'

'I know, I know. Bridie says she came back with some other fella.'

'Oh, no,' said Best, putting his hand over his eyes. 'You'd better come into the office.'

'Who,' said McLeod when they were ensconced in the branch's office, 'did Sadie come back with?'

'I don't know. I don't know.'

'Didn't Bridie tell you what he looked like?'

'She said it could be the detective who first came about Mary. A bloke with sandy hair and blue eyes.'

'Clegg,' said McLeod and Best in unison.

'But what did she want?' asked McLeod.

'I told her,' said Best, 'that as soon as she spotted the man she'd seen Mary Donovan with before she went missing that she was to come up and get me.'

'*You?* To get *you*?'

Best nodded. 'Yes.' He could see how it sounded.

'Just you.'

Best grimaced ruefully. 'I thought that since I knew what it was all about . . .'

It sounded weak, even to him.

'But,' said McLeod, 'we share all information. That was what you said when you arrived. We were all in this together. No one trying to outdo the other. All for justice.'

Best spread his hands apologetically. 'I know, I know. I'm sorry.'

'You never even mentioned this man to me. A rather important matter, wouldn't you say?'

'When did I have time?' asked Best a trifle defensively.

'When we were having our little conferences, our friendly little conferences, exchanging information over a friendly pint. Failing that, you could have left a message advising me of this most important development.'

Best nodded. 'You're right, I suppose.'

'You suppose I'm right!' shouted McLeod. 'You suppose! What's that – bloody Cockney for sod you! You've put one of my officers in danger – who knows what has happened to him – all because you wanted to get the better of the local yokels!'

'That's not true.'

Wasn't it? Maybe, in part. Had he felt that he had developed this lead so should be the one to follow it up? *McLeod didn't even know about Smith yet.* Oh God.

'The lass was set on seeing you,' said the front desk clerk, who had been called in to verify what had happened. 'She said, "I divn't want anyone else." Clegg wasn't keen to go. Not at first. Then when she kept worriting on about only wanting Inspector Best he suddenly decided to go with her.'

Silence fell over the room. Best suddenly felt deeply depressed and full of foreboding. By the way the furious McLeod was refusing to meet his eye, it was obvious that he was as well. Force and personal rivalry. The very thing they had been trying to avoid.

'Could be partly my fault,' said the clerk, obviously desperate to mollify the atmosphere.

'How do you make that out, man?' snapped McLeod.

'I told him she was het up about something.' He looked at them as for absolution, 'Well, she was.' He was almost tearful. 'You don't think anything bad has happened to them do you?'

'I sincerely hope not,' said McLeod. 'But, if it has, I can assure you *you* are *not* the one to blame.'

Searches down at the Quayside revealed nothing. Neither did inspection of the ships in dock, with the aid of the River Police – apart from anxiety among the sailors that their petty smuggling activities might be uncovered. The captains became fearful that their sailing times might be delayed or their hands taken into custody at the last minute.

No one admitted to having seen a pair answering the description of Clegg or Sadie two nights ago, heading eastwards towards Gilroy's Spirit Vaults. Best and McLeod were not surprised. Such an admission could also cause delay or attract unwanted attention.

The landlord and staff of Gilroy's had no recollection of Sadie and Clegg reaching their hostelry. Nor did they recognize the vague description of the mystery man. Their word was more reliable than that of the sailors. They were stuck there on land all the time and it was vital to keep in with the police, who could make life difficult for them should they find they had been holding anything back.

Best and McLeod came to a brief and melancholy halt in Gilroy's and sipped a whisky and a brandy respectively in an effort to warm up on the damp and chilly night.

'Might have more luck in the morning,' said McLeod in an effort to cheer himself as well as Best, who looked distraught. 'More people about then. We'll bring a posse down and frighten the life out of them all.'

A figure was hovering behind him as he spoke. A young member of the River Police – wearing a grim expression.

'I think we might have found them, sir,' he said.

They were led eastwards along Horatio Street between the Continental wharves and the derelict old houses that ran along in front of the Ropery Banks, then over the quaintly curved

Glasshouse Bridge, which crossed the thick, brown Ouseburn just below its splendid new bridge.

No thumping cranes and busy shipping here, nor granite-clad edifices, just a quiet huddle of smoke-blackened, neglected old buildings.

They turned into a narrow cobbled street that ran parallel to the river, passed the River Police Station and came to a halt outside the adjacent building.

Best had seen this building on his walks along the Quayside and thought it a most melancholy sight, proclaiming its purpose as it did with a huge and unequivocal hoarding emblazoned with the words:

DEAD HOUSE
Grappling Irons

Inside the Dead House was the very thing Best had been dreading. Two bodies resting on stone slabs while they were sluiced down to remove the river filth.

'They were jammed between some old staithes,' murmured the young policeman.

One body was obviously that of a male: squat, well-muscled and, as the clean water did its job, with hair that was emerging as sandy. The other was tiny, thin and female.

There was little doubt who they were, despite the obvious damage that had been done by immersion in a busy river, being jammed up against the river wall and hauled aboard a River Police rowing boat with grappling irons. The contents of Clegg's pockets confirmed it, as did the cheap tin brooch that spelled out the name: SADIE.

Best was devastated, McLeod in tears.

'Everything I touch turns to dust and death,' he said, then pulled himself together sufficiently to add, 'I think I should come off the case. I've been disastrous.'

'No,' said the chief constable. 'We can't have that. That would give the impression that we are beaten.'

'I agree,' said Detective Superintendent Tunnah, now back in charge. 'We must not give them comfort.' He glanced at Best. 'In any case,' he added robustly in a clumsy attempt to

157

be kind, 'you did the *right* thing telling Sadie to come and let us know when that man came again. It might have been you.'

Best wished it had. 'I can't tell you how sorry I am,' he said. 'Clegg was a good man – and as for that poor child.'

'Aye, he was,' agreed McLeod, tears springing into his eyes. 'But,' he said to Best, 'it was his own decision to go with Sadie, and it was his duty.'

Best turned his face away as if unable to bear any more of this kindness.

'We must be on the right track,' added the superintendent robustly, 'or this would not have happened.'

'Exactly,' agreed the chief constable. 'And, dreadful though it is, if it brings us nearer catching these terrible people . . .'

Best and McLeod exchanged rueful glances. And that was it. Conference over.

'What now?' said Best. 'I don't know what to do any more.'

'Of course you do,' insisted McLeod. 'We carry on where we left off as well as deciding how we can get this man identified.'

His fury had been abated by the deaths and his admission to himself that he, too, had made mistakes that other people had paid for. It saddened him to see a man like Best brought down. 'What *were* you going to do next?'

'Meet up with Smith then go to see Amelia Cook's parents.'

'Do it then, as long as you dinna overindulge in the cocoa.'

Best smiled wanly. He had explained about Smith's presence and why those in authority had thought it best to keep it secret.

'While you're seeing the saintly Amelia's parents I'll go back to beard Mrs Thomson among her sweeties. There is something she was no telling me.'

McLeod grasped Best's hands. 'You know I was angry that you asked Sadie to come to you. But it wouldna have made any difference if you'd just said tell the detectives. Clegg was in, and he would have gone.'

Best nodded, and covered McLeod's hands with his own, gratefully.

McLeod knew he should have been pleased that he was in charge again, but he didn't want to shoulder this burden alone and, in any case, he had grown fond of this flashy Londoner and wanted his friend back.

'It wasn't your fault,' McLeod insisted as he helped Best into his overcoat and tucked his scarf around his neck as though he were a small boy. 'Vengeance is what we want now, laddie. Let's go after them!'

Thirty

The tentative early morning sun helped to lessen the bite of the icy east wind cutting into Best and McLeod as they walked along Mosley Street on their way to catch an omnibus and one of the new horse trams. The pale sun also managed to force its way through the smoke-filled air to catch the beaded turrets and flying spurs of the graceful crown spire surmounting the tower of the medieval church of St Nicholas.

At another time and in different circumstances Best would have appreciated the sight.

'First spire like that in the country, you know,' said McLeod and smiled confidingly. 'Geordies say that the others, especially the one on the High Kirk of St Giles in Edinburgh, are just poor imitations.'

Best nodded absently. He longed to be alone.

As they passed St Nicholas Square McLeod suddenly grasped Best's arm and said, 'Why don't we go in here and say a prayer for Clegg and wee Sadie?' He paused, embarrassed, as Best hesitated. 'I know the place is not of your persuasion. Mine neither, but . . .'

Best did not feel like praying to any God in any place of worship, but this man was forgiving him for causing the death of his colleague so it was the least he could do.

Somehow the peace and tranquillity inside made him feel worse. There was a mellow simplicity about the place, but the font cover, pointed out by McLeod, was a spectacular confection of Gothic tracery.

They edged into a rear pew. McLeod immediately kneeled down and murmured a short prayer. Best could not even bring himself to kneel and pretend to pray but merely sat in a trance, staring ahead. When he finally turned his head to speak he was surprised and relieved to find himself alone.

He sat on and, when he allowed himself to think, wondered how to find a reason to continue. Finally, he convinced himself that McLeod was right. They must get justice and vengeance for the dead and missing. Then he could go – and not just from this town.

'You *must* forgive yourself, you know,' murmured a soft voice from the pew behind him. 'You are not responsible for all the ills of the world.'

He froze. Helen? It couldn't be. He was hallucinating! It had come to that.

He turned his head very slowly and couldn't believe what he saw. Helen, dear little Helen, all buttoned-up in a chestnut-brown astrakhan coat and fur hat, her grey eyes full of concern. Beside her on the pew lay one of her large drawing pads.

She smiled gently at him, leaned forward, reached out her hand and touched his cheek. That undid him. A sob rose in his throat.

They were back in the Cocoa Rooms and Smith was talking very quickly again. This time largely because he was in a hurry. He was out on one of his intermittent morning errands chasing haberdashery suppliers and dropping in new orders. It was a task more usually left to the boy messengers, but due to Smith's expertise in judging colour consistency and in pointing out faults in weft and weave the job occasionally went to him. But he couldn't be away too long.

'It's a treat to get out at all,' he said. 'I feel like one of them medieval monks who's been locked in his cell all day.'

'Medieval monks wouldn't have the pleasure of dancing attendance on lovely ladies,' smiled Helen.

'Anyway,' he raced on, 'nothing much seems to be 'appening that I can see. Just the usual things. Barker the floor walker is going around barking. Luke, well, that bloke is getting even stringier. Looks like he's living off his nerves. Wouldn't be surprised if one of these days he didn't lay down on one of his half-testers and pass away.'

'Hm,' said Best, forcing himself to respond. 'Could be

significant that, you know. He might have a guilty conscience.'

'Nah. He couldn't do no one in. Hasn't got the mettle.'

'You never know,' said Best. 'What about the hostel? Anything happening there?'

Smith groaned.

'Only the usual boring things. Prayers, lay preachers preaching at us, an' rules, rules, rules. Like, would you believe this?' He recited: '"No loud or unnecessary conversation at meals." Unnecessary conversation – what's that? And, do you know,' he waxed indignant, 'you has to pay a library subscription but you can't read in bed! Can't smoke in the bedrooms, neither. An' you got to be in your room by eleven p.m. Five shilling fine if you're not! What a liberty! Then it's lights out by twenty past!'

He was certainly looking paler, thought Best, losing some of that ruddy outdoor glow and a little more of his cheerful demeanour.

'Can't I come out now?' he pleaded.

'Give it a couple more days,' said Best. 'I've got a feeling something is about to happen.' He paused. 'What about that basement?'

Smith shrugged. 'Got a bit of a squint at it but couldn't see nothing promising. They're just starting the excavation. But I'll have another poke about tonight if I can – use an excuse about checking stock.'

'Don't put yourself in any danger!' Best almost shouted.

After a short, surprised silence Smith grinned. 'Nah. Course I won't. Not a sharp Cockney lad like me. You know, if I'm caught doing something I shouldn't I always pretend to be a simple Southerner not knowing about these rules. They like that. They're friendly folk, you know. Well, most of them, anyway.' He grinned conspiratorially and looked up at the clock. 'Blimey. Got to go.'

He began to stand up then stopped. 'Here, I was thinking,' he said, bending over and lowering his voice, 'about that bloke what Sadie saw – why not get the barman and Bridie to have a little stroll through Bainbridges – see if they recognize anyone?'

'Good idea,' said Best uncertainly. It was, but it might put them in terrible danger.

'You could dress 'em up a bit so they're not obvious.'

'Yes. I'll think about that.'

'Be as pleased as a dog with two tails if they picked out Barker,' said Smith. He chuckled, saluted and was gone.

Helen and Best watched him go then contemplated each other in silence for a few moments.

'How are you feeling?' she asked eventually.

'Fine, fine.' He'd girded his loins again and shut out the pain, ready to get to work. 'So, why are you here?'

It was obvious that she was here working, but he suspected other hands involved in the timing of her arrival and their 'accidental' meeting.

'I have a commission to illustrate our latest cathedral.' She opened up her sketch pad and showed him a drawing of St Nicholas's font canopy. 'The carving is really quite beautiful and unusual. I hope I've captured some of that.'

'You have.'

'Anyway, it's good to see you again,' she said, adopting his casually matter-of-fact tone, as if they were mere acquaintances bumping into one another after a long interval.

'You too.'

What was it about her that so captivated him? he wondered yet again. Compared with some of his exotic dark-haired female relatives she was almost colourless, with her mousy-brown hair, grey eyes and subdued clothing. But there was something peaceful about her very lack of female coquettishness and the womanly wiles to which a handsome man like Best had become accustomed. Maybe that was it, and the way she looked you directly in the eye.

Right from the start, when she had stormed into his office demanding to know why he was doing nothing to find her missing sister, he had realized she was a force to be reckoned with. In the ensuing investigation her intelligence and fellow sense of fun had gradually won his heart, which, ultimately, she had rejected.

She was an artist, she had explained, and women artists who married were so burdened with children and domestic tasks that they were obliged to give up painting. She loved him, but not enough to do that. You wouldn't give up being a detective for me, she'd pointed out.

They had met again while he was on the trail of Quicksilver, the man who had threatened to blow up the Police Fête being held at Alexandra Palace. Her knowledge of poetry had helped decipher the maniac's crazy letters. Meanwhile, she once again edged her way into his heart, a heart which rightfully belonged to his young fiancée, Mary Jane. Then, as though to punish him, that terrible thing had happened to the girl.

'It does seem such an odd case,' Helen said when Best had outlined their enquiries in the hope that a fresh and intelligent eye might see something they had missed.

'I'm totally confused,' he admitted.

'I must say, I can't see how the other girls tie in with Phoebe – apart from the fact that they all went missing at around the same time.'

Best nodded. 'I keep wondering whether they are really separate cases – and it's pulling me this way and that.'

'You've written this Meredith fellow off completely?'

'Well . . .' He wrinkled his nose. 'Not entirely. But I can't work out what his motive to kill Phoebe might be.' He shrugged. 'I am going to get Sir George's side of that story.'

'He could have known and bought Meredith off.'

'Exactly.'

'But that means even less reason for him to murder the girl. He'd be killing the golden goose. No daughter. No reason to pay. No sense in that.'

'Quite. Same applies if he had wanted more money and decided on blackmail.'

'It's perplexing.'

They sat in silence for a few moments.

'Do Sir George and those Bainbridge people need looking at more closely?' she asked suddenly.

'In what way?'

'Their business dealings. Might be some resentment from employees or rival firms.'

'We did wonder about that, but following it up is very difficult. These Northern industrialists and businessmen seem to have their fingers in every pie: shipping, coal mining, rail-ways, iron and steel, land . . .' He shook his head. 'So that idea got pushed to one side.'

'Hmm. A lot of potential there.'

He grimaced. 'I suppose so.'

'Business rivalry?'

'Maybe. But I really can't see how it would help anyone to murder a rival's daughter.'

'Keep him away from business at an important moment? Distract him?'

'A convoluted way to do it. Why not just put arsenic in his port?'

'Too obvious.'

Best said nothing.

'They're all in a pretty nervous state at the moment, aren't they? What with the agricultural depression and the new competition from America and Germany biting into their profits at the same time as all these new worker-protection acts are slowing them down – not to mention the workers' strikes.'

Best looked doubtful. Helen had always been interested in these things but he scarcely had time to keep informed and found it all a bit boring anyway.

'Don't forget it was the Newcastle Engineers who held the first successful shorter-hours strike, which set off all the others.'

'Was it?'

Best was dazed by all these new possibilities. He couldn't see how they would help find Clegg and Sadie's killers.

'We could take a closer look at their interests. Are they good employers? Do they own land in Ireland? There are lots of Irish around. Does a business rival want revenge or just to put them out of business?'

'Finding Phoebe in one of their beds hasn't harmed the business at Bainbridges,' Best pointed out a trifle testily. 'In fact, hundreds of people have just discovered they need a new full-tester bed.'

'Ghouls.'

The thought of ever more new avenues of enquiry wearied

him, and their conversation reminded him of one of the things about her that had irritated him. Sometimes she was too clever and, even more unforgivable, she was often right.

'I'll help you,' said Helen decisively. 'I'm in touch with lots of businessmen for this project – I can ask a few innocent questions . . .'

He stared at her in horror. 'No!' he shouted, causing other customers to look round in surprise. 'No! No! No! Keep out of this! Do you want to be the death of me!'

She smiled gently at him. 'That's the last thing I would want, Ernest. Especially now.'

Thirty-one

It was an ordinary ground-floor window in an ordinary terraced street just one step up from the 'pit rows', which were occupied solely by coal miners and their families. But this window looked straight on to a shelf piled with open sweet cartons, small jars of wrapped toffees, dummy chocolate bars, a Fry's Chocolate enamel sign and a hand-written notice urging customers to join the Christmas club.

The goods were not artistically arranged. They had clearly arrived there piecemeal some time ago and gradually acquired their fine layer of dust. But the window did provide one bright spot in a dull parade of lace-curtained windows. Some of these curtains testified to fierce regular tubbing necessary to keep them clean in this soot-laden air, as did the scrubbed and whitened doorsteps. McLeod well knew that in this sort of neighbourhood the most flattering thing you could say about a woman was 'she keeps a nice step'.

He was relieved to see that the door of Mrs Thomson's shop was tightly shut. He could talk to her in her parlour without being interrupted by an endless parade of snotty-nosed kids demanding a halfpennyworth of black bullets or a farthing poke of sherbet dip.

Return interviews went one of two ways. The person would decide that they had said far too much the first time and would stop cooperating and even attempt to retract previous statements, or the questions would stir up more memories and snippets of information, which they were now eager to impart.

He guessed that the latter would apply at least in part to Mrs Thomson, who desperately wanted her daughter Kate back. He wondered whether, this time, she would answer one particular question truthfully.

It turned out that, as the inspector had suggested, she had put her mind to recalling what she could about the fine houses that Kate had visited when assisting with the measuring up and fitting of fine ladies with fine dresses.

She was clearly embarrassed by the scratchy, ill-written piece of paper clutched in her pudgy little hand as she sat on an old rocking chair in front of her kitchen-cum-parlour cooking range.

'You'll not understand these,' she insisted. 'That compulsory schooling has come a bit too late for the likes of me!'

She read her notes out to him slowly. Sitting opposite he wrote them and her comments down.

At the finish he was a little disappointed but tried not to show it.

'She never went to Sir George Threapleton's or Lady Hester's?' he enquired casually.

She shook her head. 'Not as I recall, hinny. An' I think I would, him being so high up and that.' Her lips began to tremble. 'She used to tell me such stories about them that was in the papers.'

The tears, which had been rimming her eyelids, slowly tipped over on to her plump cheeks. 'I don't know what I'm going to do without our Kate,' she sobbed. 'She was all I had!'

McLeod realized that it might, after all, have been more sensible to come back when the shop was open. Keeping busy saved the grieving mind from dwelling on its loss.

He waited for a while, giving her time to cry herself out.

She stopped quite abruptly, looked at him over the scrunched up handkerchief with which she was dabbing her cheeks and announced bluntly, 'I've got something to tell you.'

'About who Kate worked for before she went to Perkins's?'

'Yes.'

'Well, who was it?'

'Bainbridges.'

McLeod stared at her, astonished and furious.

'Why,' he said, trying to keep the rage from his voice, 'did you not tell us this before?'

She refused to meet his eye, muttering defensively, 'It was only for three months.'

168

He said nothing but felt like striking her.

Eventually, in a rush, it came out. 'If I'd shamed our Kate she'd have been affeared to face people when she came back.'

'She was sacked?'

'Aha.'

'Why?'

'Some money went missing and they blamed her.'

'Did she take it?'

'No! Of course not! She swore to me she hadn't!'

'But Perkins took her on?'

She nodded. 'They didn't know – and I knew she'd want her old job when she came back.'

'You must have known that Phoebe Threapleton was found dead in Bainbridges.'

'Aha. But that was *different*, wasn't it? That didn't have anything to do with our lasses going missing. She was a customer and in a different class,' she insisted. 'I can't see how there's anything to tie them up!'

Neither can I, thought McLeod.

She watched him anxiously nonetheless.

'Well,' he said eventually, making a big effort to hide his exasperation, 'I suppose there's no helping it now.' He sighed. 'Just tell me everything she told you about working there.'

She did. But it didn't amount to much. Kate had been taken on as a trainee seamstress in Bainbridges Costume and Mantle workroom. She had been doing well, even learning how to use the sewing machine. Then one day she was sent on an errand to the shop's Manchester Print department. While there, a woman customer accused Kate of taking money from her purse.

Of course, there was no way of telling at this third hand whether or not Kate had been guilty, but, it seemed, Bainbridges had felt obliged to sack her. Unless they did, the woman threatened to call the police and have the girl charged. McLeod, as presumably had Bainbridges, knew she wouldn't have stood a chance against the high-powered lawyers a wealthy customer would engage.

'Our Kate said the woman only said that because her husband had been giving her the eye and she was jealous!'

169

Kate had not lived in at the shop's hostel but had been invited to a couple of their evening entertainments.

'They had a concert one night and there was a little party on another when one of the girls was leaving.'

No, she didn't have any special friends at work.

'She was so tired when she came home she went to bed early. She only went out those two times.'

As for particular men among her fellow workers Mrs Thomson could only recall tales about cheeky young messenger boys and a very strict foreman in their workroom whose name she couldn't recall. It might come to her later.

'You see,' she said finally, 'it wouldn't have made no difference if I'd told you about her first job before, would it?'

She could be right.

Bertrand Cook may still have been only on the middle rung of the business ladder but he clearly was planning to climb higher, judging by his choice of area in which to live. Brandling Village, named after one of the Tyne's biggest coal-mine-owning dynasties, was one of the three villages that together made up the superior suburb of Jesmond.

It lay on the western edge and was in a continuous state of development. Amongst handsome, self-contained estates a variety of smaller but choice villas and high-quality terraces were springing up to cater for the rising numbers of the well-to-do and professional classes. Here, they could be among their own sort and here was also the ideal place to make important connections.

Mr Cook summarily elected himself as the sole spokesman for his household. A familiar action and one that always irritated Best. In his experience the person who knows the least about what goes on in the home was the master of the house. The ones who knew most were the servants. In between, particularly in the homes of the wealthy, came the women of the family, who had little else to do but contemplate their surroundings and what took place in them.

To speak to *all* of these people was even more paramount in this instance, since by all accounts Amelia had been a voluntarily housebound young woman.

170

Best bided his time, giving his rapt attention to the rotund, shiny-cheeked banker as he told of the disappearance of his daughter. It was just as the detective officer's report had related. Amelia had been there in the evening, had left to go to her room at 9.00 p.m. but was not there the following morning when the maid took in her breakfast tray. Indeed, her bed had not been slept in.

This, surely, was the most perplexing of the missing girl cases. How could her going not be witnessed in a household made up of a man, his wife, their two almost adult sons, a cook, a scullery maid, a housekeeper, a parlour maid and a kitchen maid?

According to the detective officer's report it transpired that the two sons had been out late and Mrs Cook had gone to bed early with a headache, at 8.00 p.m. Mr Cook stayed up in the library enjoying a cigar and business chat with three male friends.

By then, of the domestics, only the parlour maid had remained on duty to keep the fire stoked up, fulfil the gentlemen's refreshment needs and fetch their coats and hats when they decided to leave – which they did at 11.30 p.m.

Then Mr Cook had gone to bed. Whether that was with the parlour maid Best did not enquire, but it wouldn't have surprised him given the appreciative glances the man was directing towards the girl's bottom as she leaned over to serve them tea.

The idea depressed him. The girl would doubtless end up pregnant and if not summarily dismissed by the mistress would probably be in need of the services of a baby farmer to look after the child. He had seen what abuses that could lead to when handling the dreadful case in Islington.

'Tell me, Mr Cook,' said Best as he balanced his cup and saucer while attempting to accept an almond biscuit, 'do you practise spiritualism?'

'Good heavens, no!' He raised his eyebrows disdainfully. 'Such rubbish!'

'I only ask,' Best continued calmly, 'because spiritualism may be an element in one of these cases. Obviously, I am anxious to find connections between the young women, which, in turn, might help solve this dreadful business.'

'Well, there are certainly no connections between *two* of these young women and my daughter!'

'I take it you are implying that there may be some between Amelia and Phoebe Threapleton?'

He shifted uncomfortably.

'I wouldn't suggest that they were *friends*,' he admitted.

'But?'

'Well, I did a little business with Mr Threapleton once or twice, and we have attended some of the same functions.'

Very much at the opposite end of the table, thought Best.

'So the girls met?'

Cook nodded carefully. 'Yes, I'm sure they did.' He shifted in his chair again. He wasn't silly enough to make claims that could easily be checked. 'But in any case we are not great socialites.' He made it sound like a virtue.

'Did Amelia attend any society balls or soirées?'

'No.' Best was gratified to see a tear start into the man's eye. The first sign of real feeling. 'Church outings and family gatherings were enough for her. She was only young, you know.'

Ah. I do know, thought Best. Young and untouched is how you wanted her to stay. I wonder what she really thought about that.

'Which church would that be?' he asked, mostly as something to say to keep the conversation going while he tackled his biscuit.

He obviously wasn't going to get much from this man who saw the world only as he wished it to be, and Best was in danger of drifting off, trying to grasp hold of something Helen had said that had been lingering at the back of his mind but refusing to come forward despite coaxing. Helen, however, was a presence. She kept coming forward unbidden. It was so good to see her despite all the terrible memories her presence brought with her.

'We're Wesleyan Methodists,' Cook was explaining. 'We are in the process of building a chapel here in the village, but meanwhile we are obliged to continue attending one in town.'

Best sat up.

'Wesleyan Methodists!'

'Yes.' Cook was startled. 'Methodism is very strong hereabouts.' He smiled weakly. 'Which makes us a thorn in the flesh of the orthodoxy.'

'And the chapel you attend in town?' asked Best, scarcely able to contain his excitement.

'The Brunswick.'

Best lowered his voice and reined in his enthusiasm to enquire, 'In Brunswick Place, just off Northumberland Street?'

'That's right.'

Cook was perplexed by Best's enthusiasm for their religion and place of worship. But Best knew only too well what this meant.

The Brunswick Chapel was attended not only by the Bainbridge family but also their staff. He had found a connection!

Thirty-two

'We should go to chapel on Sunday,' said Best.
'You'll be rather obvious,' Helen pointed out. 'A Scottish Presbyterian and a Roman Catholic of exotic appearance.'

'We only want to observe the congregation.'

'While they are observing you and any suspect is being warned off.'

Best sighed and shrugged. The woman could be irritating at times. 'We *could* just wait outside to see who attends?'

Even as he voiced it he realized it was a foolish idea. The chapel sat squarely at the end of Brunswick Place, the side street that led to it, in itself like an all-seeing eye.

McLeod grimaced and shook his head.

'So, what do *you two* suggest?'

'Well,' said Helen, 'I have a commission to draw all the town's most important buildings and . . .'

'No! No! No!' exclaimed Best, once again drawing startled glances from the other customers – this time in the bar of his hotel, the Royal Exchange.

'I dinna think he wants you to,' grinned McLeod.

Stalemate.

'In any case,' said Best more calmly, 'you wouldn't recognize any of the people concerned.'

They looked at each other helplessly.

'Smith!' Helen exclaimed suddenly. 'He says that Bainbridges have a pew there especially for the staff.'

'Of course!' Best was pleased. 'He's been complaining about joining in the evening prayers and being told that he could improve his job prospects if he attended the chapel on Sunday!'

She *was* a clever woman. No doubt about it.

174

'One problem,' McLeod put in reluctantly. 'He's no seen any of the other folk in the investigation either – only the shop workers.'

'Well, he can ask his colleagues to *tell* him who everyone is!' Best exclaimed. The pair were ambushing him! 'Meanwhile, we can concentrate on these business interests we keep meaning to follow up. That will be our excuse, anyway. Could Phoebe's death be a vengeance killing? will be the proposition. I'll go and see Threapleton and while there sound him out about Meredith. I'm still not happy about that young man.'

'I'll do the Bainbridge family,' agreed McLeod. 'And I can probe a little about the Brunswick Chapel congregation and Kate Thomson's contacts at the shop while I'm there.'

'Good,' said Best, glancing from one to another, a trace of his natural optimism returning. 'I have a feeling that everything is suddenly going to come together.'

As they began to rise from their seats a young woman and a middle-aged man passed their table on the way to the exit. The woman was Anne Meldrew, the Threapletons' parlour maid, and the man? Who was the man? He was vaguely familiar . . .

Sir George Threapleton was not exactly drunk but he was not exactly sober either – which Best deemed to be a good thing. The man wanted nothing more than to talk about his lovely daughter, Phoebe, and his wonderful wife, Sophie, and was determined that Best should join him as a drinking partner in this wake.

'You can't imagine what it is like,' he insisted tearfully, 'to lose the two most wonderful women in the world.'

Something of an exaggeration, thought Best, given that his wife had had a baby by another man and his daughter by all accounts was a spoiled minx. But that was how things were. You deified the dead, forgetting their drawbacks.

'I think I can, sir,' Best said, and went on to describe how he had lost his beloved young wife, Emma, to tuberculosis and his fiancée to a terrible death only two months before, and that this had been his fault.

'Oh, that was you! That was you!' exclaimed Sir George, spilling his drink in his excitement. 'I read about it in the papers and thought how terrible – never thinking . . . Oh, you poor man! You poor man!'

Best accepted his condolences gracefully. If he could retain this confessional fellow-feeling while preventing the exchange from becoming completely drunken and maudlin he might acquire some useful information.

After a decent interval he adopted a firmer, slightly more official tone. 'I'm hoping you can help us in our further enquiries regarding Phoebe,' he said.

'Anything! Anything!' declared Sir George.

'One of the strands we want to concentrate on now,' he explained, 'is these business interests of yours that Sergeant Clegg spoke to you about.'

'In case it was revenge!' exclaimed Sir George, unstopping the brandy flask again. 'I understand completely and will do my very best!'

Best led him through them one by one: railways, shipping, iron and steel, manufacturing and land.

It transpired that self-made man Sir George was a director of the massive Consett Iron and Steel Works, which bestrode the Durham moors like a colossus, had interests in four collieries and owned several merchant vessels and land and property in Durham, Lincolnshire, Ireland and Scotland.

There had been hiccups in dealings, disagreements over contracts and the occasional bad debt controversies but to his knowledge none of them, Sir George insisted, were of great proportion nor did they result in any vicious ill-feeling.

'Could it be,' said Best carefully, 'that rather than a business rival an employee or tenant might feel some resentment towards you?'

'Oh, I'm sure, I'm sure. They blame us for everything!' He put down his glass with exaggerated care and struggled upright in his throne-like Gothic armchair so as to hold forth. 'When I think what I have done for this town.'

Best nodded sympathetically. 'I saw in the papers what a charitable man you are.'

'And I've given them employment. They forget that!'

Best caught a whiff of guilty conscience behind all this denial.

'Take that Barkworth Colliery business.' He squared his shoulders as if for battle and glanced about him as though looking for enemies. 'Everyone knows that coal mining can be a dangerous business, don't they?'

It was not a question he really wanted answered. It *was* a dangerous business. One life for every hundred thousand tons of coal, Best had heard.

'It's the nature of the beast. Unexpected explosions, falls of stone – you can't prevent them no matter how strong your union and those laws they keep getting passed.'

The Northumberland miners' union, and to a lesser extent the Durham, had become the strongest in the country despite the owners' often underhand attempts to destroy them and their aims.

'We do our best. But that accident at the Barkworth Colliery – Act of God. Act of God. Nothing even they could have done to prevent that! Shipping's the same. Trying to hedge us in with all these laws. Take that *Hardwick* coming back from Odessa only last week with a load of barley. Her cargo shifted, she foundered and all but one were lost. Bad seamanship, cargo shifting like that. Not our fault.'

But untrained and inadequate crews and unseaworthy vessels *are*, thought Best, which why is the Merchant Shipping Act has just been passed. Unfortunately, it was difficult to enforce its rules, so the situation was taking a long time to improve even though everyone knew that the merchant shipping business was a disgrace.

'Of course not,' said Best.

'We lost our cargo and a vessel!'

Which, Best knew, would be well insured, probably leaving the owners even better off than if it had stayed afloat.

He realized that this line of enquiry was also proving futile not only due to Sir George's refusal to accept responsibility for any mishaps, but because there were too many candidates. Too many bereaved parents, wives and children might have good reason to feel aggrieved with the likes of Sir George Threapleton.

'No threats been made?'

'None. Just let them try!'

Best looked pityingly at the drunken man. They don't have to, he thought; if it was any of them who killed Phoebe they've done their worst anyway.

It was time to edge on to the subject of Meredith. Best accepted a generous refill of his scarcely touched glass of cognac merely so that Sir George would similarly partake, which he did.

Now. He took a deep breath and considered the situation. Should he go gently? Slyly? Or straight in?

Best contemplated the increasingly glassy expression in Sir George's eyes and thought, straight in. Often the best way, in any case. As Cheadle often said, 'Don't give the bastards time to think!'

'Meredith,' said Best, struggling to hold the man's wavering eye.

'Paid the bastard off,' said Sir George. 'Paid the bastard off!'

Thirty-three

The regular clinking of the cab harness provided a background to Best's hurried explanations to McLeod as to why they were heading yet again towards Meredith's residence at such speed.

'The swine knew all along!' he said. 'And as soon as he'd got Phoebe hooked he went to see Sir George.'

'Blackmail,' said McLeod.

'He'd deny it of course. Say it was just his conscience.'

McLeod frowned. 'Is that what he told Sir George?'

'Yes. Said that, now that they had grown so close, he and Phoebe, quite against his intentions, he felt it was his duty to tell Sir George.

'Then he went on to describe what a hard time he was having, struggling to set himself up in his career, and he realized now, though he hadn't thought of it before, that if he had married Phoebe his money troubles would have been at an end. But his conscience . . .'

'Sir George took the heavy hint?'

'He had no choice.'

'This means that Meredith is no longer a murder suspect.'

Best looked startled. 'I'm not so sure about that.'

'But why would he kill the goose that laid the golden egg? If she was dead, the threat of the marriage to her was gone.'

Best had given this matter a lot of thought since his alcoholic encounter with Sir George. 'By all accounts she did not *want* to let him go. Even pursued him desperately.'

'Even so,' McLeod argued, 'if he killed the lassie the reason for him to be bought off would no longer exist.'

'Yes, it would,' countered Best.

McLeod could only see the part of Best's face lit by the

glow of the cab's exterior lights and it gave no clue as to his thoughts.

'You have me beat, sonny. Why would it still be worth the man's while to kill Phoebe?'

'Because,' said Best slowly, 'he wasn't just being bought off the marriage, was he? But also from revealing the secret knowledge about Sophie Threapleton's infidelity, which the man had gone to such lengths to hide. Phoebe, with her persistence, was getting in the way of keeping that hidden. It was only a matter of time before she found out, began asking questions and dragging it all out into the open.'

McLeod considered the implications of that.

'So,' he said at length, 'her continued existence might in fact spoil the chances of continued pay-offs?'

'Yes.'

'Do you really think he would kill her for *that*?'

'There's been many a murder for less.'

'Maybe in that wicked metropolis of yours,' McLeod said dryly, 'but no here in the backward North.' He sighed. 'And even here, we need proof. Have we got any?'

Best leaned his tired head against the bouncing side of the cab, closed his eyes and said quietly, 'No.'

'That laddie will never cough up, you know.'

'You're right,' Best conceded. 'We need more.'

'Much more.'

'I wasn't thinking clearly. I was so excited about finding out about the blackmail I thought we could nail him with that and then break him down so he admitted the rest.'

'Not that laddie. He's as slippery as a basket of snakes, and a lawyer too, remember.'

'He'll admit only to facts that he can't deny, but put different interpretations on them.'

'Aye. That's right.'

'Sir George made his offer voluntarily,' said McLeod, assuming an insidious, lawyerly voice.

'Much to my surprise,' added Best in a similar creepy tones.

'I hadn't realized who my mother was when I met darling Phoebe and was shocked and horrified when I found out.'

'I confessed to Sir George only because I had fallen in love with the girl and needed his counsel.'

'I was devastated when she died.'

'You're right, we do need more,' Best admitted wryly. He knocked on the cab roof and shouted up to the driver.

'Stop, please. Turn round and take us back to Middleton Hall.'

McLeod frowned. 'Back to Sir George?'

'No. I saw him off to bed, well gone.'

'The servants?'

'Anne Meldrew.'

En route, Best learned that McLeod had faced the same problem with Emerson Bainbridge as he had with Sir George. Not inebriation. Like many devout Wesleyan Methodists he was very much against the devil drink and even regarded the theatre as the haunt of the devil.

It was in the diversity of the business interests that he had been thwarted. In this case as well as that vast shopping emporium there were coal, shipbuilding, iron and land. As with many local businessmen, he had been in on the ground floor of the phenomenal industrial growth of Tyneside, largely due to coal and the development of the railways. Like Sir George, Emerson was also a director of the Consett Iron and Steel Works.

The upshot was that tracking down business rivals or the bitter industrial victims was pointless without firm evidence of bad feeling and threats. There seemed to be none.

'On the whole the Bainbridges are well regarded locally.'

Best wrapped his scarf more snugly around him. God, it was cold up here!

At first, it seemed that the house was barred and bolted for the night. The tall windows were dark and there was no reply to repeated rings on the doorbell.

Backing away into the road, Best looked up and spotted a small lighted window at the top of the house where female servants usually lived. Eventually, the butler, who, earlier, Best had helped put Sir George to bed, appeared at the door in his shirtsleeves. He was carrying an oil lamp and wearing a surly look on his face.

On seeing Best, whom he had taken to, his expression turned to one of bemused surprise.

'Forget something, sir?'

'In a manner of speaking, Eddie, yes,' said Best. 'I forgot to have a word with Miss Meldrew.'

If he was surprised he didn't show it but then that was what butlers were paid for: imperturbability.

He showed the pair of weary policemen into the library, lit the gas lamps and said, 'I'll get her, sir.'

Best wondered how much the man knew about what had been going on. A great deal, he'd warrant. But persuading higher ranking servants to reveal all about their masters was difficult, particularly in such hard times. Many servants hailed from farming stock and agriculture was in dire straits. References were gold dust in this world.

Anne Meldrew had clearly not been in bed. Although minus her snowy apron and cap there was no sign that she had hastily donned her multi-buttoned, snugly fitting black dress.

Her manner was as perky as ever. 'Yes, gentlemen, what is it you want?'

'Just a few questions, please, Miss Meldrew.'

'Funny time of night to come asking questions.'

'We work all hours.'

'So do I, hinny, and I bet I get up a lot sooner than you do.'

'Very possibly, but when matters begin to come to a head in an inquiry we must act expediently no matter what the time,' said Best in a no-nonsense tone that even to him sounded pompous.

She said nothing, but a wary look crept into her large, dark eyes.

After the butler had left them they sat down on either side of a large oak desk that squatted in the corner of the room, Anne perching uncertainly on a smaller version of the throne-like Gothic chair.

Best realized that despite the easy familiarity of her manner she had probably never actually sat down in this room before. Doing so unsettled her slightly – which could only be a good thing.

'There are one or two matters I'd like to go over with you again.'

'Go on then,' she rejoined. 'If you have to.'

How this woman had ever kept her job he did not know. Servility seemed utterly foreign to her. Writer Richard Jeffries had lately been complaining that labouring men no longer automatically respected rank, reputation and authority. Was this attitude spreading to labouring women as well? Or did Anne Meldrew hold some sway over this family?

He recalled the hints of familiarity between her and Sir George that Clegg had noticed. Perhaps she no longer felt the need to be subservient. Maybe she had higher expectations. If so, she was even more likely to clam up than a butler with a cushy job to protect.

'O'Brien!' he exclaimed.

He had been just about to delve further into her knowledge of the affair of Meredith and Phoebe when the identity of the man he'd seen with her in his hotel had suddenly come to him in the mysterious manner that these things do. O'Brien, the Irish mechanic and unlikely member of Hermione and Florence's spiritualist circle – that was the man he'd seen her with in the Royal Exchange Hotel.

Best had only seen him fleetingly before Clegg had taken a statement from him. The realization surprised him so much that he just stopped and stared open-mouthed at the parlour maid. What was she doing in O'Brien's company? She who, supposedly, had no knowledge of Phoebe's involvement in spiritualism?

'Divn't kna what you mean,' she said, deliberately reverting to a strong Geordie accent.

'You were with him when you passed us in the Royal Exchange Hotel.'

'Oh. Is that so.'

'Would that be Henry O'Brien?' enquired McLeod. 'That fellow who's so active for the Parnell Defence Fund?'

Best now stared at him. This was all new information.

'We've been keeping an eye on them,' explained McLeod.

Anne Meldrew sat very still and said nothing.

Best felt the need to assimilate all this new information but had no wish to lose the initiative with this clever young woman. To give her time to think would be a mistake.

'You had better,' he said firmly, 'explain to us just how you come to know Henry O'Brien.'

Thirty-four

'He's my uncle!' Anne Meldrew exclaimed. 'Why shouldn't I be seen with the man!'

Oh. For a moment Best was silenced. Then he rallied. 'Just a minute. You said you didn't know where Phoebe went on a Wednesday afternoon and had no idea she was involved with spiritualism.'

'Aha. That's right.' She looked at him defiantly.

'But your uncle sometimes went to the very same seance as she did.'

'So what. I didn't know that then, did I.'

'He didn't tell you?'

'I hardly ever see the man. He lives over in Elswick and I live at Jesmond and work long hours. Anyway,' she shrugged, 'we're not that close.'

'Close enough to meet him yesterday in a hotel.'

'Why not? I didn't say I never saw him. We met halfway. He treated me to tea.'

'Did he tell you about seeing Phoebe?'

'Yes, of course he did – now. But he said he didn't know who she was then.'

'The daughter of such a well-known man?'

'Them do's are supposed to be private. She was just another young woman to him.'

Best tried another tack with this intractable young woman. 'Didn't it surprise you that a down-to-earth, practical man like Mr O'Brien was attending seances?' It had puzzled Sergeant Clegg, he remembered, even though he knew the man had lost family.

'Course not!' she almost shouted. 'So would you if you was him!'

'I don't follow you.'

'His son and the lad's wife and their bairns were on the *Cospatrick*!'

That really silenced Best. To lose them in that dreadful way. Everyone knew the terrible tale of the *Cospatrick*. The memory of it still hung in the air, particularly at this time of year.

It was Christmas 1874 when the terrible news of the frigate's fate had reached London from Madeira via the Brazilian underwater cable link.

Everyone had followed the subsequent newspaper stories and inquiry reports.

It had been the *Cospatrick*'s second run to the Southern hemisphere carrying emigrants hoping for a new and better life. New Zealand's agriculture was developing fast and needed railways to link the farms and sheep stations with the coast. To persuade men to travel to the other end of the world to build them six million acres of land were to be offered cheaply to the navvies once the lines had been laid.

One hundred and seventy-seven farm labourers and their families, who had seized this opportunity to climb out of dire poverty, boarded the *Cospatrick* at Gravesend on the 10th September, 1874, and sailed forth towards their new lives the following morning.

There was splendid new fire extinguishing equipment and various lifeboats and small craft on board but they were only sufficient to rescue around a third of the 476 people on board.

Out in the lonely South Atlantic fire had broken out and rapidly taken hold. The wonderful new extinguishers did not work properly and all the small craft, with the exception of the two lifeboats and the starboard quarter boat, caught fire. It had not helped that one boat was stored upside-down on deck and needed a lot of effort to right.

Panicking passengers swamped one of the two lifeboats, which capsized as it reached the water drowning over eighty people.

Righted again it was relaunched. Thus, only two small lifeboats carried survivors. Second Officer Macdonald was in charge of one, which held three other seamen, the baker, the emigrants' cook and twenty-three passengers.

To avoid being swamped by other survivors or having the boats catch fire the two laden lifeboats lay well away from the stricken ship but were near enough to hear the pitiful cries for help from those still on board.

It took thirty-six hours for the ship to die and then only after the stern exploded with a terrible noise which rang from horizon to horizon and caused shock waves that almost swamped the lifeboats. Those still alive on the *Cospatrick* jumped into the sea and drowned.

Ten days later, a sharp-eyed lookout on the barque *British Sceptre,* on a home run from Calcutta to Dundee, spotted Macdonald's drifting lifeboat. Exposure, hunger and thirst had caused the deaths of all but five on board. Macdonald was still alive. As were three other crew members and one passenger. The passenger and one of the crew died while on board the *British Sceptre.*

The remaining three survivors were landed on St Helena. They were picked up from there by the mail steamer *Nyanza,* which stopped at Madeira to telegraph London with the terrible news.

It was hoped that the other lifeboat may have made landfall at Tristan de Cunha, which the *Cospatrick* had passed ten days earlier. But nothing more was ever heard of the boat or its passengers. Second Officer Macdonald and two of his crew were the sole survivors from the 476 people on board.

The official inquiry had exonerated both the shipping line and the New Zealand Government Immigration Service. They decided that the fire must have been started by passengers and/or crew carrying naked lights while breaking into the cargo holds in search of liquor.

The number of small boats on board did fulfil the requirements of the Passenger Acts but it was suggested that they ought to be kept ready for launching. The possibility of carrying fewer emigrants but more lifeboats was also mooted – despite the extra expense.

'How terrible,' was all Best could think of to say, and felt foolish.

Helen could understand why Smith thought that many of the young Bainbridge apprentices, uncomfortable in their Sunday best suits and stiff collars 'didn't seem to mind' their compulsory attendance at the Sunday morning services in Brunswick Place Chapel. Apparently, some of the young live-in assistants even went voluntarily.

The place was light, warm and comfortable on this bleak December morning. The interior of the building, with its decorative plasterwork and abundance of rich brown wood, was most handsome, and the hymn-singing vigorous and uplifting.

Best of all, in the pews in the centre of the ground floor was a goodly assortment of young women decked out prettily and much more happily in their Sunday best.

These were servants of the prominent Newcastle families now occupying the boxed pews along the sides and in the tiered gallery above: the Bainbridges, the Fenwicks, the Richardsons and several others.

Only those servants who could be spared, of course. Not the cooks and scullery maids, who were busy labouring away preparing the midday meal, but the ladies' maids and some of the parlour maids.

Helen observed several discreetly coy sideways glances from behind the hymn books as 'Scatter the Seeds of Kindness' rang out to the accompaniment of the splendid organ and choir that filled the gallery apse.

The obvious prosperity of many of her other fellow worshippers bore out what she had heard about this chapel. Although Methodism had flourished in the North East due to the support of the miners and industrial workers who were weary of the Church of England's collusion with the upper classes, this particular congregation was largely well-to-do.

Maybe this creeping respectability was the reason why today's preacher, the incumbent minister, the Reverend William Hirst, rather than one from the Church's travelling circuit, could scarcely be called a Methodist ranter – a term used by their enemies in horrified response to the passion and enthusiasm of their sermons.

Helen approved of passion and enthusiasm in these matters and would even have liked to hear the rousing call that urged sinners to come forward, though she was not sure what her response would have been.

Since she had sketched the interior of St Nicholas's Church she felt it was only fitting that she should do the same for this chapel. It not only represented the prominence of the religion hereabouts but indeed was considered by many to be the Methodist Cathedral of the North and it had important historical connections with Charles and John Wesley.

When she asked permission to come to the service to take notes and capture the vibrant atmosphere she was advised to wear discreet clothing. That would have made Best laugh. He always said her clothes were discreet to the point of invisibility; she countered that, for a lone woman artist, they had to be.

It was now just about acceptable for a respectable lone woman to walk down the street, but never to stop and stare, not even into shop windows. If she did she risked being deemed wanton and deserving of unwelcome advances from predatory males. Stopping and staring was just what Helen needed to do and she couldn't always find a suitable companion to accompany her.

Anyway, Best didn't know she had come to the chapel that morning. She felt that she could scarcely suffer any harm sitting in a chapel on a Sunday morning, and might succeed in being of some assistance. To this end she had asked the Ridley Arms barman who had seen the mysterious stranger that Sadie and Clegg had followed to come along. He was to give her a nod should he spot the man in the congregation.

Smith didn't know she was there either and, so far, she had managed to avoid him lest he take fright and go and get Best. Fortunately, he was sitting ahead of her. He, too, was engrossed in trying to blend in, and endeavouring not to notice some of the flirtatious glances being sent in his direction.

She concentrated on noting good angles and deciding how she would capture the effect of all this glowing wood. Small wonder that some Methodists in favour of a return to the outdoor preaching of their founder and his followers were starting to call these 'the mahogany years' and wanted to end them.

The minister did become impassioned when it came to the message of the fast-approaching celebration of the birth of

Christ, and the full-throated rendering of John Wesley's wonderful hymn 'Hark the Herald Angels Sing!' rounded off the service splendidly.

It was followed by the typical end-of-service leave-taking, with friends and relatives greeting each other as they left their pews, and the patient lining up for a word with the minister.

So far the barman had not seen anyone he recognized among the throng. Helen dallied at the rear of the chapel, allowing others to pass to give him plenty of time to peruse all the congregation, while dodging in and out, trying to keep out of Smith's view.

Suddenly, he hissed, 'That's him!' and inclined his head towards a tall man ahead of them.

Helen grabbed his arm. 'Come on. We mustn't lose sight of him!' She began pushing her way forward, attracting some frowns and glances of disapproval.

The man was moving fast now, despite the density of the crowd.

Helen tried to follow. 'Excuse me, Excuse me,' she said into startled faces. 'So sorry, we must get out.'

As she reached the lobby she deliberately averted her head so as not to attract the eye of the minister. She pushed the barman along ahead of her.

The Reverend Hirst had, a little reluctantly she felt, given her special permission to be there. He would now doubtless be regretting his decision. He would see her as one of those typically rude Southerners he'd seen referred to in the Northern press.

It couldn't be helped.

The mysterious stranger was gone. She peered into the waiting carriages and cabs and drew more puzzled glances.

'You go that way,' she said to the barman, pointing straight up Brunswick Place towards Northumberland Street. 'I'll go down here.' She indicated the side street to her right, which led out to Blackett Street. Once there, she glanced desperately from left to right and back again, then over the road. Horse trams, carriages, cabs and people kept blocking her view. She nearly screamed with frustration.

Then, suddenly, there he was – on the other side of the road, turning right by the monument into Grey Street. Or, at least, she thought it was the mysterious man. She ran over the road, risking life and limb and causing a cab driver to curse her as he frantically reined in his horse to avoid knocking her down. Then she, too, turned right into Grey Street – still in hot pursuit.

Unbeknown to her Smith had spied her small figure causing a commotion as she pushed determinedly through the congregation and his heart had almost stopped. She wasn't supposed to be there! Best had expressly forbidden it. Then he relaxed. The DI had obviously changed his mind and allowed her to come. He was putty in the woman's hands anyway.

Thirty-five

Being Sunday there were few commercial travellers in evidence in the Royal Exchange Commercial and Family Hotel. Those who could had gone home happy in the knowledge that their goods were secure in the special storerooms provided by John Sayer, the canny landlord. This special service, his bonhomie and the hotel's central situation ensured that the place had become the commercial travellers' Newcastle headquarters.

Those who couldn't make it home, together with some of the members of the local cycling club, were mostly, like Best and McLeod, tucking into 'the ordinary' – in their case steak and kidney pie.

Once again, Best, accustomed to the inconvenience of sprawling London, was grateful for the surprising compactness of this industrial town. The hotel was at the top of Grey Street, a stone's throw from Grey's Monument and just around the corner from Bainbridges. Also close by were the Brunswick Place Wesleyan Chapel and the splendid headquarters of the Newcastle Borough Police. All a distinct advantage at this freezing time of year.

Despite this proximity neither of them had seen Helen as she hurried down Grey Street in pursuit of the mysterious man, even though they had left the police headquarters at about the same time. They had been there gathering what intelligence they could find on Henry O'Brien. Most, in fact all, of it was about his involvement with the Parnell Defence Fund.

Irish MP Charles Stewart Parnell and several fellow members of the Irish Land League had been indicted for conspiracy to stop tenants paying rent as part of their fight for fair rents and security of tenure.

'What we need to know,' said Best, spearing a piece of lamb's kidney, 'is whether Threapleton or the Bainbridges owned the *Cospatrick*.'

McLeod shook his head. 'It was part of the Shaw Savill line. I know because a friend of my cousin's was in the crew.'

'But couldn't they have been shareholders?'

'Oh, aye. But that waters the motive down a bit, does it not?' He paused and gave Best a long look. 'Unless you're suggesting he has his sights on all the shareholders?'

Best shrugged. 'Maybe just the ones he has access to – or maybe he has already struck down some of the nearest and dearest of the others and not yet been caught.'

It was a sobering thought, but somehow their speculations lacked conviction. It all seemed too far-fetched, especially as the man, by Clegg's account anyway, was very down-to-earth and sensible. But one never knew.

'Took him a long time to get around to Threapleton if that's the case,' McLeod pointed out.

'He did suffer a terrible loss, and that can fester and turn a man's head.'

Best knew that only too well.

'Were the owners deemed particularly guilty of neglect? I can't remember. Rumours about there being a lot of explosives on board I remember.'

'Certainly nowhere near enough lifeboats either.'

Their cogitations were interrupted by the arrival of the waiter carrying steaming portions of jam roly-poly.

Helen did not appear for their arranged meet and meal. She had probably become wrapped up in her drawing and forgotten the time again, Best smiled to himself. It was one of her few weaknesses.

Smith arrived shortly after they had finished eating, his dinner at Bainbridge's hostel having been placed on the table promptly at 12.30 p.m. To miss it altogether might have seemed odd, he pointed out, and, besides, to go off on his own could have been thought stand-offish.

'The food's quite good,' he said. 'But you got to eat all the meat you take.'

'Which rule's that?' asked Best jokingly.

'Eighty-seven,' said Smith. 'It's *true*,' he insisted when they all laughed and applauded him.

'You know they're very nice people, the Geordies,' he went on, 'very friendly once they get over their suspicions about Southerners.'

'How was the chapel?' asked Best.

'Well, the singing was good fun but the sermon went on and on.'

He seemed quite pleased with himself.

'And you didn't see anyone suspicious?'

He shook his head. 'No. The barman from the Ridley Arms was there but I didn't get a chance to speak to him. Might have looked a bit strange. I thought I'd try after the service but he went dashing off with Helen. Caused a bit of a commotion, they did. So I reckoned you must have it all in hand.'

Best's cup, which held what was reputed to be the finest brew of coffee in Newcastle, never made it to his lips but came to a sudden stop midway. His eyes widened in horror.

'What!' he almost shouted.

There was a tense silence. All eyes were pinned on a startled Smith.

'Er, I saw the barman being pushed along through the crowd by Helen when they were leaving and . . .' he tailed off in the face of Best's accusatory stare.

'And you did nothing to stop this?' Best's voice had sunk almost to a whisper.

'No, well, I didn't know . . .'

'You went off for your dinner with your new friends,' the volume of Best's voice was rising fast, 'and *you did nothing to stop them*!' He was shouting now. McLeod laid a restraining hand on his arm, to no avail. '*Nothing to alert me! Nothing!*'

He began looking about him feverishly, muttering, 'We must get down there! We must get down there!'

McLeod was already paying their bill.

'Get a cab,' he instructed the mortified Smith sharply. '*Now! Quick!*'

'If she dies,' Best hissed at Smith with utter venom in his voice, 'if she dies, I will kill you!'

McLeod had told the cabbie to make speed but he had second thoughts as they hurtled down the steep, icy and wind-buffeted Grey Street. His doubts were confirmed when the cab suddenly jerked to and fro almost tipping them out. A stream of expletives issued from the driver as he struggled to keep the horse upright.

He tapped on the roof and shouted up to the driver, 'Better slow down.' But the man had obviously come to the same conclusion.

Best, crouching in the corner like a wounded animal, said nothing. Wedged between them was the dismayed Smith looking as if he might burst into tears any minute.

The instant they reached the Ridley Arms Best sprang into life, catapulted out of the cab, flung the hotel doors open and ran into the lobby. By the time they had caught up with him he was in the lounge bar standing opposite a stunned barman who was struggling for coherence in the face of Best's intensity.

'I saw the man and we followed him,' he was saying. 'But when we got outside he was gone.' He hesitated, gathered his thoughts then went on. 'She sent me off down Brunswick Place and went off to the right herself.'

'Where does that lead?' Best snapped out.

'Blackett Street.'

Best shook his head.

'Near the monument,' McLeod put in.

'I didn't see the bloke again or her neither. So I came back here.'

Best suddenly sat down, hugged his arms around himself and looked totally forlorn.

'I don't know what to do,' he whispered.

'It's light,' McLeod cut in decisively, 'and there are lots of people about on the Quayside of a Sunday.'

Best stared at him uncomprehendingly.

'He wouldn't dare attack her and push her in the Tyne now,' he explained. 'He'll wait until it's dark.'

He was aware that that scenario all hung on the supposition that they had come down to the Quayside and that the man had waylaid her here but done so without drawing undue attention. He could think of no other trail they could follow, and they had to do something.

Best stirred, looked up at him and said, hopefully, 'So he's keeping her somewhere? Maybe on board a ship?'

McLeod nodded, crossing his fingers that he was right.

'But the Antwerp steamer leaves on a Saturday.'

'If it's gone.'

'What do you mean?'

'Yesterday's gales will have been keeping some of the ships port-bound and it's blowing up again now. They're all a bit more cautious since those three steam trawlers went down in the November gales.'

'Come on then!' exclaimed Best, leaping to his feet. 'Let's go!'

Thirty-six

The *Dragoon* had gone. The spot where the Antwerp-bound vessel usually berthed was empty.

While the rising wind raged noisily around them the three men stood and stared, wordlessly, at the empty dockside as if by willing her to be there she would materialize.

Eventually, McLeod shouted, 'They must have taken a wee chance this morning when they found the wind had dropped.' He paused then added hopefully, 'Now it's getting up again she might have taken shelter down river at North Shields harbour.'

Best knew by the tone of his voice that he thought this was doubtful. They would have taken advantage of the overnight drop in the wind and got going early. By now, they would be out in the North Sea somehow. God knows what would happen to Helen there.

'Doesn't have to be Antwerp,' Smith said quietly. 'Does it?'

The two inspectors turned to stare at him.

'Well, don't you remember them girls they took to Brussels – they went by Boulogne and,' he took a deep breath and kept going, 'that man Dyer said that they take English girls into Holland and France as well.'

Best and McLeod now stared at each other and then glanced along the quay at the other two Tyne Steam Ship Company vessels: the *Admiral*, which sailed between Newcastle and Rotterdam and the *Lord Raglan*, which would soon be Hamburg-bound.

Could the young man have something?

McLeod turned to him and barked out an order. 'Go to the River Police Station, tell them I sent you, and that we need every man jack of them that is available to search these two

197

ships!' He looked left and right to the other ships hugging the Quayside. 'And more if necessary.'

As Smith turned to go Best grasped his arm and murmured, 'Good idea, John George. Good idea.'

Smith was unable to speak but took off as if his life depended on it. In a way, it did. Best began climbing up the gangway of the *Admiral*.

'Shouldn't we wait?' McLeod shouted, 'until we have some help. He could slip out while we are busy looking . . .'

It was no use. The Yard man was already on board and making his presence felt.

He could see the sailors shaking their heads in answer to his urgent questions. Then the captain appeared.

'Don't sail until dawn on Tuesday,' McLeod heard him say as he reached the deck. 'Passengers don't board until Monday evening.'

'Someone could have slipped into one of the cabins while you weren't looking,' Best insisted.

'No,' said the captain, shaking his head firmly. 'They are all locked.'

'What about cleaning? They must be opened for cleaning?'

'Tomorrow. After we have finished loading the cargo. No use before.'

Best persisted, and finally the captain allowed him to check each cabin. As he passed along the passageways he kept shouting, 'Helen! Helen! Are you there, Helen?'

The captain exchanged wondering glances with a crew member. Who was this mad man?

They followed the same procedure with the *Lord Raglan* – to no avail. By then, more help had arrived and they spread out to cover all of the many ships docked at the port of Newcastle-upon-Tyne. But it was no use. There was no sign of either Helen or the mysterious man.

When they had finished, officers were posted at strategic points along the dockside while McLeod took Best off to a pub. Ostensibly, this was to plan their next move, but in reality it was to get him out of the way lest he break down in front of all these men.

He took him to the Stone Cellars, a very old riverside tavern.

The parlour was low-ceilinged, cosy, carpeted, stuffed with china ornaments and pictures and tucked away at the end of a dark corridor. Best of all it was empty.

Unfortunately, McLeod had forgotten that this public house was also the venue for most of the inquests on bodies found in the Tyne and that mementoes to that effect were scattered about the place.

Worse, in the corner of the room were some steps leading down to a door that opened on to a gallery overlooking the river. In the forefront of the view from the gallery were the River Police Station and the Dead House. A restless Best insisted on wandering out there – at the very moment that another river victim, swathed in tarpaulin, was unloaded from the police boat.

'I must go down,' he exclaimed and turned to leave.

McLeod grasped him firmly by the arm and ordered, 'No. They'll tell us straight away if it is her. What we have to do now,' he said, pushing Best back into the parlour and on to a chair, 'is think of other places where he might take her.'

Best gave him a forlorn look. 'There must be a million.'

He was right.

The dockside and the area directly behind it were crammed with potential hiding places: huts, warehouses, derelict buildings, iron works, glass works – the list went on and on.

'As soon as it's dark,' Best whispered.

'We'll swamp the area with coppers,' exclaimed McLeod. 'He won't dare go near the water.'

'He doesn't have to.'

He was right there, too. It was a melancholy fact that most men are stronger than most women and so, if desperate, can easily overpower and dispatch them.

McLeod's mind went blank. He couldn't think of a thing to say. Any suggestion that might be useful. His glance roamed around the room in search of inspiration. It alighted on the notices pinned up behind the bar detailing the prices of ales, spirits and food and announcing that there were rooms available.

He suddenly sat up. 'A room in a pub!' he exclaimed.

Best stared at him. 'What?'

'He might have taken her to a room in a pub. Why not? The simplest explanations are often the best.'

'But they'd notice she was being taken in against her will.'

'Not if she was drugged or drunk.'

That's what they did to some of the girls they took to the Continent – white slavery or girl farming as some were starting to call it.

'Of course,' whispered Best. 'Of course!'

'Might,' warned McLeod. 'Might!' But Best was on his feet, making for the parlour door.

McLeod grasped his arm again. 'You check here and at the Lamb Inn just behind the Malmo Wharf. I'll alert the others,' McLeod said. 'It's worth a try.'

Indeed it was, he reflected, as he offered a short prayer.

There followed the biggest ever search of Newcastle's riverside pubs and taverns, causing great consternation among the licensees. They could not decide whether this heralded a big crackdown on their various smuggling and other nefarious activities, a drive against prostitution as was periodically instigated by influential purity societies, or that something much bigger and more mysterious was afoot.

This despite careful explanations that all the police were looking for were two people. One a distinguished looking middle-aged man and the other a slight, mousy-haired, thirty-year-old woman wearing a simple chestnut-brown astrakhan coat and a fur hat, who may have hired a room that afternoon.

Most innkeepers were familiar with most of the ladies who did that sort of thing around here and this one didn't sound anything like any of them. And, indeed, the police had no luck at all until the skinny landlord of the Tug Boat Inn on the Milk Market, eager to please since a threat to close him down for rowdiness, admitted that he might well have just such a pair in one of his rooms right now.

It seemed an unlikely venue. Contrary to the impression given by its bucolic name the Milk Market was sited in a most squalid area and was the venue for the weekly Paddy's Market where the poor haggled over clothes that had long since seen their best.

But Best and McLeod were elated and the landlord only too delighted to put the keys of room four into their eager hands.

They dashed upstairs, banged on the door and shouted, 'Open up! Police!'

Receiving no response except some mumbling and apparent cursing they broke down the door.

On the bed, legs akimbo and minus any simple brown coat if she had ever worn one, was a woman no longer young and never beautiful. Sweating over her, a man who may have been distinguished with his trousers on, his hair less disarranged and his face not puce with effort.

The woman was not Helen.

Best and McLeod were on the right track in assuming that Helen might be locked up in a room near the river – but not in the assumption that it would be a room in a hotel or public house.

She was, in fact, captive in a tiny room in a small terraced house. This terrace, although not far from the river bank, indeed no distance from the River Police Station, was cut off from it both physically and mentally.

Firstly by an iron works and a jumble of factory and other buildings, then by an immensely long rope-works stretching out behind these buildings.

It was perfectly possible to find a way around all these obstructions by walking east or west for a few hundred yards then turning inland. But the terraces were hidden from sight by the obstructions and, thus, were effectively out of mind. Rescue was therefore extremely unlikely given the time left and the fact that Helen had not just one captor but two.

Helen realized that there was no hope for her. She cursed herself for her stupidity.

She had followed the man all along the Quayside, across the New Glasshouse Bridge over the Ouseburn and had been startled when he stopped outside a house in one of the terraces. Uncertain what to do next, she had hesitated, until, suddenly, he was before her – with an accomplice. Together they had forced her into the house from which, she now saw, there was no escape.

She gazed out of the window, made impregnable by strong bars, over a road alive with carts and lorries towards a brick-yard and clay pit where men toiled. But there was no chance of her banging on the window to attract their attention, tied up as she was.

Fear gripped her stomach, but it was for Ernest Best that her heart bled. She knew that her death would spell the end for him. Be the final straw from which he would never recover.

First he had lost his young wife from tuberculosis. Then Helen herself had refused him, and Joseph, the boy he had saved from the *Princess Alice* disaster and grown found of, had died during an epidemic of scarlet fever. Finally, his fiancée, Mary Jane, had been killed when flung from the galleries of the Crystal Palace.

He blamed himself for her death because he had not real-ized quickly enough that the vendetta being carried out against police by Quicksilver was aimed at him in particular, nor guessed the man's identity until it was too late.

As the light outside dimmed and her time grew shorter there was a knock on the door, then the one she called 'the accomplice' came in. Why he kept up such niceties heaven only knew. With a gag in her mouth she could scarcely shout 'come in' – nor could she be doing anything that he might interrupt.

He was a runtish man but, as she knew from his grip on her arms when they had taken her, he was surprisingly powerful.

'What's your name?' she asked him after he undid her gag to give her a drink of water.

'Joe.'

The fact that he wouldn't meet her eye made her realize that despite these little kindnesses he was not going to save her. Were they just to make her way easier or to make him feel better? Both probably.

It was hopeless. You must not give up, she chastised herself. Do something! But what?

What would Best do? She tried to remember some of his ideas for getting people to do what he wanted. Foolishly all she could recall was 'plant seeds of doubt – let them grow in people's minds'. But she had no time for that! Besides, what would it achieve?

'You'll hang you know,' she said instead.

'If they catch me,' he retorted, 'an' they're not goin' to.'

His teeth so crowded his mouth that they caused spittle to pile up at the corners of his lips.

He handed her a cup of water. She must make this last!

'That man who's chasing you is my fiancé,' she lied. 'The man from Scotland Yard. And he won't rest till he gets you.'

'He won't catch us. Eustace is smarter than him.' The difficulty of saying the name caused him to spit as he spoke.

What now? What now? She took a sip.

'He's taking you with him, then, Joe?' she asked casually.

He was pouring beer into a glass for himself and she saw him stop for a moment, puzzled. 'What d'you mean?' he said. Then he shrugged. 'He ain't goin' nowhere.'

'Oh yes he is.'

She felt as if someone else had taken over her tongue. When Joe failed to answer she carried on recklessly. What had she to lose.

'He's decided that it's getting too dangerous.'

She paused to let that sink in and took a sip of water. How long could she make this last?

'He's booked a passage to Rotterdam.'

Joe said nothing for a moment then exclaimed, 'Course he hasn't!' and slammed down his glass. 'Anyway, if he 'ad, how would you know?'

'He was talking to somebody while you were out.' Her mind was trying to keep pace with her mouth. Keep a step ahead of the lies she was telling so she'd know what to say next.

Seeds of doubt. Say things with confidence. What else? Make them think it was their idea . . .

'Weren't nobody here.'

'Oh yes there was. While you were out spying out the land. Taking all the risks.'

'Don't believe you,' he said sullenly. He was beginning to get angry. 'Finish your water.'

'Ask him then. Ask him!' she exclaimed desperately.

He was reaching for the gag.

'He wouldn't do that!' he shouted, dropping the gag on the floor.

Oh dear. She'd better calm him down. Shouting would attract attention. While he picked up the gag she whispered, 'You can still save yourself.'

'Nah. It's too late,' he muttered.

'No it isn't. No it isn't,' she hissed, moving her head about to prevent him fixing the gag back on. 'You could turn Queen's evidence and . . .' The rest of her words were lost. The gag was back on.

'It's too late,' he said again. 'It's no good. It's too late.'

The pub search was over. There was nowhere else to look. They paced about trying to think of what to do next. Maybe just keep sweeping the area, searching factories, derelict buildings, houses – but that was an impossible task and would take an age.

Best sat in the River Police Station looking out at the Tyne. Smith came in to be with him.

'No, you go out, son, help them. Then they will feel they have done everything they can.' As he was leaving Best looked up. 'John George,' he said, 'it wasn't your fault, son. Sorry I shouted at you. You were not to know. I want you to understand that.' He gave the boy a hug.

Smith recognized it as a goodbye.

'Time you were back with your family. I'll send you home tomorrow.'

It had grown quite dark and much too late for hope when a River Police sergeant came into the room. He removed his cap and cleared his throat as though speaking to one already bereaved.

'I know you don't want bothering now but there's this fellow here insists on speaking to you. Won't talk to anyone else. Says to tell you, it's a bit weird, but says to tell you that she sowed seeds of doubt.'

'What?' yelled Best, jumping to his feet. 'What? Where is he?'

Joe came in. As he moved into the light they could see that his hands and jacket front were saturated with blood.

'Oh my God!' yelled Best. '*What have you done? What have you done?*'

'He's saved me,' said Helen, appearing beside Joe and grasping hold of his hand. 'Him and you.'

Best looked her all over, open-mouthed. 'But the blood! The blood!'

'It's Eustace Arnold's. He was going to kill me so Joe saved me. He's dead.'

'Seeds of doubt.' Joe was burbling now. 'Seeds of doubt. That's what she said I had to say.'

Best buried his head on Helen's shoulder and wept.

Thirty-seven

'So, we are no further forward with Phoebe's murder,' said McLeod, who had been looking forward to spending Christmas Day in Edinburgh, and saw the prospect fading again.

'There's no doubt Meredith is a bastard for leading the girl on when he knew he wouldn't be able to marry her, but,' said Best, 'I don't think he killed her.'

'I don't know. I still wonder whether he might have wanted to shut her up so he could go on milking Sir George.'

'Well, he's never going to admit to it and we have no evidence . . .'

'But we can still get him for blackmail,' said Best, 'and who knows what we might uncover while doing so?'

They grinned at each other. They would both enjoy taking the smirk off that young man's face.

'If Sir George will agree, of course,' said McLeod.

'But he told me about it.'

'Aye, in his cups. He's had time to think about it now and the reasons for him paying up are the same as they'll be for him refusing to cooperate: reputation, dirty washing and all.'

That turned out to be an understatement. When they faced Sir George as he sat on his Gothic throne in his ice-cream cake of a villa, at his side was his new-found 'son'.

Meredith, the consummate actor, was wearing a piously filial expression.

While Best and McLeod had been occupied on their chase after Eustace Arnold, Meredith had been to see Sir George, begged his forgiveness and insinuated his way into the vulnerable old man's heart.

'We have realized,' said Meredith, 'that by remaining at

loggerheads we can only be losers.' He smiled unctuously at Best. 'We both loved Phoebe and we can comfort each other over her loss.'

He exchanged a sympathetic glance with Sir George.

Best felt sick. Surely, an astute and ruthless businessman like Sir George would not be taken in by this reptile?

As if in answer to his thoughts Sir George, who, Best had to admit, looked brighter and much less forlorn than on his previous visit, leaned across and patted Meredith's shoulder.

'But he blackmailed you!' Best spat out.

Sir George raised surprised eyebrows. 'I don't know where you got that idea?'

'From *you*,' Best retorted testily. 'You told me that you had "paid the bastard off"!'

The older man shook his head. 'You misunderstood me, my boy. I gave Arthur a loan to help set him up, which, under the circumstances, was the least I could do.' He smiled condescendingly at Best. 'I think we both had had a little too much to drink that night, don't you?'

Best could not bear to look at Meredith knowing that beneath his understanding smile would lurk a grin of triumph. He didn't want to be remembered in the North East as the Yard man who had been charged with grievous bodily harm on one of their upstanding young lawyers not to mention biffing an elderly public benefactor on the nose.

'We presume we can trust your discretion in this matter, Inspector?' said Meredith.

Best refused to reply so McLeod put in bluntly, 'Yes. We have no choice,' and got up.

'We can also rely on you to work a bit harder finding Phoebe's killer?' was Meredith's parting shot, which had even the mild-mannered McLeod tightening his fists.

'You realize, my boy,' McLeod said as they left through Middleton Hall's grandiose gateway, 'that dear Arthur will probably inherit.'

Best shook his head wonderingly. 'If "dear Arthur" hasn't cleaned him out before he dies.'

McLeod laughed. 'Well, at least they deserve each other.'

It was one of those rare sparklingly sunny winter days with a just bearable bite in the air. They elected to walk all the way back to headquarters.

'If you don't mind,' said Best, 'I'll deprive myself of the pleasure of returning to help investigate Sir George's murder after he has signed the will.'

'With luck, Ernest my friend, I'll have retired by then,' smiled McLeod. 'A smart lawyer like Arthur will realize he has to leave a decent interval before doing the dirty deed.'

Back to the station, tired but invigorated, they found they had visitors. Sitting patiently in the waiting room were Anne Meldrew and her uncle, Henry O'Brien.

'It's about Phoebe,' said O'Brien.

'You killed her because Sir George had shares in the *Cospatrick* company?' said Best, uncharacteristically rushing in. He was desperate to get back to Helen and to London.

'No,' said O'Brien soberly. 'It was an accident, and I don't know whether he has shares in the Shaw Savill line.'

'He had Henry's son and family evicted from their cottage and land,' Anne put in quietly and glanced sadly at her uncle, who was temporarily unable to speak, 'so they had no choice but to take up the chance of a new life in New Zealand.'

'Ah.'

Best and McLeod sat looking perplexed.

'That explains one thing,' said Best eventually, 'but not the other.'

'We don't understand,' McLeod said tiredly. 'You had reason to hate him but his daughter's death was an accident?'

'You'd better start at the beginning,' said Best.

'Phoebe was in such a state about that man Meredith,' Anne said, 'she made my life a misery. She kept harping on and on saying if only she could ask her mother if it were true that he was her half-brother. In the end,' Anne sighed heavily, 'I said why divn't you try to contact her.'

'Through spiritualism,' said Best.

She nodded sadly. 'Aha.' She sighed then took a deep breath and went on. 'What you've got to understand is how wilful

Phoebe was. She'd always had her own way and if she didn't get it she made everyone suffer. God rest her soul.' She crossed herself.

'First of all she got her Aunt Hettie to take her to the Newcastle Society meetings, but that didn't suit. She couldn't ask her mother if she had committed adultery in front of all those people. I knew my uncle went to one of those smaller circles, and he got Mr Quarrell to introduce her there.

'She seemed to be happier with that but was still too embarrassed to ask her questions and was frightened her father would get to hear of it – so she got the idea she would become a medium herself. There was no stopping her. In the end,' Anne caught O'Brien's eye and he nodded, 'we said we'd help her.'

'For a fee,' said O'Brien bluntly, 'which I gave to the Irish Land League and the Parnell fund. I felt that would be a proper diversion of Threapleton's funds,' he added dryly.

'I took some as well,' Anne confessed, holding up her hand when O'Brien tried to come in to silence her. 'I took some for a miners' welfare fund.' Her lips tightened. 'My brother was killed in one of Threapleton's mines because he refused to spend out the money to shore up some of the workings properly. Harold Luke's father died in the same accident.'

Harold Luke, the nervous deputy manager of the Beds department! Everything is knitting together in a way I could never have foretold, thought Best. Back to the vale of tears he read about on his journey north.

'You went to work for him intending to get your own back?' he asked.

'Oh, no, hinny. I didn't know then that it was mainly his mine, did I? Well,' she shrugged, 'you'd be hard put to it to work for someone around here who didn't have a finger in that pie.'

'So how did Phoebe die?'

Anne closed her eyes and was silent for a moment. 'Honestly it was an accident,' she said finally, tears starting from her eyes.

'Tell us,' said Best.

'Well, she kept trying to connect with the spirits but it didn't seem to be working so we told her just to listen to the voices in her head.'

'She was a very suggestible lass,' O'Brien put in.

'So then she said yes, she was getting some messages. But her questions weren't being answered.'

'We did begin to feel sorry for her,' confessed O'Brien. 'At first I'd just been happy to see a Threapleton suffer.'

'So you did some materialization for her?' suggested Best. They nodded.

'Well,' said Anne, 'she was getting us down.'

'She asked the spirit the questions?'

'Aha. That's right.'

'We gave her honest answers,' said O'Brien. 'Told her the truth. We thought that was only fair.'

'Just a minute,' said McLeod, 'how did you *know* the truth about who her father really was? It wasn't common knowledge.'

'Oh, it was in the servants' hall,' Anne retorted.

'Of course.'

'Well, that last time she'd insisted on being tested – tied up like she'd seen at the Newcastle Society – so she would know whether the spirits were genuine.'

'She wasn't bright enough to realize that the mediums were tied up to test whether they were acting at being spirits,' said O'Brien. 'Well, when she got the same answers she went into hysterics, screaming and shouting.'

'We were so sick of it all by then that when she began gasping we thought she was just playing up for sympathy.'

'Being dramatic.'

They glanced at each other, neither wanting to remember what happened next.

'So you left her,' said Best, ending the silence.

They both nodded.

'Not for long,' Anne insisted tearfully.

'When we came back she'd collapsed,' said O'Brien.

'We couldn't bring her back,' Anne sobbed. 'We kept trying and trying!'

'She'd got entangled in the restraints, must have suffocated,' O'Brien put in soberly.

'We just didn't know what to do with the body, then Harold—'

'Harold Luke was there?'

They exchanged glances then nodded. 'It was at his house,' said Anne.

'He suggested we pack her in a box and deliver her to Bainbridges. Then he was going to put her in a delivery crate to go to Middleton Hall.'

'They were getting a lot of new furniture from the shop.'

'We thought we would unpack it when it got there, the next morning, then put her in her bed so it would look as if she had just died of a seizure in her sleep.'

The plan had gone awry. A porter got hold of the box and took it up to the Beds department, where it would have been opened by someone else.

'So Harold stayed late, sent me a message and we put her in the full-tester.'

'He said the curtains were never drawn back,' Anne explained, sniffing. 'We were going to take her home that next night.'

'The roses,' said Best. 'What about the roses?'

O'Brien looked embarrassed. 'One for each of my family on the *Cospatrick*,' he admitted. 'It made me feel a bit better – but not much.'

'He found them in Trimmings. Artificial flowers are all the fashion,' Anne added weakly, twisting the sodden ball her handkerchief had become.

Thirty-eight

'So, what's to be done about it?' asked McLeod. 'Well, of course they could be charged with manslaughter,' said Superintendent Tunnah, 'or at the very least concealing a death – and for obstructing police.'

It was the day before Christmas Eve and a high level conference had been called in the chief constable's office.

They all nodded, but without much enthusiasm.

'Isn't there some way . . .' said the chief constable, who belonged to the same lodge as Sir George.

Usually Best would have bristled at this unspoken suggestion that they should ignore the law for the sake of the privileged. But if laws allowed ships to go to sea without sufficient lifeboats to save more than a third of the passengers and ignored negligence in mines . . .?

'I think,' he said at length, 'that we should forget that this discussion ever took place. Inspector McLeod and I should go to see Sir George, put the whole situation before him and ask him what he wants to happen.'

They all knew what that would be. Nothing. Keep the matter quiet. Particularly all that about the *Cospatrick* and his negligence in the mines.

'But what,' said McLeod, 'would we tell the newspapers, who are expecting us to arrest a murderer?'

Best blew out his cheeks, looked at the ceiling and considered the matter. They all waited. Good job I'm such a good fibber, thought Best.

'We'll tell them a lawyer's truth,' he said eventually. 'That is, the facts that they already know but with a different slant.'

'Such as?' frowned Tunnah.

'That the girl was dabbling in spiritualism because she desperately wanted to reach her mother. Everyone will sympathize

212

with that. The trio were trying to help her but didn't want to upset Sir George so held the seances at Luke's place.'

Best took a deep breath and continued. 'The excitement caused Phoebe to have a seizure and she died of natural causes. They were trying to take her body home so as to cause less distress.

'Sir George will point out that his daughter's health had always been delicate and that they have all suffered enough. He will express his gratitude to Miss Meldrew, Henry O'Brien and Harold Luke for their kindness to Phoebe and hope that the press will now leave them all in peace.'

And so it was.

'I've only just realized something,' said Best as they went through the portals of Newcastle Central Station late on Christmas Eve. 'It was probably no accident that Eustace Arnold got into my compartment on the way up here. He must have gone down especially.'

'But what would be the point?' asked McLeod as he signalled for a porter. 'Just keeping an eye on your progress?'

Best nodded. 'And to get a measure of me. He was eager to show me around and become more friendly but I resisted.'

'Wasted journey for him, then.'

'Not entirely. If I hadn't already made his acquaintance and decided he was just a harmless, jolly fellow I might have looked at him with a more critical eye.'

'Joe said he didn't know that Eustace was going to kill Clegg and Sadie,' Helen put in hurriedly.

'I'm sure he does,' said Best. 'Wouldn't you?'

'Well, he *is* telling us all about this abduction business.'

'Wouldn't you?' said Best again.

'And he could buy himself a pardon in the process,' said McLeod, putting her out of her misery. Don't worry, they won't hang him.'

'I'm sorry that I won't be here when those girls arrive back from the Continent,' said Best.

'It's going to be hard for them.'

'Better than being dead, though, isn't it?'

'You have a charming way with words, Ernest,' said Helen.

Best glanced sadly at McLeod. 'So sorry about Clegg.'

'Bad luck. Just bad luck.'

'And bad judgement.'

'Which we're all guilty of.'

'I misjudged *him*,' Best said. 'I thought he'd told Florence about me coming to her seance, but Anne Meldrew has admitted it was her.'

'Dinna blame yourself, Ernest.' McLeod shook his head. 'How were you to know? He was being difficult with you and you're only human.'

'No matter what terrible things I do people insist on forgiving me,' said Best after McLeod had left to catch his Edinburgh-bound train.

'That's because you're a nice fellow – at heart,' she added, lest he grow too proud.

They watched the Edinburgh to London express approaching the platform.

'Hope we can get a carriage to ourselves,' Best said, glancing at Helen to see her response. 'It's going to be a long night.'

'No need,' she said smugly. 'I've booked us into a sleeping car.'

Best's eyebrows shot up. 'Good Lord. I've never been in one of them.'

'Neither have I,' she admitted, giving him a saucy look. 'But you have to realize that such an arrangement comes at a price.'

'Is it very expensive?'

'I don't mean that.'

'What, then?'

The train was drawing to a halt.

'It will cost you your freedom.'

He was puzzled.

'You will have to marry me – my reputation will be compromised,' she explained patiently.

Carriage doors began to open and they stood back to allow passengers to get out.

'But you don't *want* to get married,' he said, leaning around one of them so he could see her face. Her dear face.

'Didn't,' she corrected.

'What's changed?'

'Two things. One, I'm getting sufficient work to be able to afford enough domestic help to allow me to paint.' The porter was guiding them towards the sleeping cars. 'Any manly objection to that?'

He shook his head. Truth to tell, now that he had her back he was quite incapable of objecting to anything she did.

'And the second reason?' he called as she began climbing on board.

She turned and looked down at him. 'The second reason, Ernest Best, is that I can't live without you.'

Well, well, 'Sow the seeds and watch them grow.' He grinned to himself. My luck has changed at last. Will the night be long *enough*?

Author's Note

A further successful prosecution for the abduction of English girls took place in Brussels in 1881. Josephine Butler's accusations of police involvement were published by a Belgian newspaper and provoked Lenaer, the chief of the Brussels Morals Police, to sue for libel, but the information which then emerged led to his dismissal and that of his subordinates.

The British authorities were then obliged to take the matter seriously and the House of Lords convened a Select Committee to look into the matter. Howard Vincent, the Director of the Criminal Investigation Department of Scotland Yard, gave evidence claiming that juvenile prostitution was far worse in London and little could be done about it due to the low age of consent (thirteen years). Eventually, the Criminal Law Amendment Bill, which raised the age of consent to sixteen and strengthened the anti-procuration laws, was forced through Parliament.

Scotland Yard formed a small anti-white-slave traffic branch, and international attempts to control the trade (dubbed 'mythical' by some historians and often regarded as a bit of a joke) became one of the important strands leading to the formation of Interpol.

White Slavery is again a problem but today it is girls from the ex-Communist bloc and Asia that are imported into the UK and other European countries.

Bainbridge & Co., generally acknowledged to be the world's first department store, was very much part of my Tyneside childhood. In 1953 it was taken over by the John Lewis Partnership and in 1976 moved from Market Street to splendid new premises in the Eldon Square shopping centre. The store has recently been renamed John Lewis Newcastle.